Wolf Moon

Wolf Moon

LISA KESSLER

This book is a work of fiction. Names, characters, places, and incidents are the product of the author's imagination or are used fictitiously. Any resemblance to actual events, locales, or persons, living or dead, is coincidental.

Copyright © 2017 by Lisa Kessler. All rights reserved, including the right to reproduce, distribute, or transmit in any form or by any means. For information regarding subsidiary rights, please contact the Publisher.

Entangled Publishing, LLC
2614 South Timberline Road
Suite 109
Fort Collins, CO 80525
Visit our website at www.entangledpublishing.com.

Select Otherworld is an imprint of Entangled Publishing, LLC.

Edited by Jenn Mishler
Cover design by Erin Dameron-Hill
Cover art from Shutterstock

Manufactured in the United States of America

First Edition February 2017

This one is for Ken. Thanks for coming with me on another book research adventure. Can't wait to go back to Sedona again! I love you!

Chapter One

Raven

"Damn it. No!" I smacked my hands against the steering wheel as the van sputtered and finally rolled to a slow stop on the edge of the two-lane highway. Weeks ago, I told Caldwell the gas gauge in the van was broken, but it never got fixed, and in my haste to leave town, I hadn't topped off the tank. I'd been praying I could make it to Flagstaff, safely north of Sedona, but apparently, my van had other plans. Now I was stuck in the middle of who-the-hell-knows-where Arizona. Great.

At least I was out of the Sedona city limits. Allen Caldwell, my Alpha, had some kind of supernatural GPS when it came to Pack members straying. Somehow he could focus on any Pack member and get an idea of their location. I didn't know how far-reaching his abilities were, but my sister was counting on me to get out of town and bring back the cavalry for her and the others.

I hoped I made it far enough to stay out of his reach. Outside the van, the icy January wind howled. Using my cell phone was out of the question. Just turning it on could give them a way to locate me, but I couldn't just sit and wait for Caldwell to send his bodyguards, Bo and Blake, to collect me, either.

Finally, I pressed the button for my hazard lights. Maybe a Good Samaritan would come by with a gas can—a girl could hope, right?

Hope was all I had left.

Two cars heading south zoomed past me in the other lane, and one coming north from Sedona went around me without even slowing down. So much for Good Samaritans. I broke the silence and clicked on the radio.

Music filled the interior, keeping despair and panic from settling in. The new song from Logan and the Howlers started, and I cranked up the volume, singing along.

Headlights were approaching from the north. The car slowed but didn't stop. Classic Mustang. Nice. A few months ago, I wouldn't have been able to see it in the darkness, but since being bitten by a werewolf, my human senses had been elevated to superhero level.

It might've been cool if I hadn't been trapped in the Sedona Pack.

Suddenly light blinded me from my rearview mirror. I glanced in the side mirror, narrowing my eyes. The Mustang. Whoever was behind the wheel, they'd come back for me. I grabbed my gloves off the passenger seat and pulled them on before popping open my door.

This was new, too. When I was human, I might've asked the Mustang driver to call 911 through a cracked window. Now I was strong enough to take on any human with bad intentions.

I got out, gasping at the sudden, biting cold. Behind me, a tall man got out of the Mustang. The wind brought me his scent before I could see his face. Shit.

He wasn't human. I snapped my head up, heart racing. Definitely a werewolf, but he wasn't from the Sedona Pack. He came closer, into the glow of his headlights, and my breath hitched.

His bright blue eyes locked on mine, and his chest expanded. A dark brow cocked knowingly. Oh, shit. He knew what I was, too.

I went back to the van, and his footsteps stopped. "Didn't mean to surprise you. I'm not from around here."

His voice was deep, but I didn't catch a trace of bad intentions. I was still learning to get a handle on my wolf senses, but evil had a scent, bitter and pungent, like the scorched earth after a forest fire. I'd been living with the stench long enough to recognize it anywhere.

This guy didn't reek of malevolence, but he needed to get the hell out of Dodge before my Pack changed that.

I turned around, hoping I looked casual. "My sister is bringing me some gas. You don't need to stay here."

He shrugged. "I don't mind." He started to chuckle. "Sorry. I'm trying not to be creepy, but it's really dark out here, and I'd feel terrible if I left you here and something happened."

Like an idiot, I glanced his way. Damn, he had a warm smile. But the wolves I lived with weren't bad looking, either. Better to lure in unwitting females. I reinforced my emotional barrier.

"You just passing through?"

He shook his head, resting his chiseled forearms on the roof of my minivan. "I've been living in Sedona for a couple weeks, just haven't been into town much yet."

I looked up the highway. "You're coming in from Flagstaff?"

"Yeah. Just getting my bearings."

It made no sense. I'd never seen him before, but there was something familiar about him. "Are you a hiker?"

"Nah." He straightened, tugging his jacket collar up to cover the back of his neck. "I'm a horse trainer. Working over at Valley Farms."

No doubt he was a wolf, but he seemed so...normal. Nothing like the predators I'd just escaped.

But they'd change that if they caught him. The Pack would either drive him out of town or kill him, or worse yet, infect him with their psychotic poison.

None of my business. My life was screwed enough without getting mixed up with a lone wolf. I needed to get to Reno and pray that the Pack there might help us.

He held his gloved hand out toward me. "I'm Luke, by the way."

I didn't take his hand. "I'm Raven. How long have you been training horses?"

What the hell was I doing? Small talk was not going to get me out of Arizona and safely to Reno, Nevada.

"I've been working on a ranch since high school. This is my first head trainer position."

"Congratulations." My gaze wandered over his face again. "I thought maybe I saw you on billboards or something."

A crooked smile curved his lips, and my heart thudded, surprising me. "I get that a lot, actually, but no, I haven't been on any that I know of." He glanced in each direction down the road. "Cell service is spotty on the highway. Maybe your sister is lost."

I sighed. I had a can of pepper spray, but it was in the van. "I'll check and see if she sent me a text."

I opened the van. My sister was still trapped in Caldwell's Pack, counting on me to find the Reno Wolf Pack and come back for her. The longer I stayed here, the riskier it became.

But trust wasn't something I could afford, either. I pocketed the pepper spray and walked back toward Luke, my hand clutched around the vial in my pocket.

"You seem like a good guy, so I'm going to give you a solid piece of advice. Get out of Sedona and don't look back. It's not safe for you here."

"Thanks for the tip." He kept his expression neutral, his voice so low I wouldn't have been able to hear him a few months ago.

When I was still human.

His gaze wandered over my face as he added, "Is your mate in trouble?"

"My what?" I grimaced, unwilling to imagine any of the males in the Pack as anything other than jailers. Did I give off the married vibe? Maybe he took my initial cold shoulder as being unavailable.

With his looks, he was probably used to single women falling all over him.

Confusion marred his brow. "You were bitten, right?"

"I wasn't born this way." I kept my attention on my van. "There's no mate for me. And I was serious, you should go. I won't risk warning you again."

I hated snapping at him, but if he didn't leave… I didn't want to think about what they'd do to him.

"This isn't getting us anywhere." He walked back to his classic Mustang without any fanfare. I couldn't help but watch. His jeans fit him just right, and his jacket strained across the back of his broad shoulders.

He would've been exactly my type back when I was human.

He dug around the front seat of his car and came over with a credit card in hand. "I'll buy your gas. If you don't want me to drive you, you can use this card to call a tow. I'll cancel the card tomorrow. But I'm a horse trainer, not a rock star, so you won't be able to buy a car or a trip to the Bahamas…"

I glanced down at the card. Luke Reynolds.

He hadn't been lying about his name. Wait a second. Reynolds.

My gaze rose to his face. No wonder he looked so familiar.

Now it seemed obvious. He *had* to be Logan Reynolds's twin brother. Had to be. His hair was shorter, maybe a slimmer build, but those piercing blue eyes and the strong jaw were undeniable. Now that I knew his last name, I wasn't sure how I missed it before.

He could've led with name-dropping his rock star twin brother. Instead, even when I mentioned he looked familiar, he didn't let on.

If Luke is a werewolf, Logan must be a wolf, too. The Y chromosome carried the shifter gene, so only males were born as werewolves, and they always came in sets of twins. Just like Luke and Logan.

Maybe that was why the Howlers never toured.

I lifted my gaze to his face. "You're Logan's twin brother. From Logan and the Howlers."

He raised his eyebrows with a little nod. "Yeah." He sobered. "It's freezing out here. Are you going to let me drive you to a gas station, or do you want to call a tow?"

I wasn't about to turn on my cell phone. My choices were to trust this guy, this werewolf, or wait for a human to stop. The longer I waited, the greater the chance my Alpha would find me. I shuddered and handed Luke's card back.

"I'd love a ride to the gas station. Thanks."

I went to the van to grab my purse and my phone. When I came back, Luke had the passenger door of the Mustang opened for me. I got in, and he closed the door before jogging over to his side. He already had the engine running and the heater pumping hot air. I shivered as my body defrosted.

Okay, I was *not* used to anyone putting my needs before their own.

He got in and checked for traffic before pulling away. We were headed north. Away from Sedona. The hazard lights on the van dimmed in the side mirror until we finally rounded a corner and it was gone.

I stared ahead into the darkness, trying not to notice how good he smelled.

He broke the silence first. "I've never met a female werewolf who didn't have a mate."

"Now you have." I turned to look out the window. It came out bitchier than I intended, but I was running low on trust these days. The only reason I was even in this car was because I was out of options.

"All right." He turned up the radio. His brother's song "Howling" filled the car. God, no wonder the Howlers' music spoke to me. Logan was a shifter, too. He understood how the secret kept us apart from everyone around us.

And something else occurred to me—Logan lived in Reno.

My head snapped toward Luke. "Are you from Reno? The Wolf Pack in Reno?"

He frowned, peering my way for a second. "Yeah, why?"

My heart raced like a jackhammer in my chest. Could something finally be going my way? I shook my head. "What the hell are you doing down here in Sedona?"

"I told you, I'm the head trainer at Valley Farms. My Alpha is head trainer in Reno, so I either stayed as an assistant trainer or moved away." He tightened his grip on the wheel. "Your pulse is giving you away. What haven't you told me?"

I opened my mouth, but the words wouldn't come. Finally, I managed to force out a whisper. "I was on my way to find you."

His brow furrowed. "Why?"

"My Alpha is going to lead the Sedona pack up to Nevada to wipe yours out."

He frowned, his grip tightening on the wheel. "And why would you go to the trouble to search us out and warn us?"

I swallowed the lump in my throat. "Because Caldwell has my sister."

Chapter Two

Luke

Caldwell. Despite the heater blasting in my face, I shivered.

My father's old Alpha, the man who sold out my dad and his Pack to the Nero Organization, was leading a Pack in Sedona.

"*Allen* Caldwell?" I needed to be certain.

Raven frowned. "You know him?"

"I know *of* him. He was my dad's Alpha when he was my age." I cursed under my breath. "I didn't know he was…"

"Still alive?" Raven shook her head. "Sadly, yeah, and he's after your Pack in Reno. That's how I found out you existed."

I nodded, but dread was welling in the pit of my stomach. Finding her stranded on the side of the road in the dark, it couldn't have been random. It had to be a setup. And I walked right into it. Fuck.

My Mustang ate up the curves on the two-lane highway. I'd restored her over the years. She was my pride and joy. And if I wasn't very careful, we might not be together much longer.

When we finally made it to Flagstaff, I pulled into the first gas station and got out without a word. I didn't want it to be true, but I had to face the facts. If Caldwell discovered another wolf was in his territory, what's the surest way to lure him in?

Damsel in distress. Make the damsel a werewolf, and it was a sure thing.

I paid for the plastic gas can and filled it. No eye contact. I couldn't risk it. Her dark eyes pulled me in until I forgot everything else.

That could get me killed, and I didn't plan on dying today.

After I put the gas can in the trunk, I got in and stared at the steering wheel. "Look, I know enough about Caldwell not to trust that I just happened to stumble onto a female wolf on the run to Reno to ask my Pack for help. How long has he known I was in Sedona?"

Raven shook her head. "I don't think he knows you're here."

"Right." I sighed and started the engine. My Pack had heard Sedona mentioned a couple of times by Nero jaguar shifters, but I'd never imagined they were talking about another Pack led by Allen Caldwell.

I steeled my resolve and turned her way. "I'll take you back to your van, and you can tell Caldwell I'm well armed and I'll take out any wolf who trespasses on Valley Farms land."

"I'm not bait." She pulled her hair back from her forehead. "The reason I got in your car was because I couldn't risk using my cell phone. If they find me, they'll kill me. Your Pack in Reno was my only hope of saving my sister. They still have her."

I drove out and headed for the highway. "And why would my Pack help you?"

"Good question. Isabelle and I figured if Caldwell wants to kill your Alpha so bad, it must mean you all aren't on his team with Nero." She tipped her head down, looking at her hands. "Guess we were wrong."

She seemed sincere. But she also could have been an amazing actress. I focused on the highway. "If you want my help, you're going to have to meet me halfway. How did you and your sister get into a Pack without mates?"

She hesitated for a second, her voice tentative. "I was dating this guy, Bo. I didn't know he was a werewolf. He told Caldwell I was strong, and they're trying to grow this Pack quickly, so I was marked to be bitten."

My jaw went slack. What the hell? Frowning, I glanced her way. "You were bitten just to make another werewolf?"

"Something like that."

Fuck. I shook my head. "And your sister?"

"She asked me to bite her so she'd be strong enough to protect me while we figured a way out."

"Shit." I gripped the wheel so tight my gloves squeaked. "That's not how a Pack works."

"Apparently, this Pack never got the werewolf manual."

I rolled my eyes, surprised that a smile crept up on me. "There's no manual, but an Alpha should protect his Pack, and sending wolves out to bite humans is…"

"Sick."

"Insane" would've been my word, but she'd shared enough that I didn't think this was all an elaborate trap anymore.

I just needed an idea.

The only thing I knew for sure was I wasn't going to let them kill her.

She crossed her arms. "So I guess biting people during the full moon isn't how you do it in Reno?"

"No, that's not how we fucking *do it*." My shoulders bunched with tension. I tipped my head a little. "Sorry. I'm just…" I struggled for words. "I've never heard of a Pack doing this. If humans find out shifters are real, then we're all in danger, Nero included."

Raven shrugged. "No one outside the Pack knows we exist."

"How? How do you bite humans and no one finds out?" I turned her way for a second. "You told your sister and then bit her. You can't be the only one in your Pack who turned a loved one."

"Changing Isabelle without Caldwell's approval should have gotten me killed, but he has plans for me, so instead I've been tied to his watchdogs." She shuddered, and my gut twisted with rage. "Sucks, but it's better than being dead."

A growl rumbled deep in my chest. "This doesn't make any sense. Why change a female if she's not a mate for someone in the Pack? It's a huge risk for no reason."

"They want another generation of male wolves." She paused, slowing her speech. "You don't have to be married to get pregnant."

"You don't understand." I blew out a frustrated breath. "Marriage and mates are two very different things. You could *marry* anyone. Do you even know what a mate is?"

"As far as I know, it's the raging assholes your Alpha assigns to your bed. They're your mates."

I shook my head, aching to beat the shit out of Caldwell, and I hadn't even met him yet. "Fate chooses your mate, *not* your Alpha. Wolves mate for life, and it's the same for werewolves. When you touch your mate's skin, the wolf inside you will recognize her. A werewolf treasures her as the other half of his soul. She's only bitten and changed if she wants to have his children."

She laughed, but there wasn't any joy in it. "That's a romantic fairy tale, but it's not what's happening in Sedona. The werewolves I know do whatever their Alpha commands. I've been mated to two brothers who are in a race to see who can get me pregnant first. I can't go to the police ranting about werewolves or I'll be locked in a loony bin until I shift there. Then I'd be transferred to some secret government facility someplace for experiments, like a lab rat."

She was probably right. My head was spinning. I started to slow down. Her van was right around the next corner... It was gone.

"Oh, shit." Raven gasped. "Keep driving." She slid lower in the seat. "Caldwell has a sixth sense when it comes to finding the wolves in his Pack. I must not have gotten far enough away. There's nowhere I can hide."

I gave the Mustang more gas, and she roared in answer, eating up the road. "You can stay at my place tonight. I'll call my Alpha and we'll make a plan."

She shook her head, frantic. "It'll lead him right to you."

"I wasn't lying when I said I was well armed." I didn't mention that if Caldwell brought an entire Pack against me, I'd never stand a chance.

"No." She straightened up in her seat again, her jaw set. "You should get out of Sedona while you can. Warn your Alpha. Your mate is probably worried about you anyway."

I shook my head, clenching my teeth. "I'm the only one in my Pack without a mate. That's another reason why I took the job in Sedona." I held up my hand before she could say anything. "Before you start feeling sorry for me, it's not for a lack of trying."

She laughed, the sound warming me all over. "Well, when you find her, tell her I said she's a lucky lady."

"I'm not going anywhere. I can't leave you here to get hunted and killed any more than I can pretend this insanity in your Pack isn't happening. You're right about not going to the police, but you aren't alone. Not anymore."

She stared out the passenger window. "I will be when they kill you."

"They won't be the first to try. I'm tough to kill."

Raven fought to stay awake with me for a few hours before succumbing to a fitful night's sleep on my couch. I stayed alert, watching the door with my gun in my hand. I should've called Adam, my Alpha, as soon as we got back, but in my gut I knew he'd tell me to stay out of this and…shit…the second Raven first looked up at me on the side of the highway, there was no way I could walk away.

It only got worse when she told me Caldwell was alive and ordering his Pack to bite humans. Judging by her groans and the way she thrashed in her sleep, her experience with this Pack was far from good.

As the sun came up, the tension in my shoulders eased a bit. Maybe she misjudged how powerful Caldwell's Alpha senses really were. I'd only known two Alphas in my life, Adam and his father, Malcolm, and each of them seemed to have their own powers when it came to their Pack. Adam had a knack for sensing when we were agitated or in danger, and his father could sense a lie before it ever left our lips.

Raven seemed to think Caldwell could find them anywhere, but he hadn't come for her yet.

But they'd found her van.

I shook it off. We still didn't know if it was her Pack. The highway patrol could have stumbled across it and decided it was a road hazard and called a tow. For now, we were safe. They either didn't know where she was or they'd have to wait for nightfall to make a grab for her without humans watching.

Stretching, I stood and went into my bedroom to brush my teeth and drag a comb through my hair. My day started early at Valley Farms. The ranch hands fed the horses at six a.m. every day, and by seven thirty I took the first one out of his stall.

I brought out a comforter and covered Raven. She gasped,

wide-awake and on the defensive.

Holding my hands up, I took a step back. "Just thought you might want a blanket."

She relaxed against the couch and sighed, running a hand down her face. "Sorry. I wasn't always this jumpy."

I shook my head. "You don't have to apologize. I've got some work to do, but make yourself at home—sleep, eat, whatever you need. I'll be back up soon."

A crease lined her forehead. "Keeping me here is like signing your death certificate."

"I'm not *keeping* you. I'm letting you stay. And for the record, I don't plan on having a death certificate for a long time."

I didn't tell her an idea was forming in my head. It was too crazy to speak out loud. I wanted to bounce it off Adam first. He wouldn't like it, but he'd tell me if it had any chance of working.

Before she could argue any more, I opened the door. The cold wind stung my face. "I'll be at the barn if you need me."

I walked down the path from my trainer's quarters to the stable. With ten horses that needed training, plus riding lessons in the afternoon, there was plenty to distract me from the trouble brewing on the horizon.

Since I'd been in Sedona, I'd lain low, sticking to the ranch and getting a feel for the work. This was my first head trainer position. I didn't want to screw it up.

Even so, there had been scents of other werewolves on the wind, and a random jaguar shifter a couple of times, too. For now, I had stayed under the radar.

My move to Sedona hadn't just been to take the job as head trainer at Valley Farms. Sedona was a place of interest for my Pack back home in Reno. A Nero assassin had died with the word on his lips. Now that the rest of my Pack had mates and some had children, I was the last single pack member standing. It made me the best choice to scout out Sedona.

I wasn't going to pass up the chance to get out on my own. Seeing my Pack happy with their mates was a constant reminder that I might never find mine.

So far, all I'd managed to find was Raven on the side of the highway.

I jumped off Eclipse's back and took him to the cross ties. The groom had the halter ready and finished with the horse while I walked over to the other ties, where Sabrina was already saddled and waiting. The three-year-old Morgan mare was a buckskin, a striking sand color with a black mane and tail. Rare for the breed.

I bridled her up and lifted the reins over her head. She nuzzled my chest until a smile tugged at my lips. "Good to see you, too, sweetheart."

The groom held her while I got into the saddle. "Thanks, I got her."

He stepped back, and I headed for the arena. She was a solid mare despite her young age. Nothing spooked her, and she was eager to please. One cluck of my tongue and she broke into an even-paced trot.

Since I'd been at the stable, Sabrina had made the most progress. I tried to work her last every day so I could end on a high note. She had the potential to sweep her three-year-old English pleasure division when show season came around in the spring.

As a new head trainer, every win was like a recommendation letter for future clients.

"She's looking great, Luke."

I glanced at the rail. Gabby Parks, the only daughter of Sue and John, who owned the ranch, grinned at me. She was eighteen and just starting Yavapai College here in town. Although she gave me every hint she was interested in being more than just friends, I had no intention of crossing the line with my boss's daughter.

Not to mention she wasn't my mate.

My mate was still out there. Somewhere. I was losing hope I would ever find her.

I shoved the thoughts aside. Picking at them just led to bitterness, and so far, my day hadn't been too bad considering I was harboring a fugitive from a rival Pack.

"Thanks, Gabby." I reversed direction and stopped when we reached her. "I thought you had classes today."

She stroked Sabrina's muzzle and smiled up at me. "My last class was canceled."

I scratched the mare just in front of the saddle. "Want to hop up and take her around the ring a few times?"

Gabby grinned. "Sure."

She came inside the arena, and I kicked my leg over, dropping to the ground. I grabbed the reins near the bit to hold the mare steady as Gabby walked around me.

"Could you give me a leg up?" She bent her left one at the knee.

I took her ankle and supported her knee with the other hand. Giving her a boost into the saddle was how I first discovered she wasn't my mate.

We'd touched skin to skin that day, but the wolf inside me stayed quiet. According to my brother, when I touched my mate's skin, the world would tilt. The wolf would recognize her.

And with Gabby, just like every other woman I'd ever met…nothing.

She cued the mare into a trot as I walked to the center. Back at the ranch in Reno, Adam gave all the riding lessons, but I paid attention. And when I got the job here, helping riders came to me like second nature. I enjoyed it more than I thought I would.

After work, I took refuge in the tack room and finally called my Alpha. Adam needed to know what I had planned. If this was all a trap, I'd do my best not to get caught in it, but if I failed, Adam would be my only hope of getting out.

"Hey, Adam, it's Luke."

"How's Arizona treating you?" Hearing my Alpha's voice had a profound effect on the wolf inside me. I didn't realize how close my wolf was to the surface. Apparently, I wasn't the only one shaken by the new surroundings without my Pack watching my back.

"Allen Caldwell is in Sedona. He's the Alpha of the Pack here."

Adam didn't say anything, but with my enhanced hearing I had no trouble catching the thumps of his boots as he started pacing. He sighed. "I know you don't want to hear this, but you've got to come home. Now."

I clasped the back of my neck. He was right. If Caldwell discovered me, he'd have leverage against my Pack in Reno. Against my father.

But there was a woman hiding in my cottage who had been bitten against her will. She couldn't go to the human authorities without outing us all. I was all she had, and damn it, I couldn't walk away. "I can't. Not yet."

The pacing on the other end of the line stopped. "It wasn't a request, Luke."

My wolf responded to the command in my Alpha's voice, but the human side of me couldn't turn my back on Raven.

Adam wouldn't leave her behind, either, if he were in my shoes.

"What if Caldwell is still working with Nero? We heard the jaguar assassins talk about Sedona. It was Damian's last word when he died. It can't be a coincidence. It's connected."

"All the more reason for you to come back to Reno. We can't protect you when you're in another state, in another

Pack's territory."

"They don't know I'm here yet." I took a breath and dropped my plan. "I think I have a way in. I can get more information on what they're planning." I pressed my lips together, forcing myself to pause before adding, "This Pack is really twisted, and they probably outnumber us. Big-time."

"Fuck. Luke, get your ass home. Now."

"No." I shook my head. "I took this job for a reason. Let me see what I can find out. If Caldwell is still working with Nero, this could be our chance to figure out their next move. You're expecting retaliation for Damian's death. We know Sedona has something to do with it. Maybe Caldwell is the key."

"Shit." The pacing picked up again. "I don't like this."

"You don't have to like it, but I'm being careful, and I'll keep you informed every step of the way."

Silence. Finally, Adam's voice rumbled in my ear. "Come home. I'm not asking."

I fought off the Alpha command in his voice. "I'm not a kid anymore, and I'm not leaving. Not until I have something that can help us."

"I'm sending you backup."

"You don't have anyone to spare."

"Get the intel, and then come back to Reno so we can cover you." He paused, his tone softening. "Getting involved in their Pack won't make you a hero, Luke—it'll make you a casualty."

He hung up, and I stared at my cell. Ever since Adam ascended to the Alpha of my Pack, his sixth sense when it came to each Pack member had grown. He joked about it and called it his spidey sense, but that last warning he gave me left me shaken.

How had he known I was getting involved to help Raven?

Chapter Three

Raven

I had to check in with Isabelle. If the Pack had taken the van last night, they could've told her anything. But turning on my cell phone could lead them right to me. Across the room, I spotted Luke's laptop. He'd told me to use anything I needed.

Opening the lid, I waited to see if I'd need a password. I didn't. I opened Facebook and logged him out. Once I was signed in, I clicked on Messenger.

Whatever they told you, I'm okay.

The seconds ticked by. As I reached for the mouse to log out, Messenger came to life. She was typing.

Did you make it to Reno?

Not exactly.

The door opened, and I almost jumped out of my skin. Luke held his hand up. "Sorry. Didn't mean to startle you."

"No problem." I glanced at the screen and back over at him. "Hope you don't mind. I logged you out of Facebook."

He shook his head, tugging his gloves off and setting them

on the counter. "I don't mind. Did you contact your sister?"

I nodded, facing the keyboard again. "Yeah. I don't know how much longer she'll be on."

My fingers flew on the keyboard. *I found a guy from the Reno Pack, though. Luke Reynolds. We're working on a plan. Caldwell was the Alpha of his father's Pack when they were younger. They were sent to Nero and escaped. Started their own Pack in Reno. No love lost.*

Messenger blinked as she typed her response. *If Luke's dad was part of Caldwell's original Pack and got away... If they did it once, then it's possible. We could do it again. And Caldwell's older now.*

I sighed, raking my fingers through my hair. *But the Sedona Pack probably outnumbers Luke's with all the rapid growth Caldwell has been doing.*

He'd had two more Hopi men bitten during the last full moon. We still weren't sure if he was going to let them live. The probation month in the Sedona Pack was deadly for males. If they didn't commit their lives to the man who stole theirs, he'd kill them.

Obedience or death. Those were the choices for newly bitten males and females. I chose not to die, but obedience had never been my strong suit.

I waited for her answer.

We can't keep living like this.

She was right about that. I worried my lower lip. *This isn't forever. Talk soon.*

I logged out with no idea how I could fix this for us, only a burning desire that I would do whatever it took. Until I'd been bitten, I'd had some anger issues, but I'd never wished anyone dead.

Right now I didn't *wish* Caldwell dead. I promised myself he *would be*. Somehow.

Luke was making sandwiches as I closed the laptop. "You hungry?"

My stomach answered for me. Werewolves were almost always hungry. I chuckled. "Apparently, yes, I'm starving."

He glanced my way with a crooked grin that made my stomach flutter. "Good. Grilled ham and cheese all right?"

I nodded, marveling at how easy it was to be with him. Like we weren't werewolves on the run.

He put a frying pan on the stove top. "Is your sister okay?"

"For now." I wandered into the kitchen, keeping a healthy distance from him. Habit. "Is there any chance your Pack will help us? I've got to get her out of there."

It was my fault Isabelle and I were mixed up with the Pack in the first place. After I'd dated the wrong guy and ended up a werewolf, I'd dragged Isabelle into it, too. Biting her had been another mistake. She'd demanded it, but I could've refused. The truth was, I wanted my older sister with me. Somehow I'd clung to the hope that together we could do anything. Together we could escape.

But Caldwell always found us.

"I might have an idea." Luke's voice broke through my inner turmoil. "My Alpha wasn't a fan, and you probably won't be, either, but I think it's our best chance to get Isabelle and the others out."

"I'm listening." And also trying to keep my heart from pounding out of my chest.

"How many in your Pack are loyal to Caldwell?"

I frowned, scanning through Pack members' faces in my mind. "We're all obedient, but there are probably only two that are loyal. Bo and Blake. They're his right-hand men." My stomach soured. "Caldwell gave me to them. I'm their mate."

Luke shook his head, his expression stern as he turned

my way. "No, you're not. He may have forced you to be with them, but that makes you their prisoner, not their mate."

Something in his bright blue eyes was like a balm on my battered spirit. I swallowed the lump in my throat. "I can't be certain about a few of the other born wolves, but none of the bitten wolves have any deep loyalty to Caldwell."

"Born wolves?" He cursed under his breath. "Are you telling me he's having men bitten, too?"

I nodded. "Yeah. Rapid growth. They're bitten, and he gives them the ultimatum—obedience or death."

"Insane." Luke shook it off, pacing. "So he has numbers but not strength."

I shrugged. "He trains them all."

"That's not what I mean. A Wolf Pack is strong because we love each other. We argue sometimes, but when the chips are down, I never worry I'll be facing danger alone. They'd die for me, and I'd do the same for them. No questions asked. That's loyalty. It comes from love, not fear."

Damn. No wonder Caldwell hated this Pack. They made him seem pathetic.

"So they'll come down here to help you?"

He rolled a shoulder back, flipping the sandwich in the pan. "I told Adam not to send anyone."

I frowned. "Why?"

He glanced my way. "Because I think the best way to protect my Pack, and free yours, is to take out Caldwell. No one else has to die."

"You'll never get a chance." I shook my head. "He's always protected by Bo and Blake. And if he's got them training men, he'll have another Pack member on guard."

Luke nodded and put a sandwich on a plate. "That's why you're going to bring me to him."

My eyes widened. "Are you nuts?"

He put the plate in front of me. "Think about it. If you

bring me to Caldwell, you weren't running away, and if I was in Sedona because I was leaving my Pack, I'd have inside information for him. He'd be crazy not to take me in."

My pulse raced. "This is a suicide mission."

"No, it's not." He went back to the stove. "It's probably going to involve some hell, but I'm worth more to him alive than dead."

"And how are you going to get the chance to…take him out?"

Luke crossed to the closet; he took out a duffel and opened it, exposing a couple of handguns and ammunition. "I've also got a long-distance rifle stashed in the crawl space over the bedroom. I'll figure out his schedule and find a good sniper position."

I raised a brow. This was insane, but it could work. I met his eyes. "You'll only get one shot."

"That's all I'll need."

He was confident, I'd give him that. My mind raced through possible scenarios. Could I just waltz back into the Pack? They'd found the van, but that didn't mean they knew I'd been trying to run to Reno. The plan would probably hinge on how we played my return.

And when.

I swallowed a bite of the sandwich as Luke took a seat on the couch. "Tomorrow we have a Pack meeting at Caldwell's place. He'll have his hands full. I could show up and let him know I found you and you want to arrange a meeting."

Luke tensed. "I don't like sending you in there alone."

"It'll be more hostile if we show up together. I'm already a member of the Pack. He doesn't consider me a threat."

"Maybe." He nodded, his gaze turning toward the window. "What's the meeting about?"

I took another bite. The man cooked a mean grilled cheese. "One of the jaguar shifters from Nero is coming to inspect the Pack and plan the trip to Reno." I paused for a second and added, "Caldwell will want as many of us there as possible. There's no way he'll punish me for showing up." I glanced over at Luke. "This could work."

He met my eyes. "Do you know who Nero is sending?"

"Sebastian. He's—"

"Antonio Severino's son, heir to the entire Nero organization," Luke interrupted as he stood up. "Don't mention me in front of him."

I frowned. "You know him?"

He nodded. "Yeah. And there's a good chance he won't believe I'm joining this Pack. I don't want him tipping off Caldwell."

"I'll be careful." I finished my sandwich and got up to return the plate. Luke remained silent over by the window, and suddenly uneasiness seeped into my skin. I didn't want to stay here. Although he'd been nothing but kind to me, I didn't have a good track record with men.

But I didn't have anywhere else to go.

As if he could hear me, he grabbed his gloves off the counter and headed toward his bedroom. "We can't just hide in here and wait to see if they come for you." He came back out with a jacket, beanie, and gloves. "Put these on. Let's drive to the Grand Canyon. I've heard it's only a couple hours away. We can get there in time for the sunset."

I took the clothes, trying to come up with some excuse, but he smiled, and my defenses faltered.

"I've never seen the Grand Canyon." His eyes sparkled. "Have you?"

I chuckled, shaking my head. "Nope." I pulled on the beanie. "And maybe we can stop at a store so I can get some essentials, too."

He nodded, grabbing another jacket off the hook by the door. "Sure. There's a store in Flagstaff that should keep us far from your Alpha's reach, right?"

"I hope so." The truth was, I didn't know how Caldwell's powers worked. I only knew the last two times I tried to escape he found me before I got outside the city limits. We stopped at a store in Flagstaff, and I grabbed a toothbrush, hairbrush, and some lip balm. At the checkout, I hesitated, but Luke paid the bill, saving me from using my credit card.

Luke was…too good to be true. Where did this guy come from? I kept pinching myself just to be sure he was real. Half of me expected him to use his kindness as leverage against me.

We spent the rest of the drive talking about nothing, but it never seemed forced or awkward, and gradually, I started to forget that tomorrow morning I'd be facing Caldwell again.

He parked inside the gateway to the canyon, and we put on our coats and gloves. The wind bit at my cheeks, the gusts tugging at my ponytail.

Luke came around to my side of the car, chuckling. "Coming to see the Grand Canyon in winter was probably not my best plan."

I grinned. "We just need to get our blood pumping. See you at the lookout." I spun around and ran.

The cold air stung my eyes, but the strength in my legs, the speed—I couldn't describe the rush. Not with words. Running was one of the few times I didn't hate being a werewolf. I loved the power and freedom.

As I neared the scenic viewpoint, I slowed. Luke was right behind me. I bent over, fog puffing out of my mouth with every breath.

Luke chuckled beside me. "Good thing we're the only ones nuts enough to come out here today, or we'd have people pushing us to join the Olympic track team."

Shit. I straightened up. "Sorry. I forgot about being seen. I could've exposed us all."

He shook his head, his gloved hand catching my chin until I met his eyes. "Don't beat yourself up. We're fine." His lips curved into a smile. "And you were right, I'm not freezing my ass off anymore."

Just like that, he turned toward the canyon. I followed his gaze, and my heart pounded. There wasn't a giant neon sign or any fancy marker along the edge. It didn't need it. Right there before our eyes was a time machine. The layers of history were marked in the different gradations of color along the canyon, and words couldn't describe the size. "It's massive."

He nodded. "Postcards don't do it justice."

We walked a little closer to the rim, the wind getting more ferocious with each step. He sat on a bench, and I perched on the other end.

The gusts of wind assaulted my heightened senses. I caught the scents of rabbits, donkeys, coyotes, but the most distracting was Luke. He had a clean, natural scent. Masculine and a little rough.

"Makes our problems seem tiny, doesn't it?"

His voice jarred me from my thoughts. I nodded. "Yeah. This canyon was here long before I was bitten, and it'll be here way after I'm gone."

Luke peered over at me. "If Caldwell is having his Pack bite humans and changing them, he'd have to keep them off the grid until he was sure they could be trusted. That's got to be expensive. How does Caldwell fund this Pack?"

"He doesn't trust me with that information, but I know Nero has been sending us weapons. I inventory them at the bar after hours." I shrugged. "They could be giving him money, too."

"Damn it." Luke shook his head. "We had no idea this was going on down here."

He didn't say anything more. I glanced over at him, catching my hair to tuck it behind my ear. Even his profile was strong, honorable. I swallowed the lump in my throat. "Are you worried you won't find her?"

"My mate?" He met my eyes. "Honest answer? Yeah." He focused on the canyon again. "Last man standing in my Pack doesn't help."

"Does everyone find their mate eventually?"

He leaned forward, resting his elbows on his knees. "Most do, but not everyone." He paused, his voice dropping, but I had no trouble hearing him. Werewolf perk. "My uncle never found his mate. He ended up a bitter drunk."

I crossed my arms against the cold. "Do I have a mate out there, too, now?"

He straightened up, a crease in his brow. "I think so. I've never met a female werewolf who wasn't bitten by her mate, so I don't know for sure, but the wolf is alive inside you now, and she has the same instincts mine does."

"So I could touch some stranger and my wolf would decide he's the one?" I shuddered at the thought. "What if I hate him?"

Luke laughed. Deep and warm.

He looked my way. "You won't hate him. I've seen enough of my packmates find the other half of their soul. It's not always a smooth process, but fate hasn't messed up even once." He sobered, his eyes searching mine. "Whoever he is, he's lucky, and he doesn't even know it yet."

Chapter Four

Luke

She broke eye contact, choosing the canyon over looking at me. I stared at Raven's profile, the wind tugging at her dark hair. She was beautiful, intelligent, and resilient. She had to be to have survived this Pack and then escaped it.

And for a minute, I wished I could choose my mate. Raven.

Enough. I huffed out a breath, forcing my gaze in another direction. Wanting something didn't make it real. And even if choosing my own mate were an option, we had to free her sister and protect my Pack. Tough to focus if our wolves were distracted. I needed to let it go and trust my mate was out there, somewhere.

Time to change the subject. I cleared my throat. "So did you go to college before you were bitten?"

She shook her head. "No. I used to sew. I designed costumes for cosplay, mostly." She shrugged. "I guess I dreamed about being a costumer for a theater someday." Raven glanced over at me. "What about you? Any college?"

"Nah. I love working outside with the horses. Once I started at Adam's ranch, I knew that was my path."

She smiled. Damn. She blinded me for a second. Seeing her happy strengthened my resolve. I had to help her out of this Pack.

"I've gotta ask." Her eyes sparkled. "What's it like being Logan's twin brother? Do people mistake you for him?"

I rubbed my gloved hands down my thighs. "Back in Reno they do. I used to get a kick out of the groupies, but now…" I stared at the canyon. "One-night stands aren't as exciting anymore." I chuckled. "Damn, a few years ago I never would've *dreamed* I'd be saying that."

She laughed as her gaze locked on mine. "Thanks for bringing me here. I forgot life could be so…simple."

I reached over to grip her gloved hand. "You're not going to be in that Pack much longer. This is going to work."

I wasn't sure if I was trying to reassure her or myself, but either way, I intended to see it through. Caldwell was going down, one way or another.

…

The bright morning sun blinded me as I rounded the corner of Caldwell's street. We'd talked almost all night, but I didn't feel tired. My nerves were too jacked up to sleep anyway.

I pulled over, my gut twisting into a knot. "I don't like sending you in there alone."

Raven glanced over at me. "This is the best chance for me to slide back in without any retaliation for me disappearing. He'll be distracted with Sebastian around. It'll work."

"Text me after you talk to him." I broke eye contact, focusing out the front windshield. "And don't mention me around Sebastian."

"I won't." She got out and slammed the door.

I watched her walk away, but all I could think about was Sebastian Severino.

When my brother mentioned Sedona to Sebastian a few months ago, Sebastian shut it down, ignored it like it wasn't worth discussing.

But he was involved the entire time. I shouldn't have been surprised. Sebastian always looked down on werewolves as lessers, and Nero had been kidnapping women for over twenty years, converting them into jaguars and using them for their shifter breeding program.

But even so, this was lower than I thought Sebastian could stoop. Women bitten and used as breeding stock.

How did that bastard sleep at night?

Probably better than I did.

. . .

After I got back to the ranch, I grabbed a cup of coffee and called Adam. He answered on the first ring. "Luke? Everything all right?"

Loaded question. "Sebastian is in Sedona today."

"If Nero is involved with their Pack, that's to be expected. You're lying low, right?"

"Yeah." I stared at the ceiling. "Nero is funding Caldwell with weapons and most likely money, too. They're pushing them to grow the Pack. Fast."

"Grow the Pack, as in?"

I took a swallow. The coffee hit my stomach like a bitter pill. "They're biting men and women that Caldwell thinks are strong and making them werewolves."

"You have got to be fucking kidding me."

"Gets worse." I blew out a breath. "Caldwell has his eye on Reno. I think Nero isn't going to chance us killing any more of their mercenary teams. They're sending another Pack to avenge Damian's death instead."

Adam was quiet for a few seconds. "Doesn't sound like Sebastian will be any help to us this time."

"Looks like he's on the other side of the chessboard for now."

"How soon can you get back here? We need to prepare for what's coming."

I rubbed my forehead. "There's another problem."

His pitch dropped, the Alpha command coloring his tone. "This isn't *your* Pack. Not your responsibility. Come home. The sooner we beat them, the sooner we can help the bitten wolves."

I frowned, shaking my head, struggling to break free from my desire to please my Alpha. I yanked my phone from my ear, pulling up the goofy selfies Raven and I took at the Grand Canyon the day before. Raven's smile lit up the screen.

Focused again, I put the phone to my ear and cleared my throat. "You're right, I probably can't save them all on my own, but I won't turn my back on the *one* that asked for my help."

"This isn't a game. They will kill you."

"They don't even know I'm here yet."

"I'm coming down there."

I shook my head. "You need to stay in Reno. If they come for you, the Pack needs you there."

"You can't do this on your own."

"Fine." I sighed. "I'll call Logan. If we can take Caldwell out of the equation, the Pack will crumble."

Adam paused. "I already sent Sasha down your way. She should be there later today."

I got up, frowning. "I told you I could handle this."

"I didn't say you couldn't, but members of *my* Pack don't walk into danger without backup."

I set my coffee down and rubbed my forehead. "Does

Sasha understand the situation? If Nero's in town, they could recognize her. She used to work for them, remember?"

"Enough." Adam growled. "It's done. Sasha knows the risks. And they won't know she's there until it's too late." Adam paused. "Watch your ass and wait for backup, okay? I don't want to bring you home from Sedona in a body bag."

We ended the call, and I poured another cup of coffee. If I could figure out Caldwell's patterns, I could stake out a spot for a clear sniper shot without his Pack ever suspecting. This could work. Once I had an attack plan, Sasha could help me finish him.

All I needed to do was get on the inside.

...

My cell buzzed in my pocket as I walked down the barn aisle. I pulled it free, glancing at the screen. Raven had texted me a couple of hours ago to let me know she was all right, but I was still disappointed when it wasn't her name on my phone.

I clicked to answer. "Hey, Sasha."

"Hi, Luke. Just wanted to let you know I'm about an hour away. Is it safe for me to come by your place?"

"Yeah. I'll be here."

"Good. See you soon." The call ended.

I finished checking all the horses' water buckets and headed for my cottage. So far winter in Sedona had been mild. No real snow yet, but the wind was frigid. I flipped the collar up on my coat to cover my ears.

By the time Sasha knocked on my door, I had my feet up, watching TV, trying to keep my mind off worrying about Raven. I got up and clasped Sasha's forearm in the traditional Pack greeting before I stepped back to let her in. She used to be one of Nero's deadliest assets with a handgun, kill shot at thirty feet, but now she was Aren's mate and part of my

Pack. No doubt her defection to the Pack was a thorn in Antonio Severino's side. Most jaguar shifters didn't leave Nero voluntarily.

Sasha glanced around the room and back to me. "Nice place, Luke." She sat in a chair. "How's your new job?"

I took a seat and rested my elbows on my knees. "The job is great. Can't say the same for the werewolf Pack in Sedona."

"So I hear." She crossed her ankles and leaned back. "Did Adam tell you what I'm here for?"

I raised a brow. "He told me you were going to back me up if things went to shit."

She chuckled. "That works, too." Sobering, she went on. "Once you have the intel we need, I'm supposed to drag your ass back to Reno before you get yourself killed."

I shook my head slowly. "He doesn't think I can handle this."

"I don't think it's that at all." She straightened up. "I think he sees a lot of himself in you. Hotheaded and stubborn…"

I chuckled, shaking my head. "So he knows I won't come home until I see this through."

She nodded, the corners of her mouth curving slightly. "Exactly."

I stared at my hands. "He's right." Lifting my attention to her face, I went on. "Adam told me that while you worked for the Nero Organization, you found out they were kidnapping human women, biting them, and then using them to breed new jaguar shifters, right?"

"Yeah. Antonio Severino called it his breeding program." She frowned. "Why?"

"Because Caldwell is doing the same thing here. Maybe Severino turned him on to it. I don't know. But I've met one of the women, and I'm not turning my back on her. She and her sister are trapped here, and police aren't an option without exposing all of us."

Sasha stood, a muscle in her cheek tensing. "You're kidding me. Those bastards!" She shook her head. "At Nero they locked them up in the compound. What are they doing down here? Are bitten women wandering around Sedona?"

"Not exactly." My gaze followed her as she paced my small living room. "He must keep them someplace remote until he can be sure they'll obey him." I waited for her to look at me. "And it's not just women. Men are being bitten, too." I paused, waiting for her to meet my eyes. "I'm not leaving Sedona without them."

"This is bigger than you, Luke. We need Adam and the others."

"Not yet." I shook my head. "Just give me a few days. Right now, Raven is arranging a meeting for me with Caldwell." I lowered my voice. "All I know so far is they're building this Pack to take a trip to Reno."

Her back stiffened. "If we get down here first, we can ambush them on their turf and the kids will be safe back home in Reno."

"Or we take out Caldwell and end it without risking anyone in our Pack."

"Okay…that could work." She pondered my idea and slowly started to nod. "How can I help?"

Sasha was an amazing marksman with a handgun. She was the one who taught my brother and me, but I was deadlier with a long-distance rifle. Not even Sasha or Logan could match my aim.

"Just buy me some time with Adam."

She rested her hand on her hip. "And what are you going to be doing?"

"First I'm going to try to get accepted into this Pack, and once I have a better grip on how they function, I'm going to figure out when Caldwell is vulnerable. Whatever happens, the rapid growth for this Pack is going to stop."

Chapter Five

Raven

I leaned against the wall of Caldwell's living room, trying not to draw too much attention. My night with Luke hadn't changed anything. My sister was still with the Sedona Pack, and I was back under the same roof as Caldwell and Bo and Blake King.

But Luke had reminded me what my life used to be.

It made me want that back.

I would kick myself later for allowing hope to creep into my heart, but I couldn't help it.

Before the meeting got underway, Bo caught my arm in a vise grip and dragged me into one of the spare rooms.

He closed the door and came closer. "Where the fuck have you been?"

I jerked my arm free, eyes narrowing. "None of your business. I would've been back sooner if you hadn't stolen my van."

Without warning, he backhanded me. My teeth cut into

my lower lip, the copper tang of blood assaulting my senses. And at that moment, something snapped inside me. Maybe it was being with a guy who helped me remember who I really was, or maybe I just couldn't take any more of this asshole's abuse, but I lunged at him, my fist embedding itself into his eye. Hard.

He stumbled backward. "You bitch." Before he could come at me again, the door opened. His twin brother, Blake, filled the doorway. "Sebastian's here. We need you both in the living room."

Bo got up, glaring at me as he walked out. I started to follow, wiping blood from my mouth, but Blake didn't move.

"Another stunt like that, and I'll help my brother beat the fight out of you."

There was no threat of Blake morphing into a knight in shining armor. I straightened my clothes and brushed past him into the gathering of the Pack.

Allen Caldwell's desert-inspired custom home was a one of a kind, with a deck off the second story and a picture window downstairs that opened to a private view of the giant red mountains. A peace embraced my soul when I caught the sun rising or setting over the rocks and coloring the sky.

And just when it didn't seem like the landscape could get any more beautiful, snow would be dusting the mountaintops soon.

If Caldwell wasn't such a conniving asshole, I would love coming here for a visit. As it was, I tried to focus on the outdoor view instead of the room full of werewolves.

The Pack had been growing so rapidly, I didn't know the names of all the people in the room, and one was conspicuously missing. I scanned the room again, my chest constricting. Asher was part of the Hopi tribe and owned a small tour company in Sedona. He specialized in customized hiking excursions for out-of-towners and rock climbers. He knew the terrain and the mountains of Sedona better than anyone in the Pack.

That was why Caldwell had ordered him to be bitten.

But unlike the King brothers, Asher had a problem with following an Alpha with questionable intentions. I liked that about him.

He used to come into the Wolf Pack Bar for beers sometimes when he was still human. Maybe that was how Caldwell got him in his sights. Even after all day out hiking with the tourists, he always had a friendly smile for me when I worked behind the bar.

A couple of the born males—I didn't know what else to call them—tried to help Asher come to grips with his new situation, but maybe they were too late.

My gut twisted. Had Caldwell killed him already?

Speak of the devil. Caldwell strode into the room, his arm around Sebastian's shoulder and a politician's grin on his face. Isabelle was behind him, her gaze locking on mine as she entered the room.

Caldwell scanned the crowd. "Thank you all for being here."

As if we had a choice.

Sebastian rolled his shoulder, knocking Caldwell's hand off as he stepped into the center of the picture window. His dark gaze swept the room. He probably didn't recognize everyone, either. We had thirty in the room, and I would bet money Caldwell had a few newly bitten wolves under lock and key off the property.

Sebastian was a jaguar shifter, a little different from us. He'd shift into a huge jungle cat during the new moon, and while we had heightened hearing and sense of smell, he had better eyesight, and when he moved, you never heard a sound.

Not to mention he was one of the deadliest assassins in Nero's arsenal.

He was tall, with a commanding presence, but I'd also witnessed him fade away into a crowd. Anything to get his target. He made me nervous. His deep, articulate voice and perfect olive complexion drew you in, but unlike most people, his intentions were never clear. He had no tells. At least not that I'd ever seen.

His scan stopped at me, his gaze wandering over my face. My lower lip throbbed. It had to be swollen. I reached up to touch the corner of my mouth, checking my fingers. At least I wasn't still bleeding.

A fine crease marred Sebastian's brow. His lips flattened as he glanced toward Caldwell. "I was under the impression the women in your Pack were for breeding purposes only."

Caldwell forced another used-car-salesman grin. "Raven needed to be disciplined. I'm sure you understand."

A muscle contracted in Sebastian's cheek. "I will *never* understand a Pack of wolves." His eyes met mine again. "My father is not funding this project for dogs who attack someone smaller." His gaze cut to Caldwell. "The werewolves in Reno will be much more formidable opponents than one of your females."

Caldwell frowned, his eyes narrowing as he bared his teeth. "This is *my* Pack. If Antonio isn't happy with the way I run it, then you can tell him to shove it up his pompous ass."

The corner of Sebastian's mouth twitched, but he was otherwise unfazed by Caldwell's expression of dominance. "My father is eager to move the project forward and avenge Damian's death. Do you have a projected date to travel to Reno?"

Until now, hearing Bo and Blake mention moving on Reno hadn't really meant anything. I didn't understand the stakes, but now…they were plotting to kill Luke's family, his Pack. I pressed my lips together and stayed silent, paying attention to every word.

"I can't plan that until I know more about the Pack we're facing. I assumed that was why you called this meeting. Do you have anything for me beyond, 'they live in Reno'?"

Sebastian nodded slowly. "There are seven males and six females. There are elders in their Pack as well, but they're insignificant to the cause. If they stay out of the way, they can live. The children will be collected by my father for transfer to Nero."

"We outnumber them at least two to one." Caldwell chuckled. "We'll kill the men, and the women will become part of my Pack. Spoils of war."

Sebastian's chin rose slightly, that crease growing between his eyebrows again. "Your only mission is to wipe out the males of the Pack."

"I'm not one of your father's assets. I'm his equal. I agreed to help him accomplish his objective for a price, and I'll hold up my end of that bargain. Adam Sloan will die. What I choose to do beyond that is none of your concern."

I tried not to vomit.

Sebastian crossed his arms. "I think you are sorely underestimating the battle you will face. Adam Sloan's Pack will lay down their lives to protect him and their women. And the women in the Pack are formidable, strong psychics, and two are jaguar shifters, one trained by Nero. This won't be an easy fight."

"Did you come here to insult me?"

"That was not my sole purpose in coming here." Sebastian almost smiled. "But if this mission is going to succeed, you can't go in overconfident."

"We're ready. If they've only got seven men including their Alpha, we've got them outnumbered. They won't stand a chance."

"Very good." Sebastian sobered. "One more thing. The Alpha's mate is *not* to be harmed. I will come for her and her children."

Caldwell raised a brow. "It's not like Antonio to choose a favorite like that. Does he want her for himself?"

Sebastian's lip curled, repulsed. "No."

"And you're not going to tell me why this woman is so important to him?"

Sebastian headed for the door. "Just follow your orders." He stopped and turned back. "And if you want the payments to continue, keep your wolves in check. They should practice fighting each other, not the women in their care."

The door clicked shut behind him, and for a moment, you could hear a pin drop.

Caldwell broke the silence with a hiss. "Arrogant bastard." He shook his head and scanned the Pack. "The sooner we get this done, the sooner I can tell Antonio's son to kiss my ass."

He went to the wet bar while we all remained cautiously silent. "Blake, Bo, I want you to train the new wolves. They need to work on their tracking. And get Asher to show them how to move silently."

So Asher was still alive. For now.

"Jett, you take over rifleman training."

He didn't reply, only nodded. I didn't know Jett well, but I'd heard rumors his twin brother died in some project at Nero. I wasn't sure how Jett survived. Maybe no one knew. He had blue eyes and a chiseled jaw, but he was distant. In the three months since Bo bit me, I'd never witnessed Jett smile.

But I had seen him shoot. He was scary deadly.

Luke popped into my head. Maybe I could still convince him to get out of Sedona. Maybe he could warn his Pack to leave town. With any luck, they could circle back for us while Caldwell was in Reno.

"Deacon and Dex, you two are in charge of getting all our males into fighting shape. If we end up in a hand-to-hand fight, I expect our Pack to win."

They were both black belts in more than one martial art, not to mention Deacon was moving into mixed martial arts. My stomach twisted in knots for Luke's Pack. If they only had seven males, they'd be outnumbered, probably outgunned, and if Deacon and Dex could train the others to fight like them...the Pack from Reno didn't stand a chance.

Caldwell wheeled around toward my sister. "Isabelle, stay here. I have a special project for you."

Her eyes locked on mine. I slid my hand into my pocket, fingertips brushing the top of my phone. She gave an almost imperceptible nod, but I knew she'd gotten the message. I'd relay all this info to Luke. Unless we wanted to be trapped in this Pack like broodmares, we were taking a side, and it wasn't going to be with Allen Caldwell.

The meeting was over before lunch, and the Pack dispersed to take on their new assignments. Mine was nothing new. Bartending at the Wolf Pack Bar was my life now, but hopefully not for much longer. I texted Luke to meet me at Costco. I needed to go there for supplies for the bar, so no one would suspect anything. I could tell him about the meeting with Sebastian and convince him that my plan for him to go back and warn his Pack to get out of Reno would be safer. He would be safer.

He could circle back for the rest of us. None of this was his problem, anyway.

I didn't usually primp for my daily Costco trip for the bar, but I passed it off as trying to cover the new bruise on my jaw. Bo and Blake seemed fine with it. They were spending the rest of the day training the male bitten wolves to use their new senses to track others, so I'd be able to go to the store alone.

Besides, they weren't worried I might run again. If I didn't check in at the bar, Caldwell would "reach out," as he called it. And he added a caveat this time.

If I ran again, he'd hurt my sister.

But I was planning to be right where I was supposed to be.

Without a spy camera, Caldwell would never know I was also talking to Luke.

And given the bad news I was about to dump on him, I doubted Luke would even notice the mascara and lip gloss I was wearing. I should *not* be excited about this meeting.

Didn't change that I was.

"I'm making the Costco run and then heading straight to the bar."

Bo shouted back, "Allen will be waiting for you there."

I rolled my eyes at his extremely old news and grabbed my purse. Caldwell was *always* at the Wolf Pack Bar, which was why I had been assigned a job there. He liked having me close. Or he liked that I loathed it. Either way, I was stuck.

For now. But finally there was a tiny light at the end of the tunnel, a spark of hope for a new future.

I parked at Costco and checked myself in the rearview mirror. Since becoming a werewolf, I healed faster. It wasn't like X-Men fast, but in two days, my swollen lip would probably be gone, and tomorrow the discoloration would be history. No one would guess a big, angry werewolf asshole smacked me.

Outside my car, the smell of the hot dog cart overwhelmed me. My stomach growled as I struggled to sift through the assault on my heightened senses.

Once the scent of meat was cataloged, I caught bubble gum, hair spray, hand lotion, and… A smile tugged at my lips. Werewolf.

Luke was already here someplace. I grabbed a cart and

dropped my purse in the front seat while I scanned the area. Nothing. I flashed my card as I entered, and his scent teased my nostrils. Fresher. Stronger. The closer I got to the paper products, the more I tied the unique smell to the werewolf from Reno. There was a musk about him, mixed with alfalfa and…molasses?

The horse stable.

The second I rounded the corner, Luke turned, and my breath caught. His blue eyes were piercing, his smile so handsome it was dangerous. I broke eye contact only to notice the way his jeans fit just right and his T-shirt strained to cover the defined muscles along his shoulders and torso.

I rolled up next to him, a million things to tell him, but all I could muster was, "Hi."

"Hi." His gaze wandered over my face, his smile fading. "Are you all right?"

Apparently my makeup couldn't cover up the swelling in my lower lip. I nodded. "Yeah."

He shook his head, his body tense. "Who did this?"

His voice rumbled, more of a growl.

I raised a brow. "Before you go all raging werewolf, you should see the other guy." A smile teased my lips. "He didn't expect me to fight back."

He pulled in a slow breath. "I never should have sent you in there alone."

"Enough." I rested my hand on my hip. "I need your help, not your protection."

He ran his hand back through his hair with a grudging nod. "Packs aren't supposed to attack each other."

"I think it's pretty clear, this isn't a normal Pack." I broke eye contact, resorting to reaching for an industrial-size bag of bar napkins. "I have a lot to tell you."

He took the bag from me and placed it in the cart. "All right."

"Is it true your Pack only has seven males including you?"

He frowned, crossing his arms. "Of my generation. My dad and Jason and Jared's dad are still in the Pack, too."

"Can they still fight?" I reached for a box of folded hand towels, but he caught my arm. The warmth of his touch burned through my shirtsleeve, my heart racing in answer. I met his eyes.

His tone was deep and low, so humans wouldn't overhear us. "What did Sebastian tell you at the Pack meeting?"

I swallowed the lump in my throat. "We have you outnumbered at least two to one. Our newly bitten males are being trained to track, shoot, and fight." His expression darkened, but he didn't say a word. "Caldwell wants to kill the men in your Pack and bring the females back to Sedona to be mated as he sees fit. Except for the Alpha's wife and all the children. Sebastian said they're not to be harmed. He's taking them back to Nero."

That shook him. Luke stepped back a couple of paces. "Shit." He met my eyes again. "Did Sebastian say why he wanted the kids and Lana?"

"Not that I remember."

"When will you start being missed?"

I checked my phone. "If I'm not at the bar in an hour, Caldwell will reach out to find me."

"All right." He stretched up to grab the hand towels, treating me to a nice view of his biceps. When he turned toward me again, heat rose up my neck. God, when was the last time I blushed? He made it so easy to remember being human, being me.

He started to smile. "I don't think I told you before, but you're beautiful."

I chuckled, trying to brush off the compliment, but the truth was, when he said it, I believed him. "Pretty sure I've looked better when I'm not sporting a split lip."

We finished loading up my cart with essentials and bar snacks. So weird, but being with him didn't feel awkward. I wasn't constantly on the defensive. Being with him…for the first time in a few months, I felt safe, valued even.

He left me at the checkout line. "I'll meet you at your car."

I frowned. "You don't know what I drove."

"But I know how you smell. I'll find you." His crooked grin made my knees weak.

I spent the rest of my wait in line bolstering my emotional defenses. This was no time for infatuation. There was real danger, and I needed to make him understand. He should go back to Reno and warn them. If they were ready, or even better if they left Reno, they'd have a chance. Plus, it was the best hope for the women of this Pack to escape this hell.

By the time I got back to the white minivan and lifted the hatchback, he was right there, helping me load the flats of supplies.

"You're fast."

His eyes sparkled. "I've been a wolf longer than you have."

I nodded, reminding myself of my plan. "You really need to go back and warn your Pack. I don't know when Caldwell will be headed your way yet, but I could text you once I hear something. Maybe you can convince them not to be in town when Caldwell comes calling."

"I'm not turning my back on you and your sister. If I can get Caldwell to accept me into this Pack, I can find his weak point." He paused. "Did you tell him you found me and I wanted a meeting?"

A pit festered in my stomach as I shook my head. "No."

He leaned against the bumper, obviously collecting himself. I could almost smell his frustration. "That's why he hit you, wasn't it? You wouldn't tell them where you were."

"It wasn't Caldwell who smacked me." I crossed my arms. "But none of that matters. I can't let you get messed up in this snake pit, Luke. This Pack isn't *your* problem. I don't want you risking your life."

I steeled myself and choked out, "Go warn your Pack and find your mate. Hopefully your Pack can defeat Caldwell, or at least avoid him, and we'll all get out of here without messing up your life, too."

He straightened, his jaw tight. "Sounds like you've got it all figured out."

"It's the safest for everyone." He didn't look convinced. I lowered my hands to my sides. "The last thing I need is another wolf going all Alpha on me. Please go. Be smart, not brave."

I reached for the handle on the van just as he did.

And the world tilted on its axis.

His rough hand covered mine, skin to skin, and somewhere in the shadows of my soul, my wolf howled. The sound deafened me from inside out. I lost my balance, but he caught me before I fell. Staring up at him, my vision blurred as my pupils dilated and contracted. His scent filled my lungs. And from the core of my being, every part of me recognized him.

Mine.

I opened my mouth to say something, but no words came. It didn't make sense. I barely knew him. But none of that mattered. On a primal level, there were no doubts.

His eyes searched my face, and finally he bent to kiss me. I wrapped my arms around his neck, clinging to him like a lifeline as my lips parted, our tongues tangling until I moaned into him. He tightened his hold on me, and his heart pounded like a sledgehammer in my sensitive ears. He felt it, too.

Whatever *it* was.

He growled against my lips and stumbled backward.

I struggled to catch my breath, unable to tear my gaze off his. "What the hell was that?"

"Fuck." He ran his hand down his face, chest heaving. His throat bobbed as he swallowed hard. "I'm not going anywhere. I can't let you go back there alone."

I frowned. "You don't have a choice."

"You're right, I don't."

I shook my head, completely confused.

He took a slow breath, his voice deep and dangerous. "I can't get you and your sister out yet, so I'm going in. I'm not leaving Sedona without you."

"No." My pulse raced at breakneck speed. "They'll kill you."

"Only if they think I'm still with the Pack in Reno."

At the moment the only thing I cared about was keeping him safe. I'd survived in this Pack so far; I could hang on a little longer. "It's too risky. You're not thinking straight."

He caressed the edge of my jaw, the simple touch sending tingles through my entire body. "They will never hurt you again."

"Luke, this is nuts." Just the thought of them killing him was making me physically ill. "Please."

He kissed my forehead and whispered, "You're my mate, Raven." When he moved back, intensity darkened his eyes. "And if any of them ever try to touch you again, they'll have to kill me first."

That was exactly what I was afraid of.

Chapter Six

Luke

From the passenger seat of her van, I could tell Raven wasn't happy with my decision to come with her. She didn't look at me, and her grip on the steering wheel was impressive.

I sighed. "You felt it, right? The pull of the wolf, the web of instinct and destiny weaving between us." I shook my head. "It pisses me off that those dicks hit you, but now..." I blew out a breath. "I can't explain it in words. I *need* to protect you from that. Your safety is all that matters."

She turned my way. "You know what drew me to you before we ever touched?"

I wanted to say my good looks, but I got the feeling she wasn't in the mood for humor. Plus, she wasn't really asking.

Her head bumped the headrest as she stared up at the roof. "When I'm with you, I feel like *me* again. The real me, not this werewolf I got turned into." Her dark eyes pinned me in my seat. "Please don't turn into one of them. I'm not a thing to be possessed or protected. I'm Raven Wood. You're the one who helped me remember that."

I ground my teeth, struggling to think before I spoke. "You're not seriously putting me into the same category as that excuse for a Pack you're stuck in, are you?"

"No." She faced forward again. "But it's a really fine line. And it goes both ways."

"What does?"

She let go of the wheel, her hands dropping into her lap. "I want to protect you, too. And I know these guys better than you do. If you ride in this van and go to the bar with me, Caldwell is going to kill you." Her gaze rose to my face. "I've managed to stay alive for the past three months. I can take care of myself. What I need is help getting me and my sister out. You should focus on that and keep yourself safe in the process."

I fucking hated that what she said made sense. I was thinking with my heart, so damned stoked to have finally found my mate, that I wanted every wolf in the world to know she was mine.

But she wasn't a trophy to put on a shelf.

And as much as it killed me to think one of those assholes might touch her, I'd be no use to her dead.

I cleared my throat, searching for my voice. "There's a good chance you might be smarter than me."

That almost made her smile. "Nah, I just like being around you while you're still breathing." She glanced my way. "I'm pretty selfish like that."

I laughed. She amazed me. Changed into a shifter against her will, stuck in a sick Pack, and through it all, my mate made me laugh.

Years of searching, worrying I'd never find her. And she was worth every minute of it all.

I reached across to caress her cheek; my fingers slid into her hair as I drew her closer. This time, my lips brushed hers slowly, savoring the softness, drinking in every shared breath, until my blood pulsed below my belt. I'd never been so turned on by a simple kiss.

But nothing about this was going to be simple.

I straightened, basking in the smile spreading across her face. God, she was a miracle.

And we needed one. I rubbed my hand down my face. "I can't focus." I barely knew her, but I wanted the chance to change that. "Okay, first off, drive back with the windows down. I don't want you in danger because they caught my scent in your van."

She nodded, starting the van. The windows lowered as she glanced my way. "I'll text you everything I know about Caldwell's schedule. We need to hurry. He said he had a special project for Isabelle. I don't want to think about what that could mean."

"We'll get her out." She didn't respond, so I went on. "Adam sent me some backup, so we're not alone in this. I'll check in with Sasha and call Adam and let him know about your Pack numbers and Sebastian's plans for Lana and the kids." I took her hand, and her fingers laced with mine. "And we need to figure out when to tell Caldwell I want to join his Pack."

She tightened her hold. "I'll work on it…"

"Make it soon. I can't let you go home with those bastards tonight." I needed her with every fiber of my being. The idea of letting her drive away in a few minutes was already tearing me up inside. "Text me."

If I didn't get out of the van now, I'd never let her go. I dropped her hand and opened the door. I slammed it shut and rested my forearms on the open window. "I didn't think I'd ever find you."

A barely there smile curved her lips, almost shy. "Sorry my Pack is trying to kill yours."

I chuckled, shaking my head. "Those assholes are *not* your Pack. I'll prove it to you when we go back to Reno. They're going to love you."

She gripped the wheel, facing forward, but her words were plain. "I wish I didn't have to drive away. Be safe."

I stepped back, and the van rolled toward the exit. Clenching my fists, I struggled to keep from chasing her down, watching her until the taillights vanished down the street.

She was going to be pissed when I showed up in the bar tonight, but Bo and Blake were never going to touch her again. Ever.

• • •

By the time I got back to the ranch, my entire body ached. My muscles were tight; the rush of finding my mate had mutated into a bitter rage that I'd let her go back to that twisted Pack. I went into my cottage and hit Adam's number on my phone.

"Hey, Luke."

"I found her."

A pause. I waited.

I didn't understand how my Alpha's Pack instincts worked, but he'd seemed to know when Jason bit Kilani and brought her into our Pack. I hadn't bitten Raven, so I had no clue if he'd still be able to connect her to me. I was about to find out.

The Alpha push filled his voice. "Your mate." Another pause. "Bring her home."

I started to smile. "That's my plan."

He hesitated. "She's already a wolf."

I nodded, even though he couldn't see me. "Yeah."

The pacing began on the other end of the line. "She's in that Pack. You have got to be shitting me, Luke. Don't do anything until I get there."

I shook my head. "You can't come down here." I sobered, leaning forward on the chair. "This Pack outnumbers us by two to one, and Caldwell is training them as we speak. Sebastian filled them in on our numbers. Caldwell is anxious to finish his commitment to Severino."

"They're coming for us."

"Yeah." I sighed. "And couple odd things. Sebastian didn't tell Caldwell about my dad or Wyatt. They were both in Caldwell's Pack when they went to Nero for Operation Moonlight. He would have remembered them. Why would Sebastian not mention them?"

Adam was slow to respond. "With Sebastian there's always a reason, but we probably won't find out until it's too late."

"He also told them Lana and all the Pack children aren't to be touched. He's planning on taking them back to Nero."

"Like hell he is." The pacing stopped. "What about the rest of the women?"

I swallowed the bile in my throat. "Caldwell is going to mate them to men in his Pack."

"He's going to *what*?"

"He doesn't think fate chooses mates, he thinks the Alpha makes that choice."

"So he's fucking insane."

"You called it." A sad chuckle escaped my lips. "I have a plan, but you're not going to like it." I took a breath. "I've got my rifle and my scope, and I'm going to take Caldwell out, but I've got to find the right angle."

"Does she know she's your mate? She believes it?"

I frowned, surprised by the turn in the conversation. "Yeah. We both felt it when I touched her hand."

"Then she'll protect you with her life."

I hadn't given it that much thought. "I guess so?"

"I know you want to go in and save her, but you need to

keep in mind it goes both ways. Kilani took a bullet for Jason."

"I remember."

"So before you do something crazy, think about that. If you walk into danger, you won't be walking alone."

I groaned. "You're saying if I put myself in a risky situation, I'm putting her in the sights, too."

"Sucks. But yes. She's already a wolf. Everything you're feeling about protecting her, she's got the same urges toward keeping *you* safe."

I rubbed my forehead, trying to slow my thoughts from spinning. "Caldwell has her staying with these brothers, and one of them smacked her around. I can't leave her in there alone."

He didn't fight me. His tone softened. "How are you going to protect her without getting killed?"

"All I can think of is to convince them I've turned my back on my family and my Pack. I'll give them some intel, gain Caldwell's trust, beat the shit out of the two brothers, and prove I'm her mate. Then once I find the right spot, I'll take out my target."

"Does Sasha know about your plan? She can be your backup shot."

"I don't know if Sebastian is still around, or anyone else from Nero, and if they recognize her, my cover's blown. Sasha's my last resort. I'm not pulling her into this shitstorm unless I have to." I shook my head. "I can do this on my own, Adam. I'm not the baby of the Pack anymore. Trust me."

"I do trust you. I just don't want anything to happen to you."

I stared at the ceiling. "I'll be careful, and Raven will be watching my back."

"Raven. Pretty name."

I nodded. "She's amazing. And when this is over, I'll bring her home."

"Keep me posted daily. If I don't hear from you, Sasha's going to drag your ass out. No lone wolves in my Pack. Understand?"

I chuckled. "Yeah. Talk to you tomorrow."

Since my day on the ranch didn't start until after lunch today, I didn't climb up onto Sabrina's back until just after five o'clock.

I'd gotten a text from Raven about an hour ago. Caldwell took the deposit from the bar to the bank on Mondays, Wednesdays, and Fridays, but the Monday trips he took alone. She said the times varied, but usually he waited until four o'clock in the afternoon. Good information, but not enough.

While I worked the mare in the arena, I tried to focus, but it was tough with my wolf so close to the surface. Our mate needed us—we should be with her, protecting her. My pure animal instincts didn't understand our mate was capable of watching out for herself.

I pushed Sabrina into an extended trot, the cold air stinging my face. As we came around the far end, Gabby stood at the other, leaning on the railing. She smiled as we passed by, and I tipped my head. On the second pass, she was still there in spite of the temperature dropping. Shit. I was going to have to be social.

Sabrina slowed to a walk as Gabby called out, "You're working late today."

I nodded, patting the side of the mare's neck. "Yeah, I didn't get started as early as I usually do."

"She's going to kick ass at the Carousel charity show in March."

"That's the plan." I rode Sabrina out of the ring toward the barn, and Gabby followed.

When I jumped down, Gabby was right there, closer than

I intended. I glanced her way. "Sorry about that."

As I inched past her to lift the reins over Sabrina's head, Gabby's hand touched my back. I tensed, turning slowly.

She stared up at me, her teeth working her lower lip. "So I was wondering if you wanted to go out for some coffee. My treat."

Funny how your life could change in an instant. A week ago, I might've taken her up on the offer, but today…nothing was going to keep me away from the Wolf Pack Bar and Raven.

"Sorry. I already have plans."

She raised a brow. "That didn't take long." My confusion must've been written all over my face because she added, "Good-looking single guys get snagged fast in Sedona."

I chuckled, handing off Sabrina to the groom. "Not sure what to say to that, but I appreciate the offer."

Her expression brightened a little. "Rain check?"

Shit. I hadn't meant to give her hope. "We'll see." I turned to the ranch hand with the wheelbarrow. "Be sure Sabrina gets cooled out before you put her away."

He nodded. When I looked back, Gabby was already on her way up to the main house. "Catch you later, Luke."

"Will do."

After a shower and a quick change of clothes, it was about eight o'clock when I parked at the Wolf Pack Bar. I should've sent Raven a text to let her know I was coming, but I knew she'd try to talk me out of it. Adam had already tried.

If my Alpha couldn't force his will on me, no one was going to change my course.

I got out of my Mustang and headed for the door. The Wolf Pack Bar was just out of the tourist district, a little ways back from the road. Since I'd been lying low in Sedona, this would be my first time inside. I didn't know what to expect. A public bar was bound to be full of humans, but I had no way of knowing for sure. If I opened the door and found myself surrounded, I had my story ready. As long as they bought it, I'd be in.

The tricky part would be not killing the asshole who hit my mate.

One problem at a time.

I pulled the door open.

Three werewolves. Raven looked up from behind the bar. I broke eye contact with her and focused on the other two at the bar stools. They got to their feet but didn't attack. Thankfully there were a handful of humans in the bar, too. They couldn't kill me first and ask questions later with witnesses in the bar. The two were clearly twin brothers, and one had a swollen, purplish eye.

My wolf growled, a deep, dangerous rumble from the darkest pits of my soul. The fire followed, smoldering as he came closer. This had to be the one who smacked Raven. My hands balled into fists.

The clean-shaven, uninjured brother spoke first. "This is a private club."

I glanced at the humans and back to meet his eyes. "I'm here to find Allen Caldwell."

The brothers shared a look, and the other one grunted. "You're new around here."

"Wow." I cocked a brow. "You're a genius."

He lurched forward, but his brother caught him. "Go sit down, Bo. I got this one."

I was going to beat the shit out of Bo.

His brother turned to me again, lowering his voice so the humans wouldn't be able to hear him over the music. "You're on the Sedona Pack's territory. We could kill you and no one would ever find the body."

I rolled my right shoulder, loosening my muscles. "You could *try*."

He laughed. I didn't.

He sobered. "Get out of here. We don't want whatever you're selling."

"Tell Caldwell Nick Reynolds's son is here. I'm pretty sure he'll want to talk to me."

He tried to stare me down. I waited him out. Finally he broke eye contact and stormed through a door to the back. I made my way farther inside, leaning my forearms on the edge of the bar. Bo was two stools down. I sized him up. He was about my height. Definitely a gym rat. I got my strength from moving hay bales and wheelbarrows.

No built-by-Bowflex body could compete with power that came from muscles forged from hard labor.

He glared at me, but before I could respond, Raven was in front of me. "What would you like to drink?"

Her get-the-hell-out-of-here expression was loud and clear. I pretended not to notice. "What do you have on tap?"

She focused on the taps. "Blue Moon, Howling Wolf, Red Wolf, White Wolf, Yellow Wolf, Wolf Ale, and Heineken."

"You guys really live up to your name."

She still didn't smile. "They don't call us the Wolf Pack Bar for nothing."

"Heineken. Thanks."

Her eyes lingered on mine for a second before she turned away, and suddenly Bo was right beside me. "Don't get any ideas. She belongs to me."

My gaze bored into his. "Did she give you that black eye?"

He shoved me, but I was ready for it. He wasn't. When I pushed back, he smacked the bar stool and tumbled backward onto the floor. He scrambled to his feet and started for me but stopped after only a couple paces.

I frowned, then the scent hit me. Another wolf. I turned around to find my father's first Alpha, Allen Caldwell, and he didn't look happy.

"Bo, if you break another stool I'm going to shove it up your ass. Are we clear?"

"Yes, sir." He righted the stool as Caldwell stepped forward.

"So little Nicky found a mate and had cubs."

"Yeah." I crossed my arms, hoping he'd take my rapid heartbeat as an aftereffect of my rumble with Bo and not for the lies I was about to tell. "Yeah. He and my brother are still with the Pack in Reno."

He raised a silver brow. "And why aren't you?"

"The Reno Pack killed Damian Severino. Nero is obviously coming for them, but they're pretending to be busy with their new families like it's business as usual. They're soft. I want to be on the winning side."

He grinned, clearly impressed with my lack of faith in my family and Pack. "So you're a *smart* boy."

Caldwell came closer, and Raven set my beer on the bar.

She cleared her throat. "That's five bucks."

I met her eyes, gathering strength, although her expression was less than happy.

Caldwell glanced her way. "This place needs to be emptied in five minutes. Cash everyone out and send Alexandra and Mike home."

Raven's attention flicked my way before she hustled out from behind the bar. While she made an excuse about a gas leak in the kitchen, Caldwell's gaze settled on me. "You have Nick's eyes. I heard about Malcolm's death."

I nodded slowly, not trusting myself to speak. I was prepared to lie my ass off, but I couldn't talk smack about Adam's father, our previous Alpha. Malcolm had been one of the best men I'd ever known, like a second father to me. And because of Nero, he wasn't here to defend himself.

Caldwell leaned on a stool, shaking his head. "I warned him not to make Nero an enemy, but I guess we both know who was right now."

I ground my teeth and glanced away. Raven stared at me, her lips tight. I cleared my throat and forced myself to engage again. "I'm not looking to repeat that mistake."

"You're a wise wolf." A dangerous spark lit in Caldwell's eyes. "I'm no fool, either."

The human waitress waved at Raven. "See you tomorrow."

The cook and the final couple followed her out of the bar.

Caldwell nodded to Blake, and he locked the doors behind them. "Lower the shades and call the males over here."

His tongue ran along his white teeth as he focused on me again. "You understand, I'll need to test your loyalty and obedience. If you drew the short straw to come to Sedona to spy, I'll find out."

He leaned closer, his freshly minted breath filling my nostrils. "And then I'll kill you."

Chapter Seven

Raven

"Oh, please, you've bitten human men to grow your Pack, and now a *real* wolf knocks on your door and you threaten to kill him?" All eyes were on me, and although I knew I would pay for getting involved, I couldn't stop myself.

I couldn't let them kill Luke.

As nuts as it sounded, they'd have to get through me first, and frankly, after the past three months with these bastards, I didn't have a lot to live for anyway.

Caldwell cocked a brow, and Bo snapped to action. He came at me like a freight train, but I was ready. Under the bar towel, I gripped a beer bottle. As he reached for my arm, I whacked him in the head. Glass shattered, a couple pieces catching the side of his face, leaving a bloody trail. The sudden stench of beer and blood assaulted me.

In a split second, Luke was between me and Bo. He shouted over his shoulder, "Get out of here, Raven."

Caldwell glared at me. "Seems you two have already met."

Shit. I held a hand out to Luke. "I'm not leaving without you."

"I'll be fine." He passed his phone back. "Press nine. Go."

I had no clue what he was talking about, but I jammed the phone in my pocket.

Bo got up, and Luke shook his head slowly. "You should've just stayed down."

"Fuck you." Bo wiped blood off his face. "I told you before, asshole, she's *my* mate. Butt the hell out."

He started toward me, but Luke blocked his path.

Caldwell growled. "You want to be a part of this Pack, boy, you live by our rules."

Bo came around Luke and grabbed my arm. I struggled to break free, but his grip was solid. He shoved me toward Caldwell. Luke narrowed his eyes, his shoulders tight as he stepped into Bo's path again.

Oh, shit. Did the mate thing come with telepathy or anything useful? I tried to send him the message to stay out of it. I could handle this.

He either didn't hear or was beyond caring. "Let her go," he growled.

Bo shook me a little for show.

Luke did the opposite. He hit Bo so hard in the jaw the blowhard lost his hold on me and flew backward, crashing down on one of the round cocktail tables. The rest happened so fast, it almost blurred together.

Bo got up, and Luke shoved him down again. Blake came through the back door with Asher, Deacon, and Dex. Ryker followed behind them. I grabbed a bar stool and swung it at Blake. The legs snapped, but the force of the blow knocked him back into the others.

I yelled to Luke, "Let's go!"

He forced himself back from Bo's bloody face, and we pivoted toward the door. Blake jumped Luke from behind, grabbing him around the waist. They fell to the ground, grappling. Luke threw his elbow back into Blake's ribs, then spun around, nailing him in the nose.

My skin crawled with the urge to run. Since becoming a werewolf, I'd never been exposed to this much blood. The wolf inside me crept closer to the surface. Survival instincts took over. I kicked, scratched, bit, and punched anyone who touched my mate.

We scrambled for the door, only to find Ryker blocking it. Ryker had been bitten a couple months before me, and it was easy to see why Caldwell chose him. He was massive.

Ryker clenched his fists, ready for battle. He rushed Luke, but Luke dodged to the right, sweeping his leg and landing a solid blow to his temple as he went down. Ryker lay motionless on the floor.

Caldwell rose from his stool, his tone calm and cold. "Deacon and Dex, grab Raven."

"What?" I smacked Deacon, stunning him for a second, but Dex got my left wrist, and no amount of struggle loosened his hold. I tried to shove Deacon back, but with only one hand, he barely moved except to pin my arm behind my back.

"Let her go!" Luke shouted, turning to punch Dex in the side.

Suddenly a cool blade was on my throat. Instinctively, I stopped struggling. Caldwell wasn't young anymore, but he was still damned fast. He stood right behind me with a knife pressed against my skin until a bead of blood trickled down my neck.

"Enough." Caldwell growled. "You hit my men one more time, and I slit her throat."

Ryker groaned, slowly getting up.

"You've got me." Luke opened his fists. "She doesn't need to be involved."

Caldwell looked between us and wet his lips. "I have

something better in mind. Asher, take his right arm. Ryker, the left. If he resists, sadly I'll have to kill Raven."

Luke offered them his wrists, his eyes never leaving Caldwell's face. "I'm not resisting. Let her go."

"I'm still not certain whether you're a spy, but judging by the way your hearts are both racing in perfect unison, I'm willing to bet you've touched our little Raven."

"I don't know what you're talking about." I did my best to hide my true feelings, but Caldwell had been an Alpha longer than I had been alive. He could hear my pulse and probably smell my panic at seeing Luke restrained and at their mercy. "I just didn't want to see another wolf killed. That's *all*."

"Is it now? Really?" He tipped his head toward Bo. "How about evening up the score?" To Luke, he lowered his voice. "If you fight back, Raven dies."

Bo's smile was lopsided, making him look even more twisted. He loosened up his shoulders and stepped in closer. Suddenly he slammed his fist into Luke's jaw; the scent of his blood sent my wolf into a rampage. I kicked my foot back, burying my heel into Caldwell's groin, and stomped on Deacon's foot.

Caldwell bent forward, shouting, "Blake!"

The Alpha's right hand man drew his Glock and tugged the slide back. Everyone froze. The barrel was aimed directly at Luke.

Caldwell narrowed his eyes, speaking through clenched teeth. "You will watch this and act like a *lady*, or we'll finish this with a bullet in his head."

I swallowed the bile rising up my throat.

He raised his voice. "I want to see you nod, Raven. I need to know you understand that if I kill him right now, it's *your* fault."

My eyes welled with hot tears as I stared at Luke and nodded slowly.

"Good girl." He replaced the knife at my neck and focused on Luke. "If you don't want to be responsible for her bleeding out, you won't fight back."

Luke didn't move, his blue eyes like ice.

Caldwell put pressure on the blade until a squeak escaped my throat. "Answer me, boy!"

"I understand," Luke growled.

He turned to Bo. "Continue."

Bo hit Luke in the face again and again. A single tear rolled down my cheek. Luke didn't defend himself, taking each blow and then refocusing on Caldwell. His nose and mouth oozed with blood, but he didn't so much as utter a word in protest.

I lost count of how many punches Bo threw before he stepped back, panting for air. It was over. I could finally breathe.

Caldwell growled. "Blake, take over for your brother."

Bo took the Glock, and Blake approached Luke. My chest burned with rage and desperation. "Blake, please. Don't do this."

Luke's face was a mess. One eye had swollen shut, blood dripping from his chin, but he still did nothing to protect himself. Caldwell was pushing me over the edge. I didn't want to fight anymore — I wanted to *kill*. And I would.

My words had no effect. Blake started burying punches in Luke's abdomen until he was coughing up blood and his legs gave out.

"Asher, hold him up," Caldwell barked. "We're not through here."

Asher's dark eyes met mine. He was probably a couple inches taller than Luke, definitely the tallest werewolf in the room. His black hair hung just past his shoulders, and right now his chiseled jaw was tight.

"Now, Asher." The Alpha command sank into Caldwell's

tone.

Asher's gaze fell to the floor, but gradually I realized he was shaking his head. "I can't do that." He lifted his head, fire in his eyes. "I won't."

Caldwell dropped the knife from my throat, storming toward his bitten wolf. "You will do what you're *fucking* told or I'll kill you myself."

Asher raised his chin. "If I keep helping you beat on this man, my spirit will already be dead. I'm *not* one of your dogs."

Caldwell shoved him so hard he lost his grip on Luke, and my mate crumpled to the ground. Deacon and Dex relaxed their grips on my arms, and I ran to Luke's side. Ryker released his other arm, and I cradled Luke's head in my lap.

Behind us, furniture crashed and punches were thrown as Bo and Blake put themselves between Asher and our Alpha. Finally a gunshot froze everyone in the building. Caldwell lowered his pistol, his gaze moving from man to man until his glare landed on me.

"So it's true. He's your mate."

I nodded. No sense lying now. I was ready for him to end this pain.

He shook his head, glaring at the other men around the room. "This is *exactly* why your Alpha should choose your mate. Love like this…" He gestured to Luke and me, disgust plain on his face. "It makes you weak." He pointed at Luke. "Is he still breathing?"

"Yes," I whispered.

"Good. Clean him up. Tomorrow I want him in my office by nine o'clock."

"Why would I bring him anywhere near you, you psychotic prick?"

Caldwell stopped at the back door and grinned over his shoulder. "Because I still have your sister. Be there with him, or I'll make her *wish* I would kill her."

Blake and Bo followed Caldwell out, but the others hung back. Deacon and Dex started righting the tables that had been knocked over while Asher came over from the bar with a wet rag and a bag of ice.

I took both and lifted my tear-soaked face. "Thanks, Asher."

He shook his head. "Nothing will make up for what just happened here." He laid a big, heavy hand on my shoulder. "Your mate has a strong will."

I carefully wiped the blood away from Luke's face, examining the cuts. Earlier today, I'd kissed those lips and admired his smile. Now he was in my arms, nearly beaten to death. Couldn't one thing in my life work?

Dex and Deacon knelt on either side of me. "Sorry, Raven. Our Pack didn't used to be like this."

I didn't respond. What could I say?

Ryker stayed back, muttering under his breath, "This is fucked-up."

Luke coughed and groaned in pain. "Understatement of the fucking millennium."

I stifled a chuckle and bent to kiss his forehead. "When you heal up, I'm going to kick your ass for coming in here tonight."

He stared up at me with his one good eye, his swollen mouth curving into a crooked grin. "You're all right."

I sniffled, trying not to smile. "Told you I could take care of myself."

He almost laughed, wincing. "You still have my phone?"

I had forgotten all about it. "Yeah."

"Good." His one eye that still opened drifted closed. "Did you press nine?"

"No." Maybe he was delirious. We couldn't call 911.

Werewolves couldn't risk our DNA ending up under a microscope. "We need to get you home."

"No backup." He hissed in pain, coughing up a little more blood. "You didn't call her."

I had no clue what he was talking about.

Suddenly his good eye opened again. "Where's Asher?"

"Right here." He came around to Luke's side. "You should go back to your Pack."

"No." Luke groaned and added, "I'm not going anywhere without Raven and her sister."

Asher smirked and took his hand. "You've got balls of steel, but Caldwell will let them kill you next time. You need to leave Sedona."

Luke glanced my way. "Help me sit up."

I did my best to move him without hurting his most likely cracked ribs. He slid his bloody hand up to Asher's forearm. Asher did the same.

Luke's voice was wheezy but strong. "*This* is how you greet a packmate."

Asher gripped him tighter, a smile tugging at his mouth. "I don't think Caldwell let you into our Pack yet."

Luke shook his head, his voice barely a whisper. "This isn't a Pack. This is a gang built on fear. A Pack is stronger than this."

Dex and Deacon shared a look, and my heart pounded in my chest. I needed to get Luke out fast before he completely blew his cover. Dex and Deacon were born wolves, not bitten like Asher and Ryker. Caldwell was not only their Alpha, but their father's, too. I had no idea how deep their loyalty ran, but I didn't want to risk it.

"Can you guys help me get him up?"

He growled as Asher and I put his arms over our shoulders and lifted him onto his feet. I watched his face. "Can you walk?"

"I can carry him to the van." Asher stared at me over Luke's head.

"I can walk my damned self." Luke took a couple of steps.

Stubborn mule. I shook my head. "I think we've got it from here. Thanks, Asher."

I glanced at the others, but again, what could any of us say? Caldwell had trapped all of us in a no-win situation, and Luke was a very visual reminder of our failure.

Once he was in the van and I got behind the wheel, my hands trembled, the adrenaline waning. I swallowed the lump in my throat. "I don't even know where to go."

"My place."

I started to object, but he turned his battered face my way. "If Caldwell wanted us dead, we would be. He had the chance tonight, and we're both still breathing."

He was right. I turned on the engine and followed his directions to Valley Farm. It was dark when we pulled up. Sedona had ordinances against light pollution. Not a trace of any neon signs in the city, and even the few streetlights in the tourist areas were a thick yellow hue. We were a perfect destination for stargazers.

I went around to his side and wrapped my arm around his waist to help him toward the door. Once we were inside, he sat on the couch and I plopped down beside him. The walls were stark white, not a single picture or piece of artwork. The kitchen was more of the same. Bare walls and empty countertops.

"I didn't notice it before. You haven't settled in here yet."

He shook his head slowly. "Not really."

Being here, alone with him…suddenly nervous jitters invaded my bloodstream. For the past few months, being on my own with a man never led to anything good. Luke wasn't like them. He would've given his life tonight to keep me safe.

But the fear shadowed me anyway.

I got up and went into the small kitchen area. "Want a glass of water?"

"Sure. Thanks."

I found glasses in the cupboard. "So why does Nero want your Pack exterminated so badly?"

He didn't answer. I came around with the water to find him dozing or unconscious, I wasn't sure which. But his heartbeat was strong, his breathing regular. I left him alone, figuring he probably needed to rest and heal.

I took a couple swallows of my ice water and toured the rest of his cottage. There wasn't much to see. One bedroom with a master bath, the tiny living area, and the kitchen.

"Raven?"

I went back to the sofa. "I'm right here."

A drowsy smile warmed his battered features. "Good. I think I need to go to bed."

The mention of the word made me tense. I clenched my fists without thinking. What was my problem? Luke was in no condition to want sex. I hated that the thought even crossed my mind.

I helped him to his feet. "At least it's not far."

He chuckled and his breath caught. "Hurts to laugh."

Luke sat on the edge of the bed and started to bend over to pull off his shoes. He hissed, straightening up again.

"I'll get them." I knelt down and took his shoes and socks off. Once his feet were bare, I took a step back. Nerves getting the best of me again.

"Your heart is pounding." He frowned. "What's wrong?"

Hard to hide things from a werewolf, but the ones I'd been living with never cared what I was feeling.

"It's stupid. I don't know how to explain...I just..." I stared out the door at the sofa, hoping the idiotic anxiety would go away. "All this time, I thought I was tough and had everything under control, but now we're alone and I'm..."

The bed squeaked as he stood up. I turned around to see him offering his hand. "You're terrified." I must've looked confused. He added, softly, "Fear has a scent."

I rubbed my hand down my face. "I shouldn't be. I know you're not like them. Even if we wanted to, you're too beat-up. This is all so dumb. But…"

He caught my hand, drawing my attention back to his face. "Cut yourself some slack."

I closed my eyes as he brushed a featherlight kiss to my forehead and lumbered past me. "Where are you going?"

He went and sat on the sofa. "I'm sleeping out here. You deserve to have a door you can close and a bed to yourself."

I shook my head. "You were beaten senseless tonight. You can't sleep on the couch."

He lay back and smiled over at me. "I'm settled in. If I have to move again before morning, I might cry."

I laughed, amazed he could pull off a joke after the night we'd had and even more shocked I still remembered how to laugh. I pulled my hair back from my face, my chest aching, but not from rage or sadness. Something else I wasn't ready to think about.

"If tonight didn't make you cry, nothing will."

He chuckled. "I got kicked in the jewels by a horse once. Those bastards didn't even come close to that kind of pain." He closed his eyes. "Get some sleep, Raven. More assholes tomorrow."

I rested my head on the doorframe, smiling like some lovesick teenager as he drifted off. Luke Reynolds was unlike any man I'd ever known. Even my own father walked out on me. But tonight, Luke had sacrificed his body and his pride to keep me safe. I wasn't sure how to process that.

Or repay it.

I went into his bedroom and pulled the comforter off the bed along with a pillow. When I came back out, I covered him and carefully lifted his head. He groaned but didn't open his eyes. Once he settled back onto the pillow, I pressed my lips to his forehead.

"Rest up, Luke," I whispered.

After I turned out the light, I went inside his room and closed the door. With my back against the cold wood, my legs gave out. I slid down the door, surrendering to the sobs I'd been fighting back all night.

I hugged my knees into my chest and tried to remember the last time I kissed a man simply because I wanted to, because I cared…and I couldn't.

Luke deserved so much better than me and this fucking mess I was in.

Pulling myself together, I went inside his closet and found a T-shirt to sleep in. When I took off my pants, two phones dropped from the pockets. I frowned, replaying the night. He'd handed it to me and told me to press…nine?

I picked up his phone. He didn't have the screen locked. I swiped to the phone keypad and pressed nine.

Sasha Sloan.

For some reason I expected it to be his Alpha. Why would he want me to call someone else?

I finished changing and carried both phones to the nightstand. It was after midnight, and we were safe now. There was no need to call.

But now I was curious. I slid into the bed. She probably wouldn't answer, anyway. I pressed call and put the phone to my ear.

One ring. "Luke?" She sounded sleepy, but instantly alert. "Are you all right?"

My heart raced. I was tempted to hang up, but what if she came looking for him? I cleared my throat, keeping my voice low so I wouldn't wake Luke.

"He's resting now."

Silence. But I could hear her breathing. "Who is this?"

I wanted to ask her the same question. "I'm Raven. Luke told me to call you."

"Do they have him?"

"No." I swallowed, struggling to keep my voice even. "But he's beat up pretty bad."

"Shit." She sighed. "I'm his backup. He was supposed to let me know *before* he went in."

"He surprised me, too, when he showed up tonight."

"Luke thinks with his heart more than his head sometimes."

I glanced at the door, wishing I could see him. "Are you in his Pack?"

"Yeah." She chuckled. "I married the Alpha's brother."

It was a stupid thing really, but hearing she was married settled my wolf. I wasn't usually a jealous person, but when I saw a woman's name pop up on his phone, my hackles had risen more than I realized. There was definitely something primal about this mate bond growing inside me.

"So you're here in Sedona?"

"Yes. Adam sent me to be sure Luke was safe. Tough to do when he doesn't tell me where he is."

My voice dropped to a whisper. "He saved my life tonight."

It took her a second to reply. And with my enhanced hearing, the warmth in her tone was impossible to miss. "Luke's a good man. I'm guessing you must be his mate?"

I nodded before I remembered she couldn't see me. "Yeah. I think so."

"He's been aching to find you. I'm glad something good has come out of this mess in Sedona."

Hearing myself referred to as "something good" almost made me laugh. Luke was nearly beaten to death tonight because of me. I was a curse.

I stared at the clock on the nightstand. "Sorry I called so late."

"Don't worry about it, that's what I'm here for. Can you have Luke call me tomorrow? Sounds like he could use some help."

"I will." I chuckled. "Your Pack sounds much better than mine."

"Adam's big on keeping everyone safe." She paused and added, "Thanks for letting me know Luke's home."

We ended the call, and I set his phone beside mine. An Alpha who cared about the safety of his Pack. Sounded like heaven.

I turned out the light and settled into the pillow, smiling as Luke's scent enveloped me.

Chapter Eight

Luke

My inner alarm clock still worked even if other parts of me were broken. I sat up, growling at the pain in my side. Definitely a cracked rib. With my feet on the floor, I pushed to stand.

Fuck. My feet were about the only part of me that didn't ache.

I turned on some coffee, squinting to force my eyes to focus. Seven o'clock. I had a half hour to change and maybe get a horse or two worked before the meeting with Caldwell. I would be working them from the ground with long lines today. No way was I getting up into a saddle.

But I'd be damned if I was going to let those gutless assholes mess up my job like they did my face.

While the coffee percolated, I opened my bedroom door. Raven's scent overwhelmed me. Her dark hair covered the pillow, the rest of her buried under the blankets. I glanced back at the sofa. She'd given up the down comforter last night to cover me. Warmth filled my chest in spite of the cold room. I went back to the couch, slower than I would've liked, and grabbed the comforter. She didn't move as I laid it over her, then I slipped into the bathroom.

Aw, hell. My face looked like I went a round or two with a diesel truck. My right eye was swollen shut and a deep shade of purple. I had cuts in both eyebrows that matched the two on either side of my mouth. I grabbed my toothbrush and brushed my teeth while checking for any that might have cracked or broken.

Okay, my teeth and my feet were uninjured. Small victory, but still a win.

I didn't want to think about it, but I was lucky to be able to stand. If that wolf hadn't disobeyed Caldwell's order to hold me up, I wasn't sure how much more my body could have taken.

Over the years, I'd been in more fights than I could count. That was how I ended up on the ranch working with horses in the first place, but I'd never been beaten by anyone before. Last night was the first time in my life that I didn't fight back. I couldn't. Defenseless.

It scared the living shit out of me.

I shoved the dark thoughts away. There hadn't been another way out. I needed to protect Raven.

But until now, I'd never known fear. Not really.

We'd faced Nero assassins, mercenary teams, jaguars in coffee shops, mutated werewolves, and I'd even been kidnapped by a newly bitten jaguar, but even in those situations, my confidence in my ability to survive, and in my Pack to have my back, never faltered.

Last night no one was watching my back, and I couldn't defend myself.

I ground my teeth, welcoming the ache in my bruised jaw as I struggled to box up the emotional tempest brewing in my gut.

A quick shower helped wash away some of the remnants of scents from the night before. At least I wasn't smelling my own blood anymore. I wrapped a towel around my waist and stepped out to go into my closet.

And almost bumped into Raven.

She was wearing one of my long-sleeved thermal shirts that came down to midthigh, her hair tousled from sleep, and despite all my aches and pains, I discovered another body part was uninjured.

Her gaze ran slowly up my bruised and battered body, and damn it, I wished I looked better for her.

When her dark eyes finally met mine, I tried to smile. "It's not as bad as it looks."

"You're lucky you're a werewolf." She shook her head. "No human would have survived."

I nodded, unwilling to dig around in those memories again. "I need to get a couple things done at the barn before we go to meet Caldwell."

"We can't go back there." She frowned. "If we get in the van now, we might make it to Reno to warn your Pack." She hesitated for a second. "I pressed nine on your phone last night."

I raised a brow. "And Sasha's not here yet?"

She started to smile, and I forgot all my aches and pains. Seeing her happy. That was all I wanted.

"She wants you to call her."

"Probably wants to kick my ass, but they beat her to it." I chuckled and winced.

"Maybe she can help us rescue Isabelle and get out of town."

"Sasha is deadly with her Glock, and we might be able to grab Isabelle, but it wouldn't solve the problem. Caldwell would still come after us."

Even pulling on my shirt hurt like hell. When my head popped through, I glanced her way. "This Pack outnumbers mine, plus there are little ones to protect. We wouldn't be able to stop all of them. Not alone. If I can get Caldwell to accept me, this could be a chance keep the bloodshed from ever getting to Reno."

She crossed her arms tight. "If he kills you today, your Pack is even more screwed."

"He's not going to kill me." I paused, collecting my thoughts. "If he wanted me dead, last night was the time to do it. He needs me. I didn't crack and confess to being a spy. He has to at least be considering I might really be switching sides."

Damn, I wanted to believe that. I wasn't sure who I was trying to convince more, her or me.

"You almost blew your cover to Asher."

I met her eyes. "Thanks for getting me out of there when you did." I swallowed. "He saved my life."

She nodded slowly. "Probably both our lives."

"So this Pack isn't a lost cause."

She frowned. "What do you mean?"

I took out a pair of underwear and grabbed clean jeans. "If we can trust a few of them, they might help us get rid of Caldwell. Then the Pack here in Sedona could rebuild. Those other guys said it wasn't always like this."

"Deacon and Dex. They grew up here." Her hands slid down to her sides. "They're usually okay guys, but they follow their Alpha. Their father died serving his country in some secret project at Nero. Caldwell pulled some strings to get him in, but he never came back."

Operation Moonlight. An ex–Special Forces werewolf had come to Reno hunting for Sasha a couple years ago. He was the last surviving member of that doomed squad of werewolves. Nero juiced them up to shift without the full moon. The experiment left them high on adrenaline, paranoid, and dying of brain hemorrhages.

"Do you think they're loyal to Caldwell?"

She shrugged. "I don't know. Last night shook everyone up."

"One step at a time, I guess we'll find out." I bent to kiss her temple. My lips hurt, but if she had tilted her head back, offering her soft mouth, I would've claimed her in a second. As it was, her heart was already starting to race.

She'd lived through hell. I needed to be patient. And soon Caldwell would pay for allowing Bo and Blake to treat her like garbage.

First, I had to live long enough to heal my injuries.

"I'm going to finish getting dressed. Coffee's in the kitchen, and you're welcome to come down to the barn if you want. If it's too cold, I'll be back up in time to get to Caldwell's by nine."

"Thanks, Luke."

I smiled. "You don't have to thank me. You're my mate." I ran a sore finger down her cheek. "I wish I could turn back time. If I had found you before Caldwell…"

She shook her head. "Going down that path will make me crazy."

"I'll never hurt you, Raven."

"I know." She swallowed, pressing her lips together. "I don't understand how I know, but…" She tapped her chest. "My wolf instincts are definitely on Team Luke."

I chuckled and winced, shaking my head. "We'll get through this. I promise."

Alone in the bathroom, I zipped my pants and stared at my battered face.

My hands wouldn't stop trembling.

I wore sunglasses to the barn. They wouldn't cover the cuts on my eyebrows or my bruised lips, but my shiner was mostly hidden from view. The grooms didn't say anything—at least not to my face.

After a quick call to Sasha, I took the first horse out the round pen, the smaller arena surrounded by twelve-foot-high walls. Sasha was *not* a fan of me going to Caldwell's place today, but I convinced her with the same argument I'd given Raven.

If he wanted me dead, I wouldn't be breathing right now.

Either way, I swore I would text her the address and she'd be nearby just in case. Both of us knew she'd be hopelessly outnumbered, but neither of us talked about it. Hopefully it wouldn't come to that.

I walked around the center of the ring, keeping myself lined up with the horse's shoulder. Toby was a dark bay gelding and the old man of the stable. He was already well trained. My job was to keep him in show shape.

The long lines were like extended reins, from the bit up to the rings on the harness and out to me in the center. From the ground, I gave Toby cues and watched him move through his gaits.

It also kept me from jarring my cracked rib.

Footsteps echoed up the stairs outside, and Gabby showed up on the platform. She was quiet at first. When I made Toby stop and go the other direction, she called out. "Did you get the number of the truck that hit you?"

I glanced her way for a second. "Not as bad as it looks."

Thankfully she didn't respond, but she also didn't leave. When I finished, Toby waited patiently while I coiled up the reins and I came closer to him. Once I had them tied to the harness, I walked him out.

Gabby met me at the gate and winced. "Shit. You need to see a doctor. What happened?"

The groom relieved me of my horse, leaving me with nowhere to turn. "I'll be fine. I took a fall, that's all."

She shook her head slowly. "Down more than one flight of stairs." She reached up to run her hand down my arm. "Maybe we should call the police."

"Really." I stepped back, out of her arm's reach. "It's no big deal."

Gabby frowned. "Who is she?"

I turned around, relieved to see Raven walking down the path from my cottage. "She helped me after the accident last night." Raven stopped in front of us, and I smiled in spite of the pain in my split lip. "Morning, Raven. This is Gabby. She's the daughter of the owners of Valley Farm."

Raven nodded, no trace of a smile. "Nice to meet you."

Gabby grinned. "Thanks for helping Luke." She took my hand, surprising me. "He means so much to us."

Raven's gaze snapped to mine. "I can see that." Her attention shifted to Gabby. "I better get going."

I pulled away from Gabby. "I've got to pick up my car and take care of a couple things, but I'll be back to work the rest of the horses later."

Raven crossed her arms without looking at me. "I don't want to mess with your work schedule. Gabby could take you to your car when you're finished."

Aw, shit.

Gabby lit up. "I'd be happy to!"

Shaking my head, I went to Raven's side, putting my arm around her shoulders. She tensed at my touch, and my chest tightened. Damn it. I didn't know my mate well yet, but safe to say she was pissed.

I backed off and gave her a little space. "I'll have plenty of time to finish this afternoon."

Gabby's smile dimmed a notch. "Guess I'll see you later, then." She glanced at Raven. "Nice to meet you."

"Likewise."

Raven walked ahead of me toward the van. Normally I'd have no trouble keeping up, but nothing about my current condition was normal. When we got to her van, I stood in front of her driver's side door.

She still didn't look at me. "I can't drive if I can't get in."

I sighed, my voice low. "Gabby is my boss's daughter. There's nothing between us."

She shrugged and lifted her eyes. "I know you had a life before fate saddled you with me yesterday." She shook her head slowly. "Your face wouldn't be beat to hell right now if you'd been with Gabby last night." I reached out to caress her cheek, but she caught my wrist. "I'm serious."

I dropped my hand. "You know how I told you that we recognize our mate when we touch skin to skin?"

She nodded.

"When I got hired here, I was desperate to find my mate. My entire Pack back in Reno, including my twin brother, had all touched the one woman they'd ever love." I swiped my chin, my gaze drifting toward the barn. "Until me, my uncle was the only one in our Pack who never found his mate."

Her voice was barely a whisper, but I heard it loud and clear. "What happened to him?"

My eyes burned behind the sunglasses. "He's dead. He got arrested in a bar brawl the night before a full moon. We couldn't get him released in time."

Her fingers were shaky, but she touched my hand.

I looked down at her. "He killed himself so the police wouldn't find a werewolf in his cell."

"Oh God." She tightened her hold on my hand. "I'm sorry."

I shook my head. "I'm not telling you this for pity." I cleared my throat. "I've had my share of girlfriends and lovers, desperate for that magic touch, and when I came to

Sedona and Gabby started dropping hints she wanted to be more than friends, I gave her a boost onto her horse. Grabbed her bare ankle…nothing."

I took off the glasses to be sure Raven could see my eyes. "That crazy moment when we touched and my wolf howled…" A smile tugged at the corner of my mouth. "You brought me to life, Raven. And if I die today, I'd have no regrets." I swallowed hard. "For once in my life…I'm whole. You gave that to me."

She rose on her toes to brush her lips against mine. I wrapped my arms around her, grateful she didn't stiffen. Her hands moved up my chest slowly, her touch setting me on fire. I deepened the kiss, ignoring the pain from my cuts, losing myself in her.

When she broke the kiss, her eyes locked on mine. "I'm sorry."

"For what?"

"For dragging you into this sick Pack, for getting you beat up, and for overreacting. I just…" She searched my face. "I've never met a man like you, and for a second I let her shake my faith."

My heart pounded in my ears. "Without this screwed-up Pack, we might not have met. Caldwell wanted you to think you were responsible for the beating, but that was all on him. Our bond…" I struggled for the right words. "We scared him. He's leading this Pack, but he's forgotten what makes a Pack strong. It's not fear, or strength, or power."

I cupped her cheek. "It's love, Raven. I love every member of my Pack and I would die for them." My voice caught. "You're *my* Pack now, and that bond terrifies him."

Chapter Nine

Raven

I tried to wrap my mind around Luke's words, but the broken pieces of myself wouldn't shut up. How could he accept me unconditionally so easily? It had to be the wolf instincts. I was nothing special. And if he made me believe I was…

I might never recover from the heartbreak when he left.

Pressing my lips together, I took a step back. "I don't love you."

He recoiled like I'd just slapped him. I shook my head, wishing I had a better filter to think before I spoke. "Shit. I just mean I barely know you. The wolf instincts are really strong, but even if we live through this meeting with Caldwell, and even if your plan works and you shoot him, I don't know if you like cereal for breakfast, or if you like drinking hot chocolate and watching it rain outside. My singing Disney songs in the shower might drive you apeshit."

He almost smiled. Maybe he liked cereal after all.

I struggled to find my point. "You know how you said you

were desperate when you came here? I was, too."

"What were you looking for?"

I shrugged. "Myself, I guess? My dad walked out on us when I was twelve. My mom started taking pills and washing them down with vodka." My heart raced. I'd never told anyone any of this before. I crossed my arms like it might protect me. "Isabelle was eighteen and did her best to raise me, but by the time I was fifteen I was pissed at the world."

"You ran away."

I nodded, staring at his feet so I wouldn't have to see the judgment, or worse yet, pity in his eyes. "First I stayed in Phoenix. I got a fake ID and a job, and I burned through men, searching for…" A sad chuckle escaped my lips. "Maybe if I had known, I wouldn't have ended up here."

I steeled myself and lifted my eyes. "When I turned twenty-one, I hitchhiked to Sedona and met Bo. After a few weeks, he asked me to meet him at Bell Rock during the full moon. A wolf bolted out of the underbrush. I screamed, scrambling for my car, but I couldn't outrun him. He bit me."

Luke took my hand, his voice tight. "It's not supposed to be like that. We don't attack humans and bite them. Not in my Pack. The only one you ever bite is your mate, and only if she wants to be changed. We have three women in our Pack who aren't werewolves and may never choose to be bitten and changed. It's supposed to be a special moment for a couple, not an ambush." He paused, squeezing my hand. "You getting bitten was *not* your fault."

I sighed. "It is what it is. I've been their prisoner, working in their Alpha's bar. I didn't have anyone to turn to, and no way out. I found Isabelle on Facebook. She was so excited to hear from me." I rolled my eyes. I wouldn't cry. No more tears left. "And then I ruined her life, too."

"Stop." His deep voice drew my gaze up to his. "Life happens. Isabelle made choices. You told me she insisted you bite her, right?"

I nodded. "Yeah, but if I'd never run away…"

"Then you wouldn't be who you are today."

"Exactly." I laughed. "I might still be human, maybe a nurse or veterinarian or…"

He caught my chin, his thumb brushing my bottom lip. "I want to get to know the woman, the wolf, standing in front of me right now. I don't care who she could have been—you're a survivor and that's more than enough for me."

For a second, I couldn't find my voice. I swallowed the emotions choking me. If he was right, if fate chose him for me, I didn't deserve it. Eventually he'd realize that.

"What if once you get to know me, you don't like what you see?"

He took my hand and lifted it to his battered lips. "I already know you're the only woman in the world I'd allow myself to get my ass kicked for. I'm pretty sure it can only get better from here."

I almost smiled. "Ah, so you're an optimist."

"Not until I met you."

My heart skipped a beat. "I hope you always feel that way."

We got to Caldwell's place two minutes before nine o'clock. I got out and looked over at Luke. "Bo and Blake are here." No sign of my sister's scent. My stomach twisted.

Luke nodded. "I smell them." One more breath, and he frowned. "There's a jaguar, too." He tugged his shirt down over the holster at his back. "But it's not Sebastian."

The head of the Nero Organization, Antonio Severino, was a longtime friend of Caldwell, but none of the rest of us had ever seen him. Severino always sent his oldest son,

Sebastian, to do his bidding.

He took another breath. "It's not Sasha, either."

"She's a jaguar?" I shook my head. "I'm not judging. I just…I assumed she was a werewolf."

"She used to work for Nero, but she's Pack now." Luke glanced my way. "Any reason another Nero assassin would be here?"

"We've seen a few recently, since Damian was killed. The ones who were backing him to be Antonio's heir have been helping us train to wipe out your Pack in Reno."

"Perfect." Luke slid his sunglasses over his bruised eyes and headed for the door.

I went with him, trying to slow my pounding heart. A pack of wolves could tell when someone was hiding something by their racing pulse and scent. I didn't want to be the reason Luke's plan failed.

Bo answered the door, glaring at me. "Raven." He smirked at Luke. "Your face looks sore."

Luke grabbed Bo's shirt and yanked him close so fast Bo gasped. Luke lifted his other hand. "My fists aren't injured, since I wasn't allowed to use them. If you'd like a second round, I'm ready."

Luke shoved Bo back and put a protective arm around my waist.

Before Bo could get in Luke's face again, I stepped between them. "Where's my sister?"

Bo's eyes shone with self-importance. "Alive."

I wanted to wipe the shit-eating grin off his face, but there was no time now. His lame excuse for an answer would have to be enough. "Caldwell's waiting for us."

Bo got out of our way, and I took Luke down the long hallway, praying this wasn't our last walk together.

He squeezed my hand. "We're going to get out of this. He needs us."

"You sure you can't read minds?" I glanced up at him.

He shook his head. "Just a lucky guess."

I swallowed the lump in my throat. "I'm worried about Isabelle."

"One problem at a time. We'll get her out. I promise."

I needed him to keep that one.

Luke opened the door and waited for me to pass through before he came in behind me. Caldwell was seated behind his massive cherrywood desk.

He gestured to the chairs. "Take a seat."

We sat, and he nodded to Luke. "I'm impressed you're upright today."

"No thanks to you." Luke's jaw was tight.

Caldwell chuckled. "You don't get to be an Alpha as long as I have by being weak. I had to know if you were sincere in your request to join us."

"Threatening my mate and allowing your wolves to attack me while forbidding me to defend myself doesn't seem like a great way to win my loyalty."

Caldwell raised a brow. "But it's a fine way to discover if you can follow orders."

"Hope I passed."

My palms were sweating while watching them posture.

"With flying colors." Caldwell gestured to me. "I let her stay with you last night, didn't I? An olive branch, per se."

"Not to mention I'll kill your bodyguards if they ever touch her again."

Caldwell laughed, his attention shifting my way. "He's a fighter, Raven. You could do worse."

I didn't dignify him with a response. As far as I was concerned, I'd never met a better man than Luke Reynolds. "Are we here for a reason? I need to get supplies for the bar."

"Yes, you are." He hit a button on his phone, and the jaguar we smelled earlier entered the office. "I want you both to meet Vance."

Luke stiffened for a second. The jaguar frowned and glanced over at Caldwell. "He's from the Reno Pack. He should have a scar from my claws."

"That was my twin brother, Logan, you scratched up at Tahoe."

Caldwell smirked. "Vance is here for the same reason you are. He wants to be on the winning side."

Vance stared at Luke and frowned. "You're going to help us kill your family?"

Now my armpits were sweating, too. We had to get out of here.

"Raven is my family now." Luke took my hand, tight. His palm was wet, too.

I stood. "Good to meet you, but I have work to do, and I need to take Luke back to his car."

Caldwell got up behind his desk. "You seem skittish, Raven."

I blew out a pent-up breath and prayed he couldn't see my nerves through my bravado. "You had a knife to my throat last night. Forgive me for not being happy to see you today." I gestured to the cat in the room. "And now I'm supposed to be excited to see an assassin joining our Pack?"

Vance chuckled. "I'm not part of this Pack, just ensuring Damian is avenged."

Luke narrowed his eyes at the jaguar. "I thought that's Sebastian's job."

"He's weak. That's why we were backing Damian. He would've been a stronger heir for Nero."

"Damian Severino was a psychotic lunatic," Luke growled, standing beside me.

Even all beat to hell, my mate was a hothead. I squeezed his hand. "Damian isn't why we're here."

"Raven's right." Caldwell came around from behind the

desk, his eyes on Luke. "Vance is going ahead of us to scout the area. I want you to give him Adam Sloan's address, as well as his brother's. Those are our first two targets. The rest of the Pack will fall quickly after the Sloans are dead."

Luke's grip on my hand tightened, but it didn't show on his face. "We'll talk tonight after the bar closes."

"You'll do it now." Caldwell took a step closer.

Luke's jaw tensed. "You seriously think I have their addresses memorized?"

Caldwell crossed his arms. "You have a cell phone, right?"

"Yeah." Luke dropped my hand and fished it out of his pocket, his attention never leaving Caldwell's face. "It's full of phone numbers." He glanced at Vance. "Adam's ranch is on Whispering Pines Court." And back to Caldwell he added, "And Aren just moved to a new place with his mate, so I'd have to call him to get it."

Caldwell's arms dropped to his sides. "So call. Now."

Shit. There was nothing I could do but watch. Then Luke pressed nine on his phone. Sasha. His backup. My breath caught.

Caldwell's silver eyes snapped over to me. "Am I missing something here, Raven?"

Fuck. I needed to get a grip. Luke was taking a huge risk calling her. Caldwell would be able to hear both sides of the conversation.

I shrugged. "How would I know? I haven't met his Pack." I tried to focus my breathing and added, "Forgive me for having a little PTSD after last night."

Sasha answered, and any werewolf would be able to hear her voice through the phone. I held my breath.

"Hey, Luke."

"Sasha, I'm at my appointment here, and I need your *new* address."

She paused for a second before quickly rattling off an

address in Reno. Luke snatched a pen from Caldwell's desk and jotted it down on an envelope on top of a stack of papers. "Thanks."

He ended the call and stuffed the phone back into his pocket. "Satisfied?" He handed the paper to Caldwell. "Adam's out working horses right now, but I can get his street number after work."

"They don't know you're here." Caldwell handed the paper to Vance.

Luke took my hand again. "They know I'm in Sedona for my job. They don't know you exist."

Caldwell smiled. "Good." He glanced at Vance. "When are you leaving?"

The jaguar shifter folded the paper, slipping it into his jacket pocket. "In the morning."

Luke walked me toward the door. "Then you can meet me at the bar tonight. I'll have what you need, but I can't give you any more of my time this morning. I have a barn full of horses that need to be worked while there's still daylight."

"I can admire a good work ethic." Caldwell glanced at Vance. "Be at the Wolf Pack Bar tonight."

Vance nodded. "I'll be there."

"Good." Luke reached for the door.

Caldwell's voice boomed, "One more thing."

We stopped, and I turned back. He steepled his fingers. "If you cross me, Reynolds, Raven doesn't go back to Bo and Blake. She'll be mine."

Something snapped inside me. "You son of a bitch!" I bolted forward, but Luke's hold on my hand was like iron. I couldn't quite reach Caldwell physically.

Luke's voice was soft and low and meant just for me. "We've got work to do."

I forced myself to walk away. I understood the real truth behind his words. We'd get even with Caldwell, but I needed to be patient. For now.

We walked out together and got into the van. Once I started the engine and got back on the road, I vented all my frustrations. "I hate him. I want to kill him and watch him die."

I'm not sure how long Luke let me rant like a crazy person before he glanced my way. "Caldwell's not going to be a threat much longer. I'm in now. We just need to keep our heads down until I have a clear shot."

I glanced his way. "That wasn't Sasha's real address, was it?"

He shook his head. "No. She knew we were going to Caldwell's this morning." He settled back into silence, staring out the passenger window. At the traffic light, I looked over at him, but he didn't notice. His shoulders were tense, the muscles in his arms tight.

"It seems like there's something else you're not telling me."

He shrugged. "Just a gut feeling."

I pulled into the Costco lot. "Want to share?"

"Up in Tahoe, when Damian was still alive, Logan and I trapped two Nero assassins during the new moon. Before they shifted, we overheard one of them saying Damian was getting erratic and would jeopardize them all." He met my eyes. "I recognized his voice. It was Vance."

"You think he's lying about wanting Damian to lead Nero?"

"I'm not sure, but I'm interested to ask him a few things tonight."

I raised a brow. "That's why you put Caldwell off today. You wanted to talk to Vance alone."

"Exactly." He chuckled. "You surprised?"

"That you're good-looking *and* intelligent?"

He grinned. "Right back at you."

My cheeks heated, and laughter bubbled from my lips.

"How do you do that?"

"Do what?"

I sobered. "Make me happy."

He took off the sunglasses and reached across to cup my cheek. "There is no one in the world I would rather be stuck with in this snake pit of a Pack than you."

Another smile crept up on me as I leaned in. "You really know how to sweep a girl off her feet."

His lips curved as he came closer, stealing my breath. "You're the only girl I care to sweep."

"Lucky me…" My words faded as his mouth met mine.

Chapter Ten

Luke

Her tongue tangled slowly with mine as my fingers slid into her silky hair. My heart pounded like cracks of thunder in my ears. All the aches in my body and all the danger surrounding us faded away until it was just Raven and me.

And we were enough.

She broke the kiss, resting her forehead on mine. "We should get the supplies so you can finish working the horses."

I brought my hand down from her hair, my fingertips gliding down her side, but she didn't tense. Baby steps.

"I don't want to leave you at the bar."

She smiled. "Then we're even, because I don't want you to go to the ranch, either."

I chuckled. "Gabby's not on my radar."

She raised a brow. "Bo and Blake aren't on mine, either."

"If they touch you, I *won't* be able to let it go."

"That shiner Bo was sporting came from me. I can protect myself."

"Wasn't implying you couldn't." I put my hands up in mock surrender. "I was warning you that I could blow all our work with Caldwell if I kill his right-hand man."

"And I'll blow a gasket if Gabby gets all handsy on the horse trainer."

On some level, her jealousy gave me hope. She'd told me she didn't love me. Fair enough. We didn't know each other well yet, but our partnership was growing.

And it was more than just wolf instincts.

I kissed her forehead. "I will stay out of her reach. And for the record…" I took her hand and held it up. "These are the only hands I want on me."

She laced her fingers with mine. "Good to know."

But I'd seen the brief flash of fear in her dark eyes. Part of my mate was scarred from her months with this Pack. Rage festered in my gut, but I did my best to bury it. She'd had enough angry wolves in her life. I needed to be patient, and no matter how badly I wanted her, I would have to let her make that first move.

After we got the van unloaded at the bar, we walked around back to get my Mustang.

Raven gasped as we rounded the corner.

Fuck.

I stood at the front of my classic car, taking in her damage. The headlights were smashed in, the windshield shattered, one tire slashed, and the chrome bumper was dented all to hell.

"Luke, I'm so sorry."

I took her hand, grateful when her fingers laced with mine. "It's only a car. I can fix it."

It would give me something to work my frustrations out

on other than Bo and Blake's faces. I pulled my keys from my pocket and opened the door.

At least they didn't have the brainpower to break inside. Replacing the seats and upholstery would've been a much bigger pain in the ass than popping in a new windshield and beating the dents out of the bumper.

I opened the trunk and fished out my jack and the spare tire.

Raven crossed her arms, watching me. "Can I help?"

"Sure." I popped off the hubcap and handed it to her.

She held it upside down like a bowl, and I filled it with the lug nuts. I slid the jack under the car and pumped it up.

"You're pretty Zen about all this."

I glanced up at her and pulled off the flat. "Not exactly." I grabbed the spare and a couple lug nuts from her. "I'm holding it together because I have to, not because I'm all right with any of this."

She didn't reply. I worked on tightening the lug nuts, but when I turned to take the hubcap, she met my eyes. "So you're not pissed at me?"

"At you?" I frowned, popping the hubcap back in place. As I straightened, I shook my head. "No. Why would I be?"

"They did this because of *me*."

The pain in her voice stoked the fire in my gut. I ran my hands up her arms until her gaze met mine. "They did this because they're spineless, chickenshit *bastards*. None of this is your fault. You had nothing to do with any of it."

She laughed, rubbing her forehead. "If you never came into the bar last night, you wouldn't be bruised and cut, and your car would still look amazing."

My arms slid around her as I kissed her hair. "I have no regrets about last night except that I didn't have my gun on me. I won't make that mistake again."

I'm not sure how long we stood there, but when she

stepped back her eyes no longer shined with tears she wouldn't allow to fall. "I better get to work."

"I'll be back by seven o'clock."

"See you then." She rose up on her toes and brushed a kiss to my lips that nearly brought me to my knees, not because it was hot and passionate, but because it was real.

And it was all her idea.

Damn, I could love her so easily. She just needed to let me in.

I got back to the ranch and called Adam and Sasha to update them on the new developments with Vance. I left out the part about me getting my ass kicked. Truth was, I didn't think I could get through talking about it yet. I didn't have time for fear right now. Denial was the simplest solution.

Bottom line, Caldwell had accepted me. And once I had an idea which side Vance was playing for, I'd be able to plan my next move.

I finished working the other horses, but I was slower by the end of the day. My ribs hurt like hell, and the cold air stung the cuts on my face. I was sure I'd heal up on my own in a few days. Going to the hospital wasn't an option, anyway. Being a werewolf, I couldn't risk the medical community getting a blood sample and accidentally discovering our shifter DNA.

But if I'd been back home, Jason, our Pack doctor, would've at least taped me up so I wasn't constantly bumping my damned ribs.

I did my best not to limp back up to my cottage. I needed a shower and fresh clothes, then I'd stop at the auto parts store and see about new headlights before I picked up Raven. As I opened my door, a black Jeep pulled in.

The scent hit me before they parked. Werewolves. I

recognized one of them. Asher.

I straightened up, chest out. Fuck. I ground my teeth through the pain as they came toward me. Asher's eyes were on mine as he reached out, sort of tentative. I stepped forward, clasping his forearm in a traditional Pack greeting, and a smile spread on his lips.

His grip was firm. "Good to see you on your feet."

I nodded. "Good to be here. How did you find me?"

"Raven told me you might have cracked ribs." He moved back and introduced his friend. "This is Cole. He's our Pack medic."

"You're not from around here." He came forward and clasped my forearm without hesitation. "I haven't seen wolves greet each other like this since I was a little guy."

I shook my head. "Other Packs still do."

He sobered, his bright hazel eyes flicking over to Asher and back to me. "Our Pack didn't used to beat people without letting them defend themselves, either."

I glanced between the two men. No scent of nervous sweat or racing heartbeats, but exposing my real reasons for joining their Pack could get Raven and me both killed. Although their intentions seemed on the up-and-up, I couldn't risk trusting them. Not yet.

As I turned to show them in, Gabby called from the barn, "Dr. Vega?"

We all turned as she jogged up. "What are you doing here?" She looked at me. "Is a horse sick?"

"No." Cole shook his head. "Everything's fine. I heard you had a new trainer, and I thought I'd come by and introduce myself."

The Pack medic was a veterinarian. That's how Gabby knew him. The pieces were coming together.

Cole was at least five years older than me, but the look that passed between him and Gabby was unmistakable.

They'd been lovers. Interesting.

Gabby forced a smile. "Good to see you again."

Cole nodded, stuffing a hand in the pocket of his jeans. "It's been a while." He shifted his gaze to the barn. "Probably time to worm the horses soon, float teeth. I'll check the schedule."

The awkward silence was maddening.

I glanced at Asher. "Asher, this is Gabby. Her folks own the stable."

Asher offered his hand, shaking hers slowly. "Good to meet you."

More silence. I sighed. "I better get inside and sit before I fall down. I'll see you tomorrow, Gabby."

Thankfully, she seemed relieved. "Sounds good." Turning to Cole, she tipped her head. "'Bye, Dr. Vega. Nice meeting you, Asher."

She walked back to the barn, and we ducked into my place. I offered chairs and sat on the sofa, wincing more than I would have liked. "So you're a horse vet."

"Yeah." Cole leaned forward in his chair. "I moonlight as the nearest thing we have to a doctor in this Pack."

"And you already know Gabby."

That knocked him back a little in his chair. "Yeah."

"Little young for you, isn't she?"

"That's why I ended it. She told me she was twenty. Found out through the grapevine she was just starting at community college." He shook his head. "There wasn't a future anyway, not for me."

"That's an old-fashioned notion around here, right?" I raised a brow. "I thought Caldwell picks your mates."

"It wouldn't matter." He shrugged. "He'd never choose Gabby to be bitten. Her parents are too close, and too rich and powerful in Sedona. The only ones bitten are strong females without attachments. No one to report them missing."

He crossed his arms. "Besides, my folks are true mates. I guess an idiotic part of me still hopes mine is out there."

I glanced at Asher and back to Cole. "You weren't bitten?"

"No. My brother and I were born wolves." Cole pointed to my chest. "Asher thought I might be able to tape up your ribs. Mind if I have a look?"

"Sure." I stood up, clenching my jaw to keep from moaning as I pulled my shirt free.

Asher caught sight of me and was on his feet, turning around and staring out my window. My guess was the dark black-and-blue bruises covering my torso were more of a reminder of what happened last night than he wanted to see.

Cole came closer, his cold fingers running along my bruised side. He straightened up. "I've got some tape out in my bag. I think you've got two cracks. We could X-ray it back at my office."

I shook my head. "Just tape me up. I'll be all right."

Cole went out to the Jeep for supplies, and Asher turned around. "I don't know how to make this right."

"This wasn't your fault. I don't blame you for the beating."

His jaw tensed. "I shouldn't have let it happen. I was weak. I'm better than this, or I used to be."

"Caldwell was pushing his Alpha power through his voice. Tough for you not to obey."

"I wasn't born into any of this." He crossed his arms. "I don't like being under someone else's control."

"An Alpha of a Pack isn't supposed to use his power the way Caldwell does. An Alpha's job is to keep his Pack safe, period."

Asher raised a brow. "If you know this, why are you willing to help him?"

Million-dollar question.

Through the window, Cole was digging into his vet toolbox. I met Asher's eyes and lowered my voice. "I'm only here to help Raven and Isabelle."

"How will you do that?" He checked Cole's progress, too.

My gut said I could trust Asher, and my gun on my back told me I could protect myself if my gut turned out to be wrong.

"By killing Caldwell."

Time stopped for a moment while Asher faced me again, digesting my words. Adrenaline fed every muscle in my exhausted body as I waited. His reaction would dictate my next move.

Finally a gruff whisper escaped his lips. "Killing Caldwell won't change my fate, but it could save others from it."

"I'm not asking for your help." Cole carried a bag toward the door. "If it doesn't work, we won't get another chance."

"You don't need to ask." His dark eyes narrowed. "I won't live my life hurting innocent people like a trained dog."

I tipped my chin toward the window. "What about Cole? Can we trust him?"

Asher shrugged. "Since I've been in the Pack, I've never seen him be cruel, but he grew up with Caldwell. He could be loyal to him."

The door opened, silencing our conversation. But we'd said enough.

Raven and I had an ally.

Chapter Eleven

Raven

Alexandra wiped down clean glasses and stacked them under the bar. "So who was the hottie that came in last night?"

I filled napkin holders. "His name is Luke."

"He looks like that alt-rock guy you listen to...the Howlers?"

"That's his twin brother, Logan."

She popped her head up over the bar. "No way!" She glanced at the kitchen and lowered her voice. "Don't tell Mike I said anything. He gets jealous when I freak out over hot guys."

A couple months ago, Alexandra had answered our help-wanted ad for a waitress, and within a few weeks, we also hired her boyfriend, Mike, for the kitchen. They were a good team. Maybe not a happily-ever-after team, but they definitely seemed to have achieved happy-for-now status.

"Your secret's safe with me."

She started stocking the wineglasses, hanging them

by their stems. "He seemed kind of into you." She glanced around and added, "Were Bo and Blake pissed?"

Alexandra didn't know about werewolves, and she'd never outright asked about me living with Bo and Blake, but she probably assumed I was a willing participant. I shrugged and walked back over to the bar. "I don't really give a crap."

"Good." Alexandra grinned, nodding her head slowly. "You deserve to be treated better."

Since she'd started working at the Wolf Pack Bar, I'd been roughed up a few times. I didn't try to cover up the bruises much. What was the point? It wouldn't have changed anything.

I pulled out the bowls and started adding the pretzels and mixed nuts. "Luke's a good guy."

The door opened, and Isabelle stepped inside. My pulse raced. I hustled around the bar and hugged her. Tight.

She returned the embrace, her voice soft on my ear. "We need to talk alone."

I glanced at Alexandra. "I've got to get something out of the van for my sister. I'll be right back."

"No problem."

Isabelle followed me out the back. Once we were on the other side of the van, I grabbed her hand. "Where have you been? Did Caldwell hurt you?"

"I'm fine. He needs me, for now." She put her hand in her pocket. "He found out I have my private investigator's license and has me digging into some records."

"Records? For what?"

"Birth records." She glanced around. "It's got something to do with Luke's Pack, with the Alpha's wife."

I frowned. "What the hell would her birth records have to do with anything?"

"My thoughts exactly. That's why I want you to text Luke and ask about her."

Luke. I needed to tell my sister. She was the only person

in this Pack I could trust. I rubbed my hands on my pants. "Luke's my mate."

Her brow shot up. "Your what?"

"My mate. Not like Caldwell assigns. This is…" I shook my head. "I don't really get it, either, but when my hand touched his, skin to skin, my wolf howled inside my head. I can't really explain it. The world went out of focus and then came back to me again. There's a connection. Mates are real."

Isabelle frowned. "Does Caldwell know? He'll be pissed."

"He wasn't happy." I didn't tell her about Luke's beating. I couldn't bring myself to talk about it. Not yet. "But I think he'd going to accept Luke into our Pack."

"Whoa." She crossed her arms. "Why would Luke want any part of this clusterfuck?"

I chuckled. My sister had a mouth that could make a sailor blush. For the past five years, she'd worked as a private eye and a bounty hunter for extra money. She could talk shit with the best of them.

My smile faded as I pulled in a deep breath, checking for the scents of any of the others. I met her eyes and whispered, "He's going to kill Caldwell."

Isabelle blinked, then shook her head slowly. "Good luck with that. Caldwell is always backed up by Tweedledee and Tweedledum. Those obedient assholes aren't going to let Luke walk up and murder their Alpha."

"He won't have to get close. Luke's a sniper. He just needs to know Caldwell's schedule and find a good angle."

She ran her tongue along her teeth, lost in thought for a second. "It could work, but he'll only get one chance. If he misses, Caldwell will kill him or he'll have Nero finish it for him. Either way, Luke dies."

Her words sliced through me, my heart palpitating.

"I can hear your pulse racing from here." Her head tilted slightly. "You're serious about this guy."

Was I? No question my wolf was, but where did *I* stand? "I've never met anyone like him."

She took my hand. "Raven, promise me you'll be careful. If this blows up in his face, you'll be next on Caldwell's kill list."

The thought of my own death didn't terrify me like the thought of Luke dying.

"I'll be careful."

She squeezed my hand. "One more thing. Just because Dad left, and Bo was a mistake, not all men are assholes."

I laughed shaking my head. "I would've called bullshit on that…until Luke."

Her lips curved into a barely there smile, our disappointments lingering in the shadows of her eyes. "Tell him I said to be good to my baby sister."

I rolled my eyes. "I'm far from a baby."

She draped her arm over my shoulder. "You are to me." She froze.

I caught it, too.

Blake was coming toward the van.

Isabelle whispered, "Ask Luke about Lana's father for me. I'll call you later."

She walked away, head held high as she rounded the van. I hustled after her.

Blake glared at us. "Isabelle, what are you doing here?" He rolled his shoulders back, like the sight of his broad chest would scare us.

Isabelle breezed right past him. "Working on a project for Caldwell."

He crossed his arms. "What project?"

"If he wanted you to know about it, you wouldn't have to ask me." Isabelle disappeared inside the back door of the bar.

I hustled to follow, but Blake caught my wrist. "Where do you think you're going?"

"To do my damned job." I looked down at his hand and back up to his face. "You have no right to touch me." He dropped my wrist, recoiling like I disgusted him. Good. I pushed by, adding, "You never did."

· · ·

Luke came in the door just before seven o'clock. His eyes met mine, and his smile warmed me all over. He pulled out a stool. "You're a sight for sore eyes."

His bruised eyes already looked less swollen than they had when he left. "How are you feeling?"

"All right." He rested an arm on the bar. "Asher brought Cole by the ranch." He lifted the side of his shirt just enough for me to see the white medical tape. "He checked me out and taped up my ribs."

"Good." I owed Asher one. "Your eyes look better, too."

"I'm a fast healer." We all were, but with a few humans in the bar, he kept it vague. "Any sign of Vance yet?"

I shook my head. "No. Blake was here earlier, but he's been gone for a couple hours." A guy at the other end of the bar held up his credit card. "Be right back."

"Ready to cash out?" I ran his card and returned it. "Thanks for coming in."

"Catch you later, Raven." He stuffed the card in his wallet.

I hurried back toward Luke. "Sorry about that."

"You're the reason these people come back." His lips curved in a warm smile.

"Nah." I waved off the compliment. "I don't water down their drinks like the tourist spots, that's all."

"My parents have a restaurant back home. Regular customers come back for the company, not the menu."

"Well, thanks." I swallowed, trying to imagine what his parents were like. A real family. I sighed. Another path I had no interest in wandering down right now. "Isabelle came by."

He leaned a little closer. "Is she all right?"

I nodded and lowered my voice. "Caldwell has her digging into birth records for your Alpha's wife."

"Lana?" Confusion lined his brow. "Why would he care… Oh, shit." Luke paled and pulled his arm off the bar. He gazed at the floor for a second before he lifted his gaze. "I bet Caldwell wants to know why Sebastian is protecting her."

"Maybe?" I hadn't put that together, but it was plausible.

Luke rubbed his forehead. "Or he needs some leverage with Severino."

"Leverage?"

He nodded. "We'll have to talk later."

"Later? Why?" I looked up just as the door started to open.

Luke didn't even move. "Because Vance is here."

Chapter Twelve

Luke

Jaguar shifters had a distinct scent, slick, like well-worn leather, and Vance had the added touch of aftershave. It probably wasn't an accident. Nothing fucked up a wolf's heightened sense of smell more than man-made perfumes. With enough of it, we were blinded to scents that could save our lives.

Vance stopped next to me. "Luke, wasn't it?"

"Yeah." I nodded. "Grab a stool."

He scanned the room and sat. "The Alpha and his goons aren't here?"

"Not yet." I glanced over at him, keeping my voice down. "This morning you sounded like Damian was your guy, but up at Tahoe before you shifted, I heard another story."

"How so?" He turned to Raven. "Can I have a beer?"

She nodded and gestured to the taps. "What's your poison?"

"Heineken, please."

Her eyes met mine before she smiled. "Popular lately."

While she got the beer, I turned to Vance. "I recognized your voice. You complained that Damian was erratic and putting you all at risk."

His well-practiced, easy smile faded as Raven set a beer in front of each of us.

I looked up at her. "You're going to spoil me."

She grinned, and I had to force myself to stop staring at her. I needed to focus on Vance. Turning his way, I lifted my mug. "Care to tell me why you're in Sedona fighting to avenge the asshole when you knew he was coming unglued?"

I took a drink and waited.

Vance rubbed his chin and glanced my way. "Why didn't you out me? Probably would've solidified your place here in this Pack." He lowered his voice. "But earning a place here isn't really your goal, either, is it?"

I raised a brow. "Touché."

"You're not going to give me your Alpha's address, are you?"

I shrugged. "If I do, I'll also be warning him to shoot your ass on sight."

He took a swig of his beer, swallowed, and met my eyes. "I can't tell you what you want to know."

"Then we're even." My gaze followed Raven down the bar.

Vance nudged me, and I winced. He frowned. "You're injured."

I ground my teeth. "I'm also armed, so touch me again and I'll end you."

He put his hands up. "I wasn't attacking you."

"Good." I tore my attention from my mate and back to the task at hand. "Tell me this. If you're not here to avenge Damian, why help this Pack at all?"

"Not helping…observing."

"Is that what you were doing at Damian's place in Tahoe?"

"My turn." He set his mug on the bar. "Did your Alpha send you here?"

"Not exactly." I glanced at Raven.

Vance leaned forward. "She's your mate."

I nodded, turning his way again. "Yeah."

"She belongs to the Alpha's guard dogs."

"She's no one's property," I growled. "Not anymore."

He raised a brow, his lips curving slightly. "Interesting."

I rolled my eyes. "Do they send all of you jaguars through some elitist asshole training course or something?"

He laughed, surprising me. I'd never met a jaguar shifter from Nero who wasn't attempting to kill me or someone I cared about, and I sure as shit had never heard one laugh.

"Sorry, man." Vance shook his head. "I wasn't judging you, just putting this together in my head. You must've gotten into it with the guard dogs while protecting your mate, and now you're trying to get closer to the Alpha. I'm guessing it's not to give him a hug."

I chuffed with a shake of my head. "Definitely not."

Vance shifted on the stool. "I won't get in your way, but you need to stay out of mine in return."

"I don't even know what your endgame is. How would I know if I was in your way?"

He leaned in closer. "Severino doesn't know I'm here right now, and I need to keep it that way."

I frowned as he got up and left a couple of bills on the bar.

He clasped my shoulder. "Good to meet you, Luke. I'm going to Reno to scout and report back. See you in a few days."

I grabbed his wrist. "You're working for Sebastian."

He didn't answer, but he didn't have to. If Severino didn't know he was here, Sebastian was the only other option. I kept my attention on him until the door closed.

Raven wandered back over. "Everything okay?"

"I'm not sure, but it's not shittier, so that's something."

She laughed. "Still an optimist."

God, I loved the sound of her laughter.

I finished my beer and met her eyes. "There are lots of players in the mix here."

Her eyes went to the door and back to me. "Which side is Vance on?"

"Hard to say, but not Caldwell's, and that's all that matters to me right now." I took her hand, lowering my voice. "Asher is with us."

"You told him?" She frowned. "That was a big risk."

"Not really." I shook my head. "He brought the Pack medic over because it's eating at him that he let those assholes beat on someone who wasn't fighting back. After a few questions, I laid my cards on the table."

"What now?"

I rocked one shoulder back, trying not to groan. "I need to heal up, and once I have a handle on Caldwell's schedule every day, then I'll take my shot."

"What about Asher?"

My gaze locked on hers. "If I miss, he'll get your ass out of Dodge."

"You said you don't miss." She tightened her grip on the rag.

"I don't." I finished my beer. "But I'm not taking any chances with your safety."

Her eyes glinted, narrowing. "Was I going to have any say in this plan?"

She was pissed? I blinked. "You knew the plan."

"Not the part about having me abandon you to face Caldwell alone."

I reached for her hand, but she jerked it out of reach.

"This mate thing…" She searched for words. "It goes both ways. I can't function when someone mentions you getting hurt. There's no way in hell I could walk away…" Her voice wobbled. "I'm not like that. I'll *never* abandon people I care about when they need me."

She pivoted on her heel and disappeared into the back storeroom. I dropped my head, staring at my empty mug. What the hell just happened? I got up to go after her when the door opened. The scent hit me before I turned around.

Caldwell.

He came toward me, Bo and Blake close behind. Did they go with him to take a piss, too? Finding a time when he'd be alone was going to be harder than I realized.

"Luke." He scanned the bar. "Vance was here." He took another breath. "But he's gone now. Did you two talk already?"

I nodded and gestured to his empty mug. "Yeah, you just missed him."

He fished his cell from his pocket and hit a button. "It's Caldwell. Did you get the addresses?"

Cell phones might as well be conference calls with werewolves in the room. We couldn't *not* hear both sides of the conversation. I held my breath, ready to grab my gun from the small of my back if Vance mentioned my plans.

"Yeah, Luke told me all I need to know. I'm on my way to Reno now."

"Good." Caldwell smiled. "Remember, the Alpha is mine. I want to look into Malcolm's eldest son's eyes and watch the life drain out of them."

I ground my teeth to keep from reacting.

"This isn't a kill mission. I know how to scout an area," Vance answered. "No one will know I'm here." He paused. "Thank Luke for the intel. It should save me time."

I relaxed. Through Caldwell, we both verified the other hadn't exposed us. We weren't allies, but not being enemies was close enough for me.

Raven came out to the bar, wiping it down with angry strokes. Bo and Blake stayed back.

So they weren't complete idiots.

Caldwell put his phone away and leaned on the bar next to me. "Tell me something, Reynolds. Have you met Sebastian Severino?"

Raven's gaze locked on mine. Isabelle. Caldwell had her searching for Lana's father. He was fishing.

"A couple of times. He's not a friend."

"Sebastian doesn't have friends." Caldwell chuckled, then slowly sobered, his eyes pinning me on my stool. "He seems to have an interest in your Alpha's wife."

"Lana is beautiful." It was all I could come up with. I wasn't sure where Caldwell was leading me, but until I knew, I was treading lightly.

He swiped his hand through the air. "Sebastian's a cold-blooded bastard. He's not looking for love."

I shrugged. "Sorry. I'm not sure why he'd be interested. She's a writer."

He shook his head. "He doesn't want her to write his biography, either." He tapped his finger on the bar. "No, it's got to be something Sebastian's *father* wants. Sebastian is loyal. He wouldn't work something behind Antonio's back."

Vance popped into my head. I did my best to bury it. Caldwell couldn't read minds, but my heart rate could give off a clue I was hiding something.

He glanced at Raven. "Your sister is checking into Lana Sloan's background for me."

"Isabelle's the best." Raven wiped at a nonexistent spot on the bar. "If there's a connection, she'll find it."

"But will she find it soon enough?" Caldwell's attention settled on me again. "There's nothing else about her that might make her valuable to Severino?"

I shrugged, scrambling for some crumb I could throw out

without endangering Lana. "She's a jaguar shifter. Maybe Sebastian is the one who bit her?"

He mulled it over, and I held my breath. Lana was born a jaguar shifter, the only female we'd ever met that carried the shifter gene without being bitten. And she'd passed it on to her daughter. We'd also discovered recently that Antonio Severino was her biological father.

There were plenty of reasons the head of Nero would want her.

It didn't take a genius to figure out that if Caldwell discovered any of those facts, he'd abduct Lana. She'd be all the leverage he'd need to get whatever he wanted out of Antonio Severino.

Caldwell started nodding slowly as he straightened. "You could be onto something, Reynolds." He clapped my shoulder. "I'm glad I didn't let them kill you."

I pressed my lips together, biting back a reply. With any luck, his decision to allow me to live would lead to his death. Asshole.

"Raven, you'll lock up?"

She nodded.

"Good girl." He eyed his bodyguards, and Bo and Blake fell into ranks behind him. As the door closed, Raven's coworker moved in beside me.

"Hi. I didn't want to interrupt." She offered her hand. "I'm Alexandra."

I took her hand and smiled. "Nice to meet you."

She stepped back, her voice soft. "Raven really likes you."

"The feeling is mutual." I glanced around the bar, but Raven was gone.

"I haven't know her long, but she's had a rough time with…" She looked over at the door and back. "Well, I'm just glad she's not with them anymore."

"Me, too." But where the hell was she?

Alexandra took her pad out of the pocket of her apron. "I better get back to work. Nice meeting you."

She took off and I stood up, following Raven's scent toward the back storeroom. As I stepped through the doorway, a glass shattered, followed by cursing. I found her in the corner, perched on the edge of a crate of whiskey.

"Go away." She grabbed a broom and dustpan. "I'm fine."

I shook my head. "You're not." I frowned. "Talk to me. What's wrong?"

She huffed out a breath and started sweeping up the remains of a shot glass. "I have work to do."

I caught her hand. "Did I do something wrong?"

"I can't do this now." Her watery eyes met mine. "Please."

I let her go, my chest constricting. Seeing my mate hurting…fuck. I needed to make it right, but how could I fix it when I wasn't even sure what was broken?

She hustled through the end of her shift, all business. I stayed at the far end of the bar, my eyes following her every move. Even though she loathed Caldwell, she cared about her customers in his bar. She listened to the ones who needed a kind ear. The regulars tipped her well. And her bar was spotless even when she was rushing a drink order.

While she was busy, I stepped out back to call Sasha.

"Hey, Luke. Everything okay?"

"I'm all right, but I have new information. You need to get back to Reno."

She sighed. "We've been through this. Adam wants me here. I'm your backup whether you want it or not."

I rubbed my forehead, struggling to keep my cool. "I don't have much time to explain. There's a jaguar from Nero headed up to Reno to scout the area. His name is Vance."

"Vance Park?" She groaned and added, "He's one of the few people Sebastian trusts."

"He said Antonio Severino doesn't know he's in Sedona

right now, so I figure he's working for Sebastian, but I have no clue what he's after, and he's headed for our territory." I jammed my hand in my pocket. "I'm in here, and there's a jaguar assassin headed to Reno. They're going to need you more than I am."

"Adam's not going to like this."

"I know." I lowered my voice even though my sense of smell told me I was alone. "But Caldwell is poking around Lana's background. I think he wants leverage against Severino."

That was all she needed to hear. We ended the call and I slipped my cell phone back in my pocket. Knowing Sasha would be back protecting the Pack in Reno, a small weight lifted off my shoulders. Now I could focus on Sedona and trust my family in Reno would be safe. For now.

I went back inside and waited for Raven's attention. When the last humans stepped out into the darkness, I got up from my stool and walked behind the counter.

Raven turned before I could touch her. "Let me send Alexandra and Mike home."

I waved to her coworkers as they left and grabbed a rag to help Raven wipe down tables. "Can we talk now?"

She peered my way, her dark hair framing her face. "We're either a team or we're not. There's no in between for me."

"We *are* a team." I straightened up, giving my ribs a break. "What's this about?"

She stalked over to me, getting in my face despite our height difference. "It's *about* you making a plan behind my back to force me to abandon you when you need me most." Her voice hitched a little. "You fill my head with all this mate crap, and then I find out you've got another plan you didn't bother to include me in."

I shook my head. "It wasn't like that. I just need to know that no matter what happens, you'll be safe."

"And you don't think I need to know that about you, too?"

I sighed. "I'm not planning on missing my shot, but if it happens, I don't want them to take it out on you."

"If it happens, then we get out of town. Together."

I stared at her for a moment. My mate was strong and fearless, and damn it, she was right. I'd been so focused on her safety, I didn't even consider her feelings. Shit.

"I'm sorry, Raven. I'm new to this whole mate thing, too. Thing is…" My heart thudded like a bass drum in my ears. "Seeing a knife at your throat, I…" My voice cut out, my eyes burning. "I've never lost a fight before. My confidence is… shaken."

She pressed her palm over my heart. Her dark eyes met mine. "You didn't lose anything. They put us in a no-win situation."

"If he had hurt you…"

"But he didn't." She slid her arms around my waist, and I pulled her close. Her warm breath caressed my chest. "All that shit he said about mates making you weak." She tipped her head up toward me. "You were right. We scared him."

She searched my face. "We're stronger together. We can't let him shake us." The corners of her full lips curved. "And if you made a deal with Asher to get me out of town, he would have to kill me to keep me from being at your side."

Chapter Thirteen

Raven

He bent to claim my lips, and I moaned as my tongue found his. In the months since I'd been in Sedona, I'd forgotten desire and want. And never in my life had passion seared so hot through my veins. I ran my hands up his chest, lacing my fingers behind his neck. He tilted his head, deepening the kiss until my entire body hungered for him.

I'd thought this part of me died the day I was bitten.

He growled against my mouth, "I'd carry you home if I thought my ribs would hold out."

I chuckled, resting my forehead on his. "How about if we drive there instead?"

"Deal."

We finished locking up the bar and went out back to the lot. His Mustang already had new headlights and a new windshield. I glanced up at him. "Wow. You're fast."

"Nah. Those were the easy parts. Straightening out my bumper is going to be a tougher job." He went to the passenger door and opened it. "Can I drive you home?"

God, had anyone *ever* opened a door for me before? Luke managed to keep me talking as he drove us to the ranch, but when he turned out the headlights, dread coiled in my stomach. He took my hand.

I didn't pull away, but I didn't lace my fingers with his, either.

He glanced over at me. "I'm not expecting anything."

"I hate this." I let go of his hand. "I wanted you, I did. I *do*. It's just…"

Luke popped his door, bathing us in the dim dome light of the Mustang. "Me, too, but I waited my whole life to find you. I'll be here as long as it takes for it to feel right."

I did *not* deserve this guy.

Inside his cottage, he went to the kitchen and opened the fridge. "Do you want anything to drink?"

"Do you have any soda?"

He held up a can of Dr Pepper and a can of Coke.

"I'll take the Coke."

He came around and sat with me while we cracked open the sodas. He clanked his can to mine and smiled. "Here's to the future."

A future. For so long, I hadn't allowed myself to picture it. Didn't want to. But now I was sitting beside Luke Reynolds, battered and bruised, but still certain we'd weather this storm. Where did that kind of confidence come from?

I took a couple of swallows. "How are you feeling?"

He shrugged. "I'm not ready for a yoga class, but if I don't bend too much there's no pain. Why?"

Before I could stop myself the words slipped from my lips. "Are you up for a little hike and maybe some stargazing?"

He set his can on the table. "What did you have in mind?"

"The vortex. You can see the entire galaxy up there. More stars than you ever knew existed." I glanced at the door. "But it's pretty cold out. It's probably a dumb idea."

A crooked smile warmed his face. "Let's do it."

I collected the pillows and Luke pulled his sleeping bag and a blanket out of the closet. We stopped for bottled water on the way and made our way to Cathedral Rock. Once he parked, we grabbed our stuff and started hiking. Between the moonlight and our animal instincts, we negotiated the trail without any falls.

At the top, I took the sleeping bag from Luke and laid it out. Then we dropped the pillows.

He smiled and shook his head. "It's made for stargazing up here."

I nodded. "When the weather is warmer, they actually have vortex yoga classes up here." I took his hand. "Can you feel the energy here?"

He was stoic for a minute before he tipped his head down toward me. "Yeah, it's just below the surface, primitive and untamed."

"Exactly." My heart pounded. "When I first came to Sedona, I came up here and wished on the stars. It felt magical."

"What did you wish for?"

I shrugged. "Dumb things. Money, a job, a nice guy. Nothing spectacular."

"You think wishing works?"

I hadn't thought about it before, but I did have a job, and I was holding Luke Reynolds's hand. I chuckled. "Maybe it does."

We lay down on our backs and pulled the blanket up over us. I probably would've frozen to death when I was human, but now I ran hotter, plus Luke seemed to raise my body temperature a few notches.

He held my hand, his attention on the tapestry of stars above us. "This was a good idea."

I glanced his way. "Except for the cold wind."

His head turned. "I run a little hot anyway." He stared up again. "Full moon in a few days. Where does the Pack shift?"

"We usually leave our cars in the Bell Rock parking area and hike a couple miles out, then shift."

"And Caldwell?"

"He's there, too. Bo and Blake usually change first and guard him while he shifts. Then we run."

He lifted my hand to his lips. "This is your last run with this Pack."

"One way or the other."

He rolled on his side. I did my best not to let on that I noticed he winced. "Remember how I confessed my confidence is a little shaken?"

I turned so I was facing him. "Yeah."

"If this is going to work, we have to trust that it will. We have to trust each other."

"Trust is tough for me." I stared into his eyes.

He nodded slowly. "I know, but I'm asking you to trust me anyway."

"I don't know how."

He cupped my cheek. "There's no manual." His gaze wandered over my face. "But I'll start. I've only known you a few days, but your laughter heals me. When I wake up, I want you to be the first person I see, and when I ice Caldwell, I want to take you back to Reno to meet my Pack."

He kissed my lips, his skin warm in spite of the cool winter wind whipping past us. His whisper would have been lost on me before, but now I heard every word. "What do you want, Raven?"

I tried to speak a couple of times, but the words caught in my throat. Instead I kissed him, hard, all my pain, my fear, and my desire blended into a tempest of want.

Luke. Luke was what I wanted.

I rolled him over, our tongues entwining together until my body ached for the same closeness. He growled into the kiss, and I pulled back. "Oh God, am I hurting your ribs?"

He smiled, his arms still tight around me. "What ribs?"

I grinned and caught his lower lip between my teeth, my hips pressing against his, and when his erection pulsed against me, there was no fear. I surrendered to the yearning for closeness. For Luke.

Pushing his shirt up, I wished like hell I could feel his skin instead of the medical tape. His hands slid under my jacket and inside my shirt. My nipples tightened as his fingers explored my skin.

He whispered, "Are you too cold?"

I rose up over him, popping the button on his jeans. "What cold?"

He grinned and rolled me over so he could be on top. His lips trailed down my neck, his warm breath tingling against my skin. "I don't have a condom."

I moved my fingers to his zipper. "I'm on birth control."

Once his fly was open, I slid my hand inside, stroking him. His teeth brushed my shoulder as he fumbled with my jeans. His lips teased the sensitive skin just below my ear. "You make it tough to concentrate."

"Good." I lifted my hips so he could push my jeans down. In spite of the dropping temperature, my body was on fire. Once our pants were off, he settled between my legs.

The tip of his erection brushed against me, making me writhe to get him inside me. His hand slid between us, his rough fingertip toying with me until I gasped his name. He dipped his finger into me and groaned into the kiss. I ran my hands down his back to grip his ass tight.

That was all it took.

He drove his hips forward, connecting our bodies. For a second, time stopped. We were all that was left. He broke the kiss and stared down at me, unspoken questions in his eyes.

My heart pounded against my ribs as I lost myself in the ocean of his eyes. "You're mine," I whispered, wonder in my voice.

He nodded slowly, his hand caressing my cheek. "I am." He kissed me as he pumped into me, deep and slow. "And you're mine."

Our tongues swirled together, savoring, like the slow grinding of our hips. My fingers tightened in the back of his hair. The yearning for release grew. He pulled back, growling my name as his thrusts came faster.

Hearing my name on his lips while the endless blanket of stars surrounded his head dizzied me. I was drunk on the pleasure, the freedom, and the safety of his arms. Sex had never been like this for me. Perched on the edge of oblivion, I didn't want it to end.

He rocked up onto his knees, gripping my thighs as he ground deeper into me, his gaze locked on mine. "I wish I could make this last all night."

"Me, too." I gasped, my inner muscles starting to contract around him.

He freed one hand, his fingers splayed across my abdomen as his thumb toyed with me until I cried out his name. His thrusts carried me through the aftershocks until he finally surrendered, exploding with his head tipped back toward the stars.

I stared up at him, trying to memorize this moment. Every sensation. Making love on a mountain in the moonlight, under the galaxy of tiny lights. Wild and free. And deep inside me my wolf howled, claiming her one true mate.

And the bond between us pulled tighter.

Chapter Fourteen

Luke

When I could move again, I forced myself back so I could help her get her pants back on before she froze. Once Raven was protected, I got my jeans on and lay beside her. She rested her head on my chest as I wrapped my arms around her and kissed her hair.

At the top of the red mountain, in the vortex of energy, alone with the stars, it was easy to imagine the danger had passed. There was so much I wanted to say, but the words wouldn't come.

So I held her close, waiting for my pulse to fall back into a normal rhythm. Raven lifted her head. "That was amazing."

I ran the back of my finger down her cheek. "It'll be even better when we're not freezing our asses off."

She laughed, her dark eyes sparkling in the moonlight. "I wish I had met you sooner."

"You may not have liked me." I slid my hand up her back. "I had some anger issues."

She raised a brow. "Why?"

"It sounds stupid now, but Malcolm, my first Alpha, made me and my brother quit playing sports when we got to high school. I spent most of my teen years bitter and angry. When it exploded into fights and brawls, his son, Adam, put me to work on his horse ranch."

"Why did Malcolm make you quit?"

"We were too fast, too strong, and too aggressive." I shook my head. "I get it now. Even in middle school we were getting a reputation. Teams would gun for us, double-team us, and high school would have been worse. Plus, if we got injured and they took us to a hospital…"

"One blood sample could've exposed shifters."

"Yeah." I nodded. "But I don't think Malcolm realized that his decision would affect us the way it did. Some kids were pissed we weren't playing for the high school team. They knew we were good, and we couldn't tell them why we quit, so we got called everything from chickenshits to pretty boys. Logan had his guitar and channeled the rage into his music, but I didn't."

I met her eyes. "I channeled it into punches."

"You could've killed a human kid."

"Maybe." I ran my finger along her jaw. "Adam made sure it didn't come to that. He saved me when my parents couldn't seem to."

"Will I get to meet Adam?"

"Definitely." I kissed her hair, my lips curving into a smile. "I already told him about you. He's looking forward to having us home."

"What's your home like?"

"Nothing special. I had an apartment, but I gave it up when I moved here. Maybe we can find one together when we get back to Reno." I paused and lifted my head a little. "When this is over, do you want to stay here?"

"No," she answered quickly. "I don't have any good memories here."

I hated seeing the pain in her eyes. Catching her chin, I waited for her gaze to find mine. "We'll make new memories."

"I'd like that." She rested her head on my chest again. "Any idea when we'll go?"

"Not yet. This Pack won't head north until Vance gets back. Until then, I'll be watching Caldwell"—I rolled her over, grinning down at her—"and doing my best to sweep my mate off her feet."

She wrapped her arms around me. "Your mate has never been swept off her feet before."

"She's way overdue, then." I kissed her lips long and slow.

When I opened my eyes, she was staring up at me. I cupped her cheek. "Everything okay?"

"I wish I was better for you."

I frowned. "How so?"

She shrugged. "Until I met you, I survived and I thought I was tough. Sex was a manipulation tactic. I just…" She shook her head. "Being with you is different."

"Good." I clenched my jaw, fighting the anger gnawing at my gut. "You're a survivor. You did what you had to do." I brushed my lips to her forehead, wishing like hell I could go back in time and save her. "And just because we made love tonight doesn't mean I expect anything from you." A smile curved on my lips. "I'm not saying I don't want to do it again, because I do, but…"

I searched for the right words. "I can't go back and fix the past—all I can do is promise you that from now on, your consent, your wants, and your needs will always come first with me."

A tear rolled down her face as she pulled me down to her. Her kiss was needy, her fingers tight in my hair. My tongue passed her lips, as I cradled the back of her head in my hand.

She moaned, coaxing a growl from deep in my chest. When she broke the kiss, we were both breathless.

Her voice was tender, no sign of the bravado she usually hid behind. "I hate this fear that creeps up on me, because I *do* want you. And even though we haven't known each other very long, there's this certainty in my heart that you would never hurt me. But the uneasiness eats me up sometimes." She swallowed, her cool fingers tracing my lower lip. "I know tonight on a sleeping bag outside in the cold was far from ideal, but being in a bedroom…bad memories."

"I'm okay if we never get busy in a bed."

Laughter bubbled from her lips. "With you, it could be fun."

"I'm all about the fun."

"Good to know." Moonlight sparkled in her eyes. "We should get out of here before we freeze."

I couldn't have agreed more. After I helped her up, we collected our gear and hurried back to the car. Back at my place, I put water on and opened the cupboard. "I have coffee or hot chocolate."

"Hot chocolate sounds great."

She turned on the TV while I took out a couple mugs. We watched a movie, sipped cocoa, and although she snuggled in close to my chest, we kept our clothes on. When she dozed off, I nuzzled her hair, breathing her in.

Until now, I'd been living to protect my Pack and my family, fighting battles for them. Everything was changing. The woman in my arms, my mate, was my focus. I wanted to make her happy and keep her safe.

I clicked off the television and rested my head back on the couch, staring at the ceiling. In the dead of night, doubt crept up on me. This was my first job as a head trainer, my first time away from the safety of my Pack, my first time losing a fistfight, and the first time my heart ever engaged with a woman.

What if I couldn't protect her? What if I lost everything?

With my Pack at my back and nothing to lose, I'd been bulletproof. Now I had something precious, and I'd fight with my life to defend her. But what if it wasn't enough?

In the darkness, my fingers trembled in her hair. This was fear.

And I fucking hated it.

...

Snow dusted the ground overnight, decorating the red rock mountains surrounding the ranch. Just when I thought Sedona couldn't get any more beautiful. Damn.

Like back home in Reno, this was a polite snow. Enough to look stunning, but you didn't have to shovel it.

I was just finishing up working the horses when Raven came down to the barn. She was bundled up in one of my big jackets, her hands hidden in the pockets. She smiled, and my heart lifted.

"Hey, stranger," she called out. "Almost done here?"

I nodded and came over to kiss her cheek. "Yeah, just about. Are you heading to the bar?"

She shook her head, a spark of mischief in her eyes. "Nope."

I raised a brow. "Really?"

"I called Caldwell with a horrible cough. I'm sick today."

"He bought it?" I chuckled.

She shrugged. "He's really distracted with getting the Pack ready for the trip to Reno, and since I'm not a piece on his chessboard at the moment, he said he'd have Ryker fill in for me."

"He bartends?"

She grinned. "Not as well as I do, but he's passable."

I put my arm around her shoulder, walking back toward the barn. "So did you have something in mind to do while you're sick today?"

She stopped. "I've always wanted to ride a horse."

My heart thudded in my ears as a smile crept up on me. "You've come to the right place."

"Think you could teach me?"

"Definitely." I winked, enjoying her grin.

When we got back to the barn, the grooms were packing up. I picked up a halter and pulled Sally out of her stall. She was a retired show mare, and of the entire stable, the steadiest for beginning riders.

I snapped her into the cross ties and grabbed the brushes. Raven was in front of her, stroking her forehead. I circled the currycomb on Sally's neck until her upper lip extended out, quivering. Raven giggled, and I warmed all over despite the cold weather.

"Here, you can start at her head and work your way back." I handed her one of the brushes.

"Like this?" She brushed in short strokes, glancing my way.

"You're a natural."

Sally stomped a foot, and Raven jumped. Her cheeks flushed. "Sorry. I haven't ever been around horses. Does it show?"

"I stand by my first answer."

I moved to the other side, and Raven peered over Sally's back at me. "How are your ribs?"

"Better." I kept brushing. "I rode a couple of the horses today, so that's an improvement."

"Your face is healing up, too."

It was a dumb, small thing, but it still surprised me to have someone looking out for me. I dropped the brush back in the grooming bucket and fished out the hoof pick. Beside Sally, I ran my hand down her front leg. She picked it up and I held her hoof with one hand, cleaning out the underside with the pick.

Raven came around to watch. "Do rocks get in there?"

"Sometimes. I'll clean them again when we finish just to be sure she's okay. Horses depend on healthy hooves."

Once she was cleaned up and ready to go, I grabbed Raven's hand and led her to the tack room. She took a deep breath and smiled. "Sometimes having heightened wolf senses doesn't suck."

I grinned. "I love the smell of clean leather, too." I handed her a saddle blanket and pulled the smaller western saddle off the rack.

Raven's eyes lingered on my chest, and again an unfamiliar pride swelled inside me. Catching my mate admiring my body was almost as good as seeing her cheeks flush with color when she realized I caught her looking.

She headed out first. The sway of her hips gradually grew until she glanced back over her shoulder. "Good to know I'm not the only one distracted."

I chuckled, shaking my head. "I'd have to get my head examined if I wasn't."

She put the blanket on Sally's back. Almost in the right spot. I held the saddle in one hand so I could move the blanket up a couple of inches before I swung it up on her back. When I bent over to reach under the mare's belly for the cinch, I caught Raven's eye. The fire in her stare had blood pumping to my groin.

I cinched up the horse and walked toward my mate. The corners of her mouth struggled not to smile as she backed up. I pursued her until her back pressed against the stall door. I planted my hands on either side of her head, leaning into her, but not quite close enough to taste her lips.

Her eyes shone, her voice a breathless whisper. "I know you can hear my heart."

I nodded. "It's racing."

She wet her lips, tempting me beyond all reason. "Your fault."

"Not sorry…" I kissed her again, coaxing her to open to me.

She moaned as my tongue found hers. I wanted to strip her naked and take her right here, but at the same time, she was worth savoring. With my hands still anchored on the cool wood siding of the door, I deepened the kiss. Raven tasted like chocolate and cream.

Her cold hands slid under my shirt against my hot skin. She gasped into my mouth. "Sorry, my hands are freezing."

I shook my head, growling against her lips. "I don't care."

She explored my back, tentative at first. I forced myself to keep my hands on the wall, allowing her to do the touching. Temptation had never been this hot. Her fingertips came around to my abs, her palms gliding up my chest.

Her touch sent an inferno through my body. I'd taken the wrapping off my ribs when I showered this morning. Now I was fucking overjoyed I did. Raven's exploration was almost more than I could take. My jeans were uncomfortably tight now that I was hard enough to cut diamonds.

I pressed hot kisses down her neck. She tilted her head, opening herself to my affection as her hand moved lower, cupping my erection through my jeans. The scent of her arousal hit my senses like a freight train. I pushed back against the wall, lifting my head to meet her eyes.

"I can't take much more teasing."

She shook her head slowly. "Me neither."

I kissed her lips again, addicted to her taste. "Should I stop?"

She answered me with a hungry, urgent kiss. I bent to lift her into my arms. My ribs ached with the effort, but my need for her overshadowed any pain. Sally stood, docile in the cross ties, while I carried my mate back toward the tack room.

Chapter Fifteen

Raven

The scent of leather told me where we were without opening my eyes. Luke cradled me in his arms as he kicked the door closed behind us. He lowered me to the floor and broke the kiss long enough to lock the door.

"The horse…"

"Sally won't mind waiting a few minutes." He pulled his shirt off, treating me to a view of his chest.

The bruises were already fading. His torso was lean and chiseled. These weren't the bulky muscles of a gym rat like Bo and Blake. Luke worked all day lifting saddles and bales of hay and pushing wheelbarrows. His body was chiseled by hard labor. Honest.

The cold air had his nipples in tight points, but the temperature wasn't having any effect on the tight fit of his jeans. I reached out to unfasten the top button on his Levi's, and his big hands ran up my arms to my shoulders, his gaze locked on mine.

With each button, his erection pulsed until I could stroke him through his boxers. The hunger in his eyes fueled my desire to take him farther. He made no move to stop me, giving me the lead.

Part of me waited for the disconnect, for my mind to go elsewhere, my body to go through the motions to get it over with, but it never happened. I opened his jeans and slid his boxers down over the curve of his ass, my nails teasing him until his hips tipped toward me. I wrapped my fingers around his length, relieved my hands were warmed up.

His piercing blue eyes slid down to my hand and back up to my face. The desire in his gaze fed my yearning to pleasure him. Not because he demanded it, or because I needed him to go to sleep, but because I…

I swallowed the lump in my throat and lifted my eyes to meet his. My mate. That was enough.

When I kissed my way down his chest, his fingers clutched the back of my hair, sending a shiver through me.

My lips brushed his skin. "I'm hot in this jacket."

He made quick work of the zipper. I pulled back enough for him to help me out of it. He tossed it over one of the saddles while I picked up where I left off, teasing his nipple with my tongue. A growl vibrated from his chest, and my pulse raced.

I stroked him slowly, watching his face as I made my way down his abs, following the fine line of dark hair below his navel. From under my lashes, I watched the pleasure play out on his face as I took him into my mouth.

"Raven." He groaned, his fists tight in my hair. God, my name had never sounded so amazing.

I took him deeper into my mouth as one hand slipped around to cup his ass, encouraging him forward. His head fell back, eyes drifting closed as he worked his hips. He pulsed against my tongue, gasping. "Enough."

Like hell it was. I rose up, our mouths fusing together. He didn't hesitate to open my pants and shove them down my body, steadying me as I stepped free of them. If it was cold anymore, I didn't notice. He ran his hands down my thighs, bending slightly, then I was weightless in his arms. He turned around, pressing my back to the wall as he entered me.

"God, yes!" My nails dug into his back, tingles shooting through my entire body.

He kissed down my neck to my shoulder, pounding his hips into me harder and faster. One hand moved from my thigh, his fingers moving between us, rubbing me in time with his thrusts until I was writhing, aching for release.

His teeth brushed my earlobe. "Come with me."

That was all it took. My inner muscles clenched around him until he followed me right over the peak. For a few seconds, we were frozen against the wall of the tack room, struggling to breathe.

Finally, Luke chuckled, lifting his head. "I need to put you down before we fall down."

My legs were like rubber in the best kind of way. I wet my lips, smiling up at him. "You're very sexy when you lift saddles like they weigh nothing."

He kissed my forehead. "And just so you know…" He met my eyes. "I lift saddles multiple times a day."

I raised a brow. "Is that a challenge?"

"Nah." He bent to hand me my jeans. "Just thought you might want to know."

I laughed, grabbing my underwear and shaking it out. "I guess that crosses me off the list for assistants. You'd never get anything done."

He grinned, pulling his pants back up. "I'm not complaining."

"Good thing." I nudged him, marveling in how easy it was to be with him.

Once we were bundled back up, he grabbed a bridle off the hook and opened the tack room door. The cold air shocked me. I wiped the sweat from my brow before it froze and followed Luke back to the horse. He was right. She didn't seem to notice that it took us a long time to find a bridle.

He took the halter off and slid the bit into her mouth before slipping the leather bridle up behind her ears. The entire time, he mumbled to Sally, talking to her like she understood. Maybe on some level she did.

When we turned toward the arena, Gabby was walking toward us. I didn't know her, and I tried not to rush to judgment, but she'd held Luke's hand the first time I met her, so…I didn't like her much, to say the least.

She shined a megawatt grin in our direction. "Hi, Luke. And it's Raven, right?"

I pushed my lips into what I hoped resembled a friendly expression. "Right, and you're Gabby?"

"Yes." As she came closer, her smile faded a little. "Luke, are you feeling all right?"

He nodded, his eyes meeting mine before looking at her again. "Feeling amazing, actually. Why?"

"You're sweating."

Oh, dear God, I almost laughed.

"Am I?" Luke swiped the back of his hand across his forehead. "I gave Sally a good grooming. I guess it warmed me up."

She raised a brow. "It's freezing out."

He shrugged. "Yeah, but I'm not cold anymore, so…"

Gabby finally glanced at me. I'd already wiped the sweat from my forehead, but her eyes narrowed anyway.

"Raven, you're flushed, too." I could almost see the lightbulb go off over her head. She knew. Pressing her lips together, she looked at Luke. "Just wanted to be sure I'm on your schedule for a lesson tomorrow?"

"Yep. Ten o'clock, right?"

"Perfect." She didn't smile. "Thanks. I'm going inside before I freeze my ass off."

She turned and hustled for the house before Luke could reply. She was definitely working her ass, too, but when I looked over at Luke, it was me he was watching.

I grinned. "What?"

"She wasn't happy." His eyes sparkled with mischief.

"If she had come down five minutes earlier…"

"I would've been the unhappy one." The corner of his mouth curved into a crooked smile. "I don't like being interrupted."

In the center of the ring, Luke gave me a boost up into the saddle. It was much higher than I expected. I didn't know what to do with my hands, so I held on to the saddle horn like my life depended on it.

Luke smiled up at me. "You can ease up on your grip. You're gonna hurt Sally's feelings. She protects her riders."

I rolled my eyes. "Tell her I meant no offense."

He handed me the reins and showed me how to hold them, then he adjusted my feet in the stirrups, and never once did he lose his patience with my lack of knowledge.

Giving my heel a little tug, he looked up at me. "Keep your heels down. It's a good habit to get into. Someday when you're on a horse with more spirit than Sally, your feet won't accidentally slide all the way through the stirrup."

"And that would be…bad?"

He nodded. "Yeah. If you fell off and your foot was caught in the stirrup, you'd be dragged along the ground until the horse stopped."

Visions of my head being pummeled by horse hooves and

smashing against rocks had me gripping the reins with white knuckles.

Luke patted my calf. "Sally's not going to run off with you."

With the patience of Job, Luke showed me how to turn and stop, and Sally followed my commands like a pro.

Finally, he grinned up at me. "I think you're ready to take her out to the rail."

"The what?"

He pointed to the fence around the arena. "The rail."

"By myself?" My heart picked up again.

"You've got this. I have faith in you." He smiled, and the warm lines around his eyes melted my insides.

I made sure my heels were as far down as I could get them and clucked my tongue. Sally walked ahead toward the rail, and as we neared it, I pulled the left rein and she turned, walking along the edge of the arena.

Nothing could've wiped the smile from my face. I called out to Luke. "I'm riding!"

"You are. See if you can ease her into a jog."

"A what?" My smile might've faltered just a little.

"Squeeze your legs into her. Gently at first."

"What if she runs?" My pulse surged.

"Then you'll pull back on the reins like we practiced."

God, I wanted to hold onto the horn of the saddle so bad. "What if she doesn't stop?"

He walked from the middle, closer to the rail, to me, his voice deep and even. "Then I would get in front of her and stop her for you." He waited for me to meet his eyes. "I'll never put you on a horse that might hurt you."

I nodded slowly. *Luke knows horses. Trust his judgment.* Trust. Ugh. Until today, my sister was the only person I ever allowed myself to count on.

"Maybe walking is enough for today." Luke's voice

scattered the fog in my brain, and while his words were clearly letting me off the hook, they had the opposite effect.

I tightened my legs into her sides and clucked again. Sally moseyed into a two-beat gait. It was a little faster and bouncier than her walk, but not by much. Once I was sure I was going to stay in the center of the saddle, I glanced toward Luke and the smile on his face. Shit. I wasn't sure I'd ever seen anyone look at me that way. Pride. I focused straight ahead, blinking hard. I was *not* going to cry.

Chapter Sixteen

LUKE

I almost felt bad for pushing her, but Sally was the best lesson horse at the barn. Raven was in good hands. Back home, Adam once told me that half of my job when giving a riding lesson was to be a coach, to encourage the rider to try something new, even though they might be hesitant or a little afraid.

But the moment Sally eased into a slow, steady jog, Raven grinned, and damn…I was proud of her. She'd been scared, but the second I gave her an out, she pushed herself. That was the same strong will that kept her from crumbling in this sick Pack. It was a hardheadedness I could certainly relate to and respect.

And I was proud to call her my mate.

Despite her hesitation, she was a natural up in the saddle. Her back moved with the mare's gait. She didn't tense up and bounce. Her posture was upright and straight, too, her shoulders back. I gave her a couple of pointers, and she was quick to adjust.

"Ease back on the reins and tell her to walk."

Once they were walking, I came toward the rail. Raven stopped Sally, and I rested my hand on Raven's thigh. "Sorry I pushed you so hard."

She laughed and shook her head, rolling her eyes. "It was all worth it in the end."

"You're a natural."

Her face flushed a little. "Well, I didn't fall off, so that's a win to me."

"Not even close. You were rock solid up there." I grabbed Sally's bit to hold her still while Raven slid down.

We led Sally back to the barn, and I took the saddle off, enjoying the way Raven's gaze wandered over me. While I put the tack away, she started brushing Sally. As I walked back toward her, my heart swelled. Seeing her grooming the mare, talking to her softly…I rubbed my chest.

I saw a future. Our future. Someone to share my passion with.

"Luke? Are you all right?"

Her voice snapped me back into the present. I nodded, tongue-tied for a second.

A crease lined her brow. "What's wrong?"

I shook my head and took her hand, pulling her in close so I could wrap her in my arms. She stared up at me with questions in her eyes, but I wasn't sure where to start. I opened my mouth and whispered, "We're going to get out of this Pack."

The worry around her eyes faded, and her throat bobbed as she swallowed. "And then…"

"We make our future. Together."

Determination shone in her dark eyes as she rose on her tiptoes and kissed me, but calling it a kiss didn't do it justice. She tightened her fingers in my hair, pulling me down to her as her lips parted and her tongue swirled slowly with mine, the warmth of her mouth a sharp contrast to the cold wind gusting through the barn aisle.

I stepped toward the stall door, and she followed my lead until I had her pressed against it. Her pulse was racing in time with mine until Sally pawed in the cross ties and Raven jumped.

She gasped, and I chuckled. "I think Sally wants her treats."

Raven slid her hands down my chest, her lips curving into a gentle smile. "I know we have this wolf-mate thing going on, but that kiss had nothing to do with instincts."

"No?" I raised a brow.

She shook her head. "No. That was all me." She swallowed, her voice softening. "I want that future, Luke. This is the first time I've ever had one."

Her admission left me aching inside. I ran a cool finger down her cheek. "I'm sorry I didn't find you sooner, but you have my word, you definitely have a future. And if I play my cards right, I hope you'll share it with me."

Sally snorted behind us, and Raven laughed. "You better show me how to give her goodies."

I took Raven's hand and led her into the feed room. Inside, we kept an industrial-size bag of carrots. I grabbed one and snapped it in half, handing the bigger piece to Raven. She followed me back toward Sally, who was already stretching her lips in anticipation.

"Hold it up like this, but keep your fingers out of the way." I let Sally have a bite. "See?"

Raven nodded.

"The last bite she can grab from your open palm. No fingers." Sally snatched the end piece from my hand and crunched, her ears already pointed at Raven.

"Like this?" She glanced my way and I nodded. She held the carrot out, and Sally took a greedy bite. Raven squeaked.

"Did she bite you?"

She shook her head. "No, just surprised me."

Raven offered the carrot again, more confident this time. Once Sally had polished off her treat, I led her back into her stall and turned her loose. When I turned around, Raven smiled. "I'm freezing. How about you?"

I took her hand. "Let's get inside."

Raven's cell rang the second we sat on the couch. I recognized Isabelle's voice and tried not to eavesdrop, but with our hearing, I would've had to wait outside if Raven wanted privacy. Her hand on my leg told me to stay put, and I wasn't going to argue.

"Are you with Luke?"

Raven met my eyes and nodded. "Yeah. What's up? Are you okay?"

"So far. Luke should warn his Pack that Caldwell's planning on heading to Reno Monday."

I laid my hand over Raven's and squeezed. I'd need to take my shot sooner than we realized.

Isabelle went on. "Luke, I assume you can hear me, right?"

"Yeah."

Raven groaned. "No weird werewolf eavesdropping. I'm putting you on speaker." She held the phone in front of us. "Okay, we're both here."

"Perfect. Luke, did you know your alpha's mate, Lana, was orphaned? Abandoned on the steps of a church in San Antonio?"

My pulse raced enough that Raven looked over at me. I trusted my mate with my life, but I barely knew her sister. And I didn't like the direction these questions were going in. "Why does Caldwell care about any of this? None of it matters now."

"I think it does. He wants to me to find out who her birth parents are."

I frowned. "Can you come to the ranch? We should talk in person."

"I think I can make that happen." She paused. "Raven, you're not at the bar?"

Her eyes met mine, and she smiled. "Nope. Ryker is taking my shift tonight."

There was a pause, followed by a slow chuckle. "Good for you, Rave."

I gave her the address, and Raven ended the call. She set her phone on the arm of the couch and met my eyes. "Your heart was racing. What's going on?"

I ran my hand down my face and stared up at the ceiling. "Your sister is really close to making some dangerous connections between my Pack and Nero." I lowered my gaze to meet hers. "Can I trust her not to give it to Caldwell?"

Raven stiffened. "Isabelle is the only person in the world I trust."

She was defending her blood—I could relate—but the jab reminded me that my mate didn't trust me yet. Patience wasn't easy. I was ready to lay down my life for her.

I got up and went in the kitchen for a beer. "Want anything?"

She shook her head. "I'm okay."

I twisted off the cap and took a sip. "I didn't mean to piss you off, but what I'm about to tell you is information that could jeopardize my Alpha's family."

"Maybe it's better if it stays a secret."

"No." I set the bottle on the counter. "You're my mate. No secrets between us." I pulled in a slow breath. "You trusted me today on that horse. And I'm trusting you now."

"Riding a horse isn't in the same league with secret

information about Nero."

I laughed, but not because she was funny. My frustration level was rising, but I couldn't put my finger on the reason. "Trust is trust. I'm not putting levels on it. You trust me or you don't. Simple."

She frowned. "Is that what this is about?"

Was it? Hell if I knew.

Raven crossed her arms. "You're upset because I told you Isabelle's the only person I trust."

"I'm not." Was she right? "I haven't earned your trust yet. I get it."

She stared up at the ceiling, pressing her lips together. My heart pounded. What the hell was I missing here?

"But you have, Luke." Her voice dropped a notch. "You were almost beaten to death when Caldwell threatened my life. You've got a plan to give us a chance at a future." She sniffed. "I've never met a man like you. I…" She shook her head. "My dad walked out when I was twelve and never looked back…" She wiped her nose, focusing on her feet. "And it hurt so bad, I promised I'd never trust another man. That rule has saved me many times."

I abandoned the beer and knelt in front of her, ignoring the nagging ache in my ribs. Her gaze met mine as I took her hands. "I didn't mean to hurt your feelings."

"You didn't." She rolled her eyes with a humorless laugh. "I'm sorry fate cursed you with an insane mate."

"Hardly." I chuffed. "You're the strongest, most amazing woman I've ever met."

"I'm trying to tell you that I'm terrified if I let myself trust you, you'll realize I'm not worth the effort. I don't think I could survive it if you walked away."

I opened my mouth to speak, but she pressed a finger to my lips.

"I'm telling you that in spite of my best efforts, I *do* trust you, Luke."

We stared at each other, the truth lain out bare before us. I reached up to cup her cheek, unsure of what to say, but somehow, my heart must've known all along.

"I love you, Raven." I swallowed, surprised by my own honesty and praying she wouldn't sprint away as fast as her legs could carry her. "I've never spoken those words to anyone but my family. I don't toss them out without meaning them."

I searched her eyes, my voice dropping to a whisper. "Because of you, I can see a future, and I want it. I'll fight for it and for you."

She wiped the corner of her eye before a tear could escape.

A car engine snapped me to attention. In a heartbeat I was on my feet, reaching for my gun. "Get down."

She frowned. "It's probably Isabelle."

"Until I know for sure, hide." I peered through the mini blinds and added, "Please."

She sighed but did as I asked.

My pulse slowed, training winning out over worry for my mate. A black car rolled up behind my Mustang. I waited. A woman got out. She was a little taller than Sasha, longer hair. I pulled in a breath. Werewolf. It had to be Raven's sister.

I released my pent-up breath. "I think it's your sister."

Raven went to the door and smiled as she opened it. I hadn't met Isabelle in person yet. Seeing her with Raven, the resemblance was undeniable. They had the same smile, same nose. Isabelle was at least four or five inches taller than Raven, and instead of dark eyes, Isabelle's were bright green.

They hugged while I put my gun back in the holster on the table. Isabelle glanced my way. "Good to see you're protecting my baby sister."

"Just being sure it was you."

Isabelle came my way and held out her hand. I reached

farther up to grip her forearm. "This is a true Pack greeting."

She tightened her hold on my forearm and almost smiled. "Good to finally meet you in person, Luke." She laid some file folders down, and her gaze wandered over my face. "Not a warm welcome into the Pack, huh?"

"Should've seen me yesterday." I chuckled. "Friendly bunch."

"Caldwell's influence." She shook her head. "I can't stay long. Why couldn't we talk this over on the phone?"

"Because you're digging into dangerous territory, and I'm pretty sure Caldwell hasn't warned you about it."

She pulled out a chair and sat. Her bright green eyes flashed with defiance. "Before I got sucked into this Pack with Raven, I worked as a PI and a bounty hunter. Checking adoption records is hardly my most dangerous assignment."

Raven came over and took a seat between us, clearly not taking a side.

I sat down, too, leveling the playing field. "Raven trusts you, so I will, too, but this can't get back to Caldwell."

Her gaze flicked to her sister and back to me. "I have no loyalty to Caldwell."

"I assume he has you digging into Lana because Sebastian ordered him not to hurt her."

She nodded. "As I understand it, Caldwell is looking for leverage to hold over his old friend Severino. Once this mission is done, he wants to be sure he doesn't turn into a loose end."

I pulled out my cell phone, clicking on the gallery. "Lana is Sebastian's half sister. Her mother was killed shortly after her birth."

Since I'd moved to Sedona, I hadn't opened the pictures on my phone. Seeing their faces made me ache for my Pack and my family. Home. I scrolled through and clicked on the picture of Lana and Adam with their twins, Madeleine and Malcolm. They were laughing together in the barn at Whispering Pines. Happy times.

Light-years from Sedona.

I slid the phone over to her. Isabelle stared at the picture and met my eyes. "Same father as Sebastian." She shook her head slowly. "Shit."

"Exactly." I nodded. "If Caldwell found out she's Severino's daughter…he'd use them as leverage."

She glanced at the photo again. "Does Severino know about his grandchildren?"

"Sadly, yeah. I think that's why he's so anxious to have Caldwell wipe us out. I think avenging his son's death is just an excuse to rally the troops. He really wants Madeleine."

Now they were both looking at me. I was already dipping a foot in the water. Time to dive in. "Lana was the product of a Nero breeding experiment. They were pairing up psychic female humans with jaguar men to see if they could produce shifters without being bitten first. What he was really hoping for was female jaguar shifters."

Confusion lined Raven's brow. "Caldwell told us the shifter gene is carried in the Y chromosome. Females have to be bitten and converted."

"That's how it's always been." I pointed to Lana. "But Lana was born a jaguar shifter, and she passed it on to her daughter. We have another woman in our Pack who gave birth to twin boy werewolves without ever being bitten. Seems to us that if the psychic ability is strong enough, a human woman can give birth to a shifter without being bitten."

Isabelle studied the pic and went back to the file. A crease marred her brow. "So Nero was conducting these experiments twenty-seven years ago?" She closed the file and sat back in her chair. "If he knew it worked, why hasn't he just rounded up female psychics and bred more?"

I shrugged. "I think he wants to. Nero funds a boarding

school that specializes in helping girls with psychic gifts. Brightwood Academy."

Raven frowned. "That sounds familiar."

Isabelle nodded. "Our mother graduated from Brightwood."

Chapter Seventeen

Raven

I sat between Luke and my sister, and judging by the looks on their faces, I was missing a big piece of the puzzle. Maybe my brain was still on overload from Luke telling me he loved me. I struggled to box up the emotions and focus on my sister's words.

"Mom graduated from a school for psychic girls?"

Isabelle nodded slowly. "Apparently."

"Wait…" Luke ran his hand back through his hair. "You two didn't know she was psychic?"

I shrugged. "Mom was a mess on many levels, but if she was psychic, she never told us."

Isabelle got up, crossing her arms. "What if that's why she fell apart?"

Luke took my hand under the table, and somehow the rough strength in his touch buoyed me, keeping me from sinking into memories I didn't want to relive.

"Believe me, she was psychic." He reached for his cell

phone with his other hand, clicking off the screen. "They wouldn't have allowed your mom to stay in the school if she didn't have abilities they could measure."

"And then Nero let her move away and get married and have kids?" Isabelle shook her head. "No way."

"I don't understand it, either." Luke sat back in his chair. "But we can only handle one problem at a time. You need to be sure Caldwell doesn't make the connection between Lana and Nero."

"Done." Isabelle nodded. "I can give him the birth records showing she was abandoned as an infant and bounced around the foster care system. She's attractive. I'm sure he'll jump to the conclusion that Sebastian wants her for himself. If he asks my opinion, I'll back up the theory."

"Thanks." Luke got up from the table. "I need a way to get closer to Caldwell. If he's planning to take the Pack to Reno after the full moon, I don't have much time to plan my shot."

My gut twisted at the thought of Luke anywhere near Caldwell, but he was our best hope of getting out of this alive. I had to trust he could do this. There was that word again.

I swallowed the anxiety and looked over at him. "We need to show Caldwell you're good with guns and rifles. Then, when Bo or Blake is incapacitated, he'll choose you to protect him."

I regretted the words the second they left my lips.

Isabelle glanced at Luke. "It could work."

Luke's hand rested heavy on my shoulder. "The problem will be taking out Bo or Blake. If I do it, Caldwell will know he's being set up."

Isabelle raised her hands in mock surrender. "I would *love* to put a bat to their kneecaps, but Caldwell's got me on a short leash digging up dirt for him."

"Asher." I tipped my head back to look up at Luke. "You

said he'd help us, right?"

"Good idea. I'll talk to him."

Isabelle's phone buzzed; she checked the screen and sighed. "His ears must be burning. Caldwell wants an update. I better go."

I embraced my sister. "Be careful."

"Always." Isabelle stepped back and looked at Luke. "Keep her safe."

He nodded. "I will."

After Isabelle drove away, Luke and I sat on the couch in silence. It should've been awkward, but it wasn't. Something about being with him calmed me. For once there wasn't an expectation. Only acceptance.

He glanced my way, a smile toying at the corners of his mouth. "So."

I laughed, rolling my eyes. "How do you do that?"

He grinned. "Happy is a good look for you."

"It's all new for me." I reached over to cup his cheek. "All of this is."

"I know." He caught my hand and brought it to his lips. "Sorry we were interrupted."

And here it was. Luke bared his soul. He shared how he felt. I opened my mouth, but words didn't come. I cleared my throat and managed a whisper. "Other than my sister, you might be the only person who ever loved me."

His smile faded as he lowered my hand. "That's about to change."

"How so?"

"My parents are going to love you, and my Pack…" His expression warmed. "They're going to be crazy about you."

I chuckled. "How can you possibly know that?"

"Because I don't need to be psychic to know they're all worried about me. No one wanted me to leave Reno." He shook his head, his blue eyes searching mine. "I wasn't whole. Everyone in my Pack had found their mate, the other half of their soul...and me?" He glanced at the window. "Seeing them just amplified the fact that I might never find mine. I might never be able to fill the emptiness in my heart."

Instinctively, I squeezed his hand until he looked at me. "What happens to wolves who don't meet their mate?"

He clenched his jaw and broke eye contact. He leaned forward, elbows on his knees as he clasped his hands together. "I told you about my dad's twin brother, my uncle Niko. He was so angry that he never found her. The night before the full moon, he got into a bar brawl. We couldn't get him out of jail in time."

He faced forward again. "So being the last lone wolf in my Pack was a constant reminder of Uncle Niko. I couldn't stand seeing the concern in their eyes." He shook his head and rested his hand over mine on his shoulder. "They could have a parade in your honor when we get home."

Somehow, he had me smiling again. "I can't wait to meet them."

I expected him to press me for my feelings, but it didn't come. He loved me, and there didn't seem to be a string attached. Maybe he trusted the wolf bond would bring me around. Or maybe, just maybe he loved me enough to give me space. I wanted to pinch myself to be sure this was real.

Luke sucked in a breath and got up. "First we need to get out of here. Alive." He looked my way. "Do you have Asher's number? Can he meet us here?"

"I'll text him right now."

"Good." He headed for the bedroom. "I'll call Adam and bring him up to speed back home."

I admired his backside as he moved across the room.

When he glanced back and winked, my cheeks flushed with heat. He chuckled and closed the door.

And for the first time in years, a warm feeling crept through my heart. I wasn't ready to say the words out loud yet, maybe I never would be, but either way, I was falling hard for Luke Reynolds.

...

Asher came through the door as the sun was sinking behind the red mountains. There was no mistaking his Native American heritage. Not only did he walk tall and proud, but there was a spark in his dark eyes, a connection with everything around him, a peace. Being near Asher grounded you. He was proud without being burdened with the vanity of pride.

Luke got up and clasped Asher's forearms. A true Pack greeting, according to Luke. Caldwell wasn't big on traditions. Our Pack didn't have any except fear.

Asher nodded in my direction. "Raven. You're not at the bar."

I shook my head. "If Caldwell asks, I have a terrible head cold."

He chuckled, more like a deep rumble. "All right." His attention shifted to Luke. "We have to act fast. Blake told us to be ready to move on your Pack after the full moon Sunday night."

"Isabelle told us. I already warned my Alpha, but we need to keep him from leaving Sedona." Luke rubbed his hands on his pants. "So I need a favor, but it's a big one, and I won't blame you if the answer is no."

Asher raised a brow. "If it will help get rid of Caldwell, I'm in."

Luke met my eyes and then back to Asher. "I've got to be closer to Caldwell…"

He hesitated, and I stepped in. "We need Blake or Bo incapacitated so Luke can take his place at Caldwell's side."

The corner of Asher's mouth pulled up into a crooked smile. "I would be happy to help, but why do you think he'll pick Luke? He'd probably choose Dex or Deacon, even me, before he'd trust a new wolf from Reno."

Luke picked up his holster from the table. "Leave that to me."

"Pointing a gun at him isn't going to work."

Luke chuckled. "That comes later." His free hand slid around my waist. "I'm a sharpshooter. Raven's going to plant the seed with Caldwell, and then when he needs backup, I'll be there."

Asher crossed his arms over his broad chest. "What's your fallback plan if it doesn't work?"

We didn't have one.

"Then I'll come up with a plan B, but it'll work." Luke shrugged. "With one of the King brothers out of the way, he'll need me. It'll work."

Asher dropped his hands to his sides. "If it doesn't, things are going to get messy. There won't be time to regroup. I'll have to finish the other King brother, too, while you make your move on Caldwell."

Doubt swelled in my stomach until my pulse pounded in my ears. The male wolves turned in my direction.

I put my hands up. "I know, I know. I'll keep my cool with Caldwell, but for now, let me freak out a little. Forgive me for hating both of your plans."

Luke tightened his hold on me. "We're going to make it through this." He glanced over at Asher. "All of us. Can you get rid of one of his bodyguards before the full moon?"

Asher nodded. "Bo likes to think he's an expert climber. I'll take him out tomorrow. He can break his own leg. This time I won't be fast enough to save him."

"Good." Luke's arm left my back. "As long as he doesn't suspect foul play, Caldwell won't, either."

"I have a request, too."

We both looked at Asher. He lifted his chin. "Caldwell is a sadistic prick, but he's still the Alpha of this Pack, and once he's gone, there are innocents who need to be protected, women and children. We've got to be sure we can gain control of his assets."

I nodded slowly. "Isabelle is working for him right now. I'll see if she can dig into his records and find a money trail we could use." I met Asher's eyes. "You're a good man."

He rolled his shoulders, shrugging off the praise. "Most of us have sins because of this Pack. I just want to end the suffering." He glanced at Luke. "I'll text Raven when it's done."

"And I'll delete the text once it comes in."

He nodded. "Deal."

Luke approached, and they clasped forearms. "Thanks, Asher."

As Asher's Jeep fired up outside, Luke turned to face me. "I'm going to need Caldwell's number."

"Why?" Tension bunched in my shoulders, and I deleted my earlier text to Asher, covering our tracks. There would be no going back now.

"I'm going to see if I can get him to meet me at the shooting range tomorrow."

I glanced up from my phone. "I thought I was going to mention you were good with a gun."

"I'm rethinking it." He came over and sat beside me. "Adding me to his bodyguard detail needs to be his idea. If he senses you're pushing him…" He shook his head. "I can't let any of this touch you. Sorry."

I stopped scrolling on Caldwell's number. "I don't want you getting hurt, either."

"I won't."

I sent up a silent prayer that his confidence wouldn't get him killed. God, I ached at the thought. He was the only bright spot in my life, and I wasn't about to give him up. Not if I could help it.

Chapter Eighteen

Luke

Caldwell didn't answer. He probably didn't recognize my number. I left a voicemail and waited. Raven kept busy in the tiny kitchen area. I couldn't see what she was up to, but my gut said she was just distracting herself.

I didn't have enough food in there to make a whole meal, so…

My phone buzzed, and I answered. "Luke here."

"Luke. Did Raven give you this number?"

I hated hearing Caldwell say my mate's name. "Yeah. Is that a problem?"

"Not at all. Did you have something to report?"

"No." I pulled my gaze from Raven's back to the window. "I'm headed to the shooting range in the morning. Wondered if you'd meet me there."

He paused. "What for, exactly?"

My pulse quickened slightly, making me grateful I'd called him. He wouldn't be able to hear it over the phone. "I thought

I passed your test, right? I'm in your Pack now."

He chuckled, a slow, calculated laugh. "True, but I didn't expect you to want my company."

I ground my teeth, yearning to punch the shit out of something. "You're the Alpha. I'm good with a gun. Just figured it'd be safer to be an asset than a liability."

Another pause. "Little Nicky raised a smart boy. All right."

When I ended the call, I turned around to find Raven watching me. She crossed her arms. "I don't like this."

"I don't, either, but it's going to work. I can feel it."

"What if he shoots you? An 'accident.'" She made quotes in the air.

"He can't shoot me in public, especially not this close to the full moon. If they arrested him…"

"…he'd never take that risk." She exhaled, shaking her head. "So what's my part in this?"

"Did you text Isabelle about checking out Caldwell's holdings?"

She nodded. "Done."

"Then all you have to do is open that bar tomorrow like nothing's changed."

She put her hand on her hip. "So you'll be with Caldwell shooting guns, Asher will be with Bo in the mountains, and I'm just supposed to bartend?"

"Caldwell has been an Alpha for a long time. His senses about his Pack are heightened. We need to stay under the radar, and we do that by keeping up appearances. If he starts to suspect anything, this won't work."

She sighed and came over to me. "Swear to me you'll be all right."

I tugged her into my arms and kissed the top of her head. "You have my word."

But adrenaline was already pumping through my veins.

If anything went wrong, I wouldn't have my Pack to back me up this time.

And it wasn't just *my* life on the line anymore.

...

I woke up early and showered while Raven dozed. We shared the bed last night. Nothing intimate, but watching her sleep in my arms…damn. She hadn't said she loved me in words yet, but seeing her resting peacefully against my chest told me all I needed to know. She trusted me.

Now I had to be sure we stayed alive long enough for me to earn her love.

When I got out of the shower, the scent of chocolate and bacon mingled until my stomach was grumbling like a grizzly bear. I pulled on some jeans and wandered out of the bedroom.

Raven smiled at me as she turned off the burner. "You have eggs, bacon, and hot chocolate."

I pressed my lips to her temple. "Thanks, beautiful."

She chuckled and grinned up at me. "Anytime, handsome."

I snatched her up and spun her around the room, enjoying her laughter. Yeah. *This* was what I was fighting for. I set her back on the ground and kissed her forehead.

"What was that for?" Raven asked.

"Just glad you think I'm okay to look at."

A playful glint sparked in her eyes. "You're much better than *okay*."

"Good to know…" I bent to claim her lips.

Her hands slid up my chest as we deepened the kiss. I boosted her up on the counter and settled my hips between her thighs. Why the hell did I put jeans on?

She pulled back, running her finger along my jaw. "You should eat before you have to go."

"You taste better than bacon."

She tipped her head back laughing. "You're laying the flattery on pretty thick."

I nuzzled her neck. "Is it working?"

Her fingers slid through my wet hair, but her laughter was gone. "Be careful today, okay?"

I straightened up, my gaze locked on hers. "I will." I tucked her hair behind her ear, memorizing every curve of her face. "This is going to work."

It had to.

Caldwell parked as I was walking into the range. I waited, grateful for the gun in my shoulder holster and the other at the small of my back. I'd feel even better if Sasha was nearby, Glock at the ready, but the Pack needed her more. I could handle this. Caldwell wouldn't risk an altercation in public, but ever since the beating, he made me wary. I'd never be in his presence unarmed again.

Blake trailed a step or two behind him. I glanced from the bodyguard to Caldwell. "No Bo today?"

He shook his head. "He's rock climbing with Asher. Sebastian said the Pack in Reno runs up in Lake Tahoe, too. Can't hurt to be ready to climb if we need it, right?"

Hearing him talk about hunting my Pack turned my stomach. I swallowed the bile building in my throat. "Yeah."

We rented lanes and went inside. I jammed in the earplugs and checked my bag for the extra clips of ammo. Shooting at an indoor range was tough on a werewolf's heightened sense of hearing and smell, but I resisted the urge to invite Caldwell to an outdoor range. It might open us up to rifle shooting, and while I wanted him to see me as an asset, I didn't want him to realize I was even deadlier with a rifle and scope.

I sent the target out to twenty feet, grounded my stance, and fired off my entire clip in rapid succession. After the first few empty shells flew out of my Glock, Caldwell's scent grew in intensity. He was watching. Good.

The gun clicked. Out of ammo. I pressed the button to bring the target in. Not bad. Every shot hit the heart. Only a small hole remained. Caldwell raised a brow. "Impressive. How are you at thirty feet?"

I hung a new target and sent the carrier out to thirty feet. I stared at the target as I slammed the clip into the Glock. Taking my stance, I pulled in a slow breath, slowing my pulse, slowing time, getting focused.

I emptied the magazine, one shot after the next again. Gunpowder stung my nostrils, but my work was done.

"Holy shit, boy." Caldwell clapped my shoulder. "Bring that target back in."

I fought the urge to brush his hand away. The target rolled back in, and his eyes widened. My shots were right on point. One in each eye and the rest right between them.

Caldwell lifted his gaze from the target to my face. "I'm glad I didn't let them kill you. You could be valuable here." He turned to show the target to Blake. "You and your brother should get some pointers from Luke."

With any luck, Bo was getting pointers of his own from Asher right now.

I cleaned my gun and swept up the casings in my area. Caldwell slapped my back. "Come grab some food with us. My treat."

"Nah, I've got horses to train. Thanks for the offer, though." Truth was, I didn't know how much longer I could suck up to the asshole without tipping my hand.

"I appreciate your work ethic, but you'll be on the road to Reno soon. Who will exercise those animals then?"

I focused on my task, putting my gear away, anything

to keep my heart rate steady. Lying wasn't something I had much experience with. "I've got a groom who'll exercise them for a few days while we're gone."

When I straightened up, Caldwell's eyes gleamed. "I'm looking forward to seeing your papa's face when you're fighting at *my* side."

I snatched my bag up and headed for the door. "I'll be at the bar tonight."

"Still watching over your *mate*. Keep in mind she's only yours because I allow it to be so. She can be back with Blake and Bo with a wave of my hand."

I couldn't fucking take it. I dropped the bag and rushed the bastard, pinning him to the wall. Before I could throw a well-deserved punch, a cold gun barrel pressed to my temple.

"Let him go, asshole," Blake growled.

I gave Caldwell a little shove as I backed off. He chuckled, shaking his head, but his eyes were icy, calculating. "Don't piss me off, Reynolds, or I'll put her back in bed with the King brothers, and I'll make you watch. Hell, we all will."

My chest heaved with aggression, but I didn't surrender to it. I was outnumbered here. But the tide was changing—the Alpha just didn't know it yet.

It almost scared me how much I was looking forward to putting a bullet in him.

I called Raven when I got back to the stable. I didn't tell her about Caldwell's threat. Instead, we made a date for target practice. If Caldwell ever tried to make good on it, I was going to make damned sure Raven could protect herself just in case.

Hard work at the barn always helped me burn off some of the fire of rage inside me, and by the time I finished riding Sabrina, the ache to beat the shit out of Caldwell had dulled. I needed to be patient. The wheels were in motion.

It was getting dark, the temperature sinking fast as I pulled into the Wolf Pack Bar. The second I opened the door, Raven's scent greeted me, calming the beast inside. The full moon was in two days. My wolf was close to the surface, and Caldwell was not his Alpha.

Raven came out from the back, her eyes met mine, and her smile erased all the frustrations of the day. I crossed the tavern to sit at the bar.

"What can I get you?"

I smiled. "God, it's good to see you."

She glanced around the bar and back to me. "Are you all right?"

"I am now." I took a slow breath. For now, we were the only werewolves in the bar. "Any word from Asher?"

She shook her head. "I'm starting to worry."

Her cell phone buzzed. She pulled it out from her apron pocket and smiled. "His ears must've been burning." She read the text. "He thinks Bo broke his ankle."

"Couldn't happen to a better guy." Relief washed through me. "I'll take that beer now."

Around closing time, Ryker came through the door. Most of the humans had left; only Alexandra and her boyfriend remained. He nodded to me and then focused on Raven. "Bo took a bad fall."

"Good." He didn't seem surprised by my mate's reaction. She met his gaze. "And Asher?"

"He's fine. He tried to pull Bo up, but he lost his grip…" He shrugged his shoulder. "Asher's strong, but Bo's a brick."

I leaned in. "Caldwell's not blaming Asher, is he?"

"Nah." Ryker almost smiled. "He knows Bo's a meathead." He sobered. "Caldwell sent me to get you. He needs to see you at the hospital right away."

"Hospital? You're shitting me."

He shook his head slowly. "Compound fracture and Cole wanted them to set it."

I glanced at Raven. "I don't like leaving you here."

She rolled her eyes. "I've got Alexandra and Mike here. I'll be fine."

I focused on Ryker again. "Is Blake at the hospital, too?"

"Yeah." He nodded. "He's with his brother."

That settled me a little, but I didn't know Ryker. He'd been upset after the beating, but I wasn't ready to trust him on that fact alone.

Raven reached across the bar and took my hand. "Luke, I'll be *fine*. Ryker can help me lock up, and I'll meet you back at your place."

I stared into her eyes, her message clear. This was the opening we needed. I finally nodded and stood up, eyeing Ryker. "If anything happens to her…"

"Easy, dude." He chuckled. "Raven and I are friends. I won't let anyone near her."

"Good." I walked around the bar and pulled my mate into my arms, unsure of what her reaction to my public display of affection might be, but I needed to touch her, to know she was all right.

She slid her hands up around my neck, a smile warming her lips. "I'll see you at home."

Damn, I loved the sound of that. I bent to kiss her, her taste taming the wolf inside me. I whispered, "Be careful."

"You, too."

I forced myself to back away and turned for the door. Ryker straightened as I passed, but I stopped and held out my arm. He stared at it and reached for my hand. I shook my head, clasping his forearm. "Like this." He took my lead and gripped my forearm, too. I started to smile. "This is how a *real* Wolf Pack does it."

We released each other, and Ryker grinned. "You're

shaking things up around here." He glanced at Raven and back to me. "Watch your back."

"Thanks, man."

I went to the door, glancing over my shoulder at Raven as I walked out.

Hospitals were hell for werewolves. I couldn't figure out why Caldwell would risk allowing a Pack member to step into one. All it would take was a routine blood sample to expose our DNA to human science. It was a stupid mistake for an Alpha.

Cole was with Caldwell. They both stood up as I approached. I crossed my arms, keeping my voice down. "This is risky."

Caldwell poked my chest. "Do you honestly think I don't know that?"

Cole came between us, cool and collected. "Blake is with his brother. They've informed the hospital staff that their religious beliefs forbid them from any care beyond resetting the bone."

I rolled my eyes. "If he starts coding, they're going to have an IV in his arm and his body on the table, religious beliefs or not."

Cole crossed his arms. "I already checked him out. He's not going to code, but if he wants to keep that foot, we need to be sure he's getting blood flow to the area."

I tried to let it go. This wasn't my Pack, not my place to say. But it risked exposing all of us. "How soon can we get him out of here?"

Speak of the devil—a tall human in blue scrubs was headed straight for Caldwell. "You're Mr. King's uncle?"

Caldwell nodded, his eyes taking on an uncharacteristic concern. "How's my nephew?"

"It's a nasty break, but we got it set and casted. I realize it's not ideal with your beliefs, but he really should consider orthopedic surgery to repair the ankle."

Caldwell shook his head. "We appreciate your concern, but we can care for him."

The doctor did not look convinced, but he didn't push the point any farther. "He wouldn't allow me to give him any pain medication, so he's going to be sore for a while."

"Can we take him home?"

The doctor sighed. "That's what I came to talk to you about. I would recommend he spend the night just so we can keep monitoring the pulse in his foot."

"Won't be necessary. Cole here has first aid training. Bo will be monitored closer by us than an overworked staff of nurses anyway."

The doctor heaved a sigh and signed some papers on his clipboard. "I'll get his discharge paperwork finished up. It'll just be a few more minutes."

As soon as the doctor was out of earshot, Caldwell cursed under his breath. "I'm not holding off the trip to Reno."

Cole glanced at me and back to his Alpha. "Blake isn't enough protection on his own. If you run into a fight half-cocked, this will be over before it starts."

"I know that. Why do you think I sent Ryker to tell Luke to get his ass over here?" He glared at Cole and finally focused on me. "Reynolds, you're going to shadow Blake this week."

Cole's jaw slackened slightly, but he covered the shock quickly. "You sure you don't want Dex or Deacon? They know this Pack and…"

Caldwell shook his head. "You haven't seen this kid shoot. And he took more of a beating than any of you ever have, and he's still standing. He's proved his worth."

I took a slow intake of breath, willing my heart rate to stay even as I nodded. "I'll need to work the horses at the stable first, but I can hook up with Blake afterward."

He slapped my back. "Fair enough." He glanced at Cole. "Bo may not have a job to come back to after his leg heals up."

More likely he wouldn't have an Alpha to come back to, but I kept that to myself. For now, I was in.

Chapter Nineteen

Raven

I got back to Luke's place and clicked on the television, hoping for a distraction from worrying. My cell chimed.

Hey, beautiful. I'm in. I start with Blake tomorrow. On my way home.

I quickly fired back.

See you soon.

I hit send, and my phone started ringing. I didn't recognize the number. Frowning, I answered. "Hello?"

"Is this Raven?"

The voice sounded familiar. "Yeah, who is this?"

His tone warmed. "I'm Luke's brother, Logan. Good to meet you."

Logan Reynolds, lead singer of Logan and the Howlers, had called *me*. I shouldn't have been starstruck. His twin brother was my mate. Someday we might even be family.

But still. Logan's music had helped me survive since I'd been bitten. Hearing him wail about pain and regret saved me in a lot of ways.

"Raven?"

His voice popped me back into the moment. "Yeah, I'm here. Sorry. Just surprised to be talking to you."

"Adam gave me your number."

I finally placed the name. "Your Alpha." I frowned. "Wait. How did he get it?"

"The only way Luke could keep Adam from getting involved down there was to give him as much information as he had. Like your number, in case he didn't check in."

A smile crept up on me. I hadn't met Adam yet, but I liked him. "And how did *you* get it?"

"I checked in with my brother yesterday, and he spilled that he found his mate."

I sat on the couch and tucked my legs up under me. "I thought you said Adam gave you the number."

"Yeah. Luke wouldn't give it to me because he knew I'd call you."

I laughed, shaking my head. "So I shouldn't tell him we've talked?"

His tone softened. "I didn't call to ask you to keep secrets."

"Then why *did* you call?"

He paused. "Because he's my twin brother, I can sense Luke's in trouble. He doesn't want me to get involved, and I don't want to blow his cover, but if he gets in over his head…" He cursed under his breath and started again. "Thing is, Adam's responsibility is to the Pack first. He's the Alpha. I get it, but my brother is my blood. I can't just sit back and do nothing."

Now that I could relate to. "You're a good brother." I glanced at the door. "I'm worried, too, but Luke's right, you can't come down here. If Caldwell caught your scent, he'd turn on Luke."

"What if he turns on him anyway and no one's there to have his back?"

"*I* have his back." I gulped at the admission. I hadn't even hesitated.

He was quiet for a moment and finally chuckled softly. "Sounds like you do. I'm looking forward to meeting you in person. Do me a favor?"

I nodded even though he couldn't see me. "Sure."

"Keep this number in your phone. And call me if you need me. Any time, okay?"

"I will." I swallowed the lump in my throat. "Luke's already made a few allies here. He's not alone in this."

"Good to hear." He sighed. "If you choose to tell him I called you, tell him I love him, and he better get his ass home soon."

I smiled. "Will do."

"Thanks for looking out for my brother." He paused. "I'm glad he found you."

"I am, too."

"See ya, Raven."

I ended the call and set my phone aside. The familiar purr of Luke's Mustang rolled up outside, and my heart raced. I went over and opened the door. His lips fused to mine as he kicked the door closed behind him. He walked me farther inside, one hand sliding up my back and the other moving down to pull my thigh up.

Then I was weightless as he lifted me up and I wrapped my legs around his waist. Our tongues swirled slowly, teasing me until I ached for more. I tangled my fingers in his hair, enjoying the growl in his chest. He placed me on the kitchen counter and finally broke the kiss, his voice a deep, low rumble.

"I missed you."

I smiled, staring into his eyes. "You've only been gone a couple hours."

"I know, but..." He caressed my cheek. "Being with Caldwell..." He shook his head. "I've killed to protect my Pack. But this..."

He backed away, staring at the floor and shaking his head. When he met my eyes again, the strain was plain to see.

"I *want* to kill him." He broke eye contact. "He's hurt so many people. My father and his Pack, you, your sister, and the men and women he's ordered to be bitten to increase this Pack's numbers."

Luke lifted his right hand. "I'm aching to pull the trigger. What the hell does that mean? Is he turning me into what I hate most?" His gaze raised to meet mine. "When I'm with you, I'm Luke Reynolds, horse trainer. But when I'm with him..."

I slid off the counter and crossed to him. Taking his hand in mine, our fingers entwined. "When you're with him, you're facing evil. You're protecting me, your Pack, and the rest of this Pack." My voice wobbled. "We can't go to the police with this, and it won't end until he's dead."

He nodded slowly. "I know."

"Then what's wrong?"

He tightened his hold on my hand. "Without my Pack, my Alpha, my brother...you're my lifeline. If I cross the line between defender and murderer—"

"No." I rested my hand flat over his heart. "Don't you dare call yourself that." I swallowed the lump in my throat. "You are the most decent man I've ever known, and you're our best chance to save my sister. Caldwell is a sadistic madman. If you didn't want to end his existence, then I'd be worried. You don't want to kill him because of bloodlust or hunger for power. You want to protect everyone."

He wrapped his arms around me, holding me tight. I

embraced him, listening to the strong, steady beat of his heart, and whispered, "The fact that this is bothering you is proof you're nothing like Caldwell."

He kissed my hair. "I love you, Raven."

I moved back enough kiss him. It was tender and slow this time. Sharing the emotions I couldn't quite put into words yet. I backed him up toward the sofa, my hands sliding under his shirt.

He growled into my mouth, "I need you."

I tugged my top off and pulled him down onto the sofa. "I need you, too."

His weight settled over me, and we escaped all of the danger and fear as the rest of the world faded away.

Chapter Twenty

Luke

I woke up before the sun came up. Raven was still sleeping on the sofa, and I tucked the blanket around her before heading for the bathroom to grab a shower. The horses had to be worked early today so I could meet Blake. Caldwell had sent me a text sometime last night with an address. I wasn't sure what to expect, but I'd be watching for quiet places where I could take my shot without risking being seen or hitting innocent people.

Rooftops were best, but I'd take whatever I could get at this point.

I bent to kiss Raven's cheek and quietly slipped out to the barn. The horses lifted their heads as I walked through the barn aisle between the stalls. The frigid air stung my cheeks. I took refuge in the tack room. Inside, the scent of leather mixed with the faint scent of sex. A smile curved my lips at the memory.

Grabbing a halter, I forced myself to get moving. The

sooner I got done, the sooner I could find the optimal spot to fire my rifle and end all of this.

I dived into my work, allowing my apprehension and dread to fade into the dark corners of my mind. The cool air had a couple of the geldings amped up, snorting and spooking at their own shadows. Once I got them warmed up and sweaty, the excess energy faded and they settled in. By the time I pulled myself onto Sabrina's back, Raven had come around the corner into the barn.

She was bundled up in one of my jackets. "You snuck out this morning."

I chuckled. "Nah, just wanted to let you get some sleep."

"Thank you." She stepped to the side as I rode the mare past her. "Mind if I watch?"

I shook my head. "As long as you don't freeze."

She followed us out to the arena. I tried to keep all my attention on the mare, but I couldn't help glancing over at Raven.

She smiled. "She's beautiful."

"Yeah." I nodded, cueing Sabrina to canter. Once her gait shifted to three beats, I glanced at Raven again, and called over. "She's going to do some winning this season."

Sabrina chose that moment to jump sideways, away from the rail. I kept myself square in the saddle. Barely.

I chuckled, shaking my head. "I may have spoken too soon."

After her workout, I rode Sabrina back into the barn and left her in the groom's capable hands. I walked toward the cottage with Raven at my side.

She looked up at me. "I didn't get a chance to tell you Logan called me last night."

I stopped in my tracks. "How did he get your number?"

"He said you gave it to Adam in case he didn't hear from you."

I shook my head. "He better not come down here. If Caldwell found out he was here…"

"That's what I told him." She paused. "He was glad to hear you've got some allies here."

I met her eyes. "I wanted him to come down here. It was tough to turn him down."

"You miss him."

"I do, but it's more than that. I'm used to us working together. With Logan at my side, we're invincible—or at least it feels that way." I struggled for words, my shoulders tight. "I'd give anything to feel that confidence again. This uncertainty is killing me."

The honesty fanned the smoldering anger in my gut. This fear inside me…I fucking hated it. I reached for the door and held it open for Raven. She passed me by and sat on the sofa.

"Can I tell you something?"

I closed the door and took a seat beside her. "Sure."

"If you weren't afraid right now, I'd be worried about you."

I leaned my head back, staring at the ceiling. "I need to have a clear head."

"And you will." She rested her hand on my thigh. "Being too confident makes you sloppy. Fear will keep you alert and ready. Use it."

I glanced her way and shook my head. "You're amazing."

She shrugged off the praise. "Don't know about that, but I've managed to stay alive."

I lifted her hand and kissed the back. "I better get out of here."

"Where are you meeting Blake?"

"He and Caldwell are going to be waiting for me at the Store-It-Yourself across the 89."

Raven tensed. "Be careful. He doesn't use that place to store records and furniture."

My gut twisted into a tight knot as I pulled into the empty parking lot. From the outside, the storage facility looked like any other, a large building with pull-down metal doors covering each of the small units. But according to my mate, Caldwell didn't rent space to the public.

The units were full of bitten men and women, some with children.

Caldwell grinned as I approached. "Right on time." He glanced over at Blake. "Show him around and then meet me in the office." Caldwell focused on me again. "Give me your gun."

Fuck. "I thought you wanted me to protect you, right?"

He nodded slowly. "And I won't be with you, so there's no need for you to be armed."

My pulse raced before I realized it. I took a step back. "The last time I was unarmed with Blake here, I got the shit beat out of me while you held my mate at knifepoint. I have good reason to keep my gun."

Caldwell raised a brow. "I have security cameras all over this facility. If Blake so much as lays a finger on you, I'll shoot him myself." His bright gray eyes shifted to Blake. "Is that understood?"

Blake nodded, and Caldwell smiled. "It's settled then." He held out his hand. "Now give me the weapon."

I shook my head. "Only if Blake is unarmed, too." Cold sweat rolled down my spine, and Raven's words echoed through my mind. *Use the fear.* "If I wanted to kill you or Blake, I could have shot you both as soon as I got out of my car."

Caldwell's eyes narrowed like a human lie detector. I ground my teeth and kept my gaze locked on his. Finally his expression lightened. "I doubt we'd be that easy to kill, but

I see your point." He gripped my shoulder, hard enough to pinch the nerves. I fought to keep any sign of pain from my face. His voice dropped to a menacing growl. "I'll be watching the cameras."

He walked toward the main building, calling back, "Be in the office in an hour."

Blake watched him go and turned for the storage units without a word. I followed, bracing myself.

But nothing could have prepared me for this.

There were three women in the first unit, all werewolves, and two of them were now mothers to twin boys. Shit. Caldwell was breeding wolves. In captivity, no less. No mates, no family, no Pack. Just bite them, assign them to bitten males, and bring more shifter children into the world.

Nero had a similar breeding project for jaguar assassins. But more jaguar shifters meant more trained killers and more money for Antonio Severino. What could Caldwell be after?

Blake stood aside. "Recreation time. No funny stuff."

The women passed me by, but the last one looked up at me, her jaw set. She wore her black hair in a single braid down her back, and her features were soft, kind. "Who is the new guy?"

Blake answered, "This is Luke. Bo took a fall, so he's filling in."

Her dark eyes flashed as her gaze met mine. "Fuck you, Luke."

She hustled to catch up to the others while Blake chuckled. "Don't mind Kaya. She's a wildcat. Literally."

I glanced his way. "Her scent is wolf."

He nodded. "Yeah, she was bitten, but some of the natives here were skin-walkers. Caldwell didn't know when he chose her."

"So she's a wolf and…"

Blake reached up for the door. "During a full moon, she's

a werewolf, but the rest of the month she can shift into a lynx. She's the reason we had to cage in the rec area. That cat can climb like a monkey. We almost lost her."

"So locking them up is the answer?"

Blake pulled the rolling metal security door back into place and headed for the next unit. "Caldwell keeps all the women with children inside for their own safety. We can't have them going to the police. They could expose us all."

"She didn't look like she had any kids."

"He has plans for the skin-walker wolf." He unlocked the next door. "If she gets back to the tribal lands, we may never find her again. They protect their own."

Just like a Wolf Pack should.

He drew his handgun as he lifted the security door. Three men spun around. Blake kept his gun aimed on them. "Rec time."

A tall blond man stepped forward. "I've done everything Caldwell asked. When do I get out of this cell?"

Blake tipped his gun in the direction the women went. "Keep training, Gage. Make yourself useful, and you'll be on the trip to Reno."

"Who is this?" Gage was my height and wearing shorts and a camouflage tank that made it obvious he'd been spending his time in the cage doing push-ups and crunches. Damn.

"I'm Luke." I didn't draw my gun. Instead I approached him and clasped his forearm.

"Stay back, Reynolds," Blake cautioned, his gun on Gage.

I kept a tight grip on Gage and glanced over at Blake. "These men are wolves now, like you and me. They're not your enemy."

Blake slid his finger over the trigger. "Back away."

I took a step back. "Good to meet you, Gage."

He and the others jogged down the alley toward the rec

area. Once they were gone, Blake got in my face. "You don't know what the hell is going on, so stay back and shut the hell up, or get the fuck out of here."

"Why don't you explain it to me?"

He holstered his gun, gesturing to the row of storage units. "Caldwell and Severino wanted an army to storm Reno. Caldwell chose his soldiers and mates for the men, and we changed them. Now they're being trained."

I frowned. "You seriously think this is training? You have them locked up like prisoners."

"Until we're certain of their loyalty, they stay here."

I clenched my fists. "How long was Asher kept here?"

"Six months."

I struggled to keep the shock off my face. "How? He has a business, right? What if his family reported him missing?"

Blake rolled his eyes. "Please, Reynolds, we're not stupid. Caldwell background checks all of his chosen ones before we're given the order to bite them."

"That's why Bo bit Raven."

He shrugged. "He was already dating her, told Caldwell she didn't have parents, and he gave him the okay."

"What about her sister?"

He shook his head. "She never mentioned her. We didn't know about Isabelle until Raven bit her."

I crossed my arms. "So you're all right with all this?"

"I'm loyal to my Alpha, and I believe in his vision. We'll be the largest Pack in North America."

I puffed out a breath, biting back the real words that I ached to say. "Sorry. I wasn't prepared to see all this, I guess."

Blake nodded. "That's why Caldwell wanted you here."

"He thinks I can't take it?"

"How the hell would I know?" Blake led me to the next door. "I'm not paid to think. I do what I'm told."

I kept my mouth shut and counted another eight men, four

more women, and one more set of twin boys. Fuck. Suddenly I understood Asher's concern about the "innocents." There were a lot of mouths to feed here.

How had Caldwell gotten to this point? Biting humans and keeping them caged like animals…this was insane.

Once everyone was out, Blake walked me to the recreation area. In the center of the compound, screened in with chain-link fencing even across the top, there was a basketball court, a swing set, and wagons.

My Alpha's twins popped in my head, and my chest tightened. Madeline and Malcolm ran free and played on his horse ranch. These kids had never been out of a cage.

I smelled Caldwell before his footsteps approached from behind. He draped an arm around my shoulder. "We've grown our numbers faster than any other Pack in the country."

"There's no strength if you have to keep them locked up."

He chuckled. "You're still using your father's old-school thinking. Look at the bigger picture, Reynolds. If we stay with the old ways and wait until that fated mate happens to cross our path, our race will always be outnumbered. Humans will always be a threat."

He pointed to Gage on the basketball court. "But if we choose the strongest male and female humans and change them, we grow our numbers. The next generation grows faster, too, and soon…"

I stepped away from him. "An entire country of werewolves."

"No. Definitely not." He shook his head. "Not everyone will be chosen to be a shifter. We'll be the elite, the top of the food chain, and we'll have the power. No more hiding in the shadows. Humans will bow to us. This is the future, boy."

My hands trembled with adrenaline. I stuffed them in the pockets of my jeans. "So why bring me here?"

"Because I want you to understand that winning the

battle in Reno is only the beginning."

"What does Nero think of your plan?"

"Antonio is paying for a large Pack, and I'm delivering. That's all he needs to know for now."

There was a better than average chance Sebastian didn't even know this place existed.

Caldwell turned my way. "After the full moon, I want you to choose three of these men and teach them to shoot. How are you with a rifle?"

I pulled in a breath, willing my body to stay calm and my heart rate steady. "I'm all right, I guess."

"Good. Antonio told me one of his jaguar females is part of the Reno Pack now. Sasha?" He paused, but I didn't answer. "She's rumored to be deadly accurate with her handguns. If we can neutralize her while staying out of her range, we'll be one step closer to the Alpha."

I glanced at the recreation area. "Will they be changing with us during the full moon?"

Caldwell chuffed. "And risk them running off? No."

I frowned. "Where do they shift?"

He started to smile. "In their units."

I shook my head, unable to hide my disgust. "Wolves need to run. This…"

"This way they earn their run. When I decide to bring them in, they understand the consequences if they cross me."

He patted me on the back. "Reynolds, keep watch for a minute. Blake, I need you."

He and Blake walked toward the office, and I fought the urge to rush all these people out to freedom. It wasn't that simple. Now that they were changed, we had to be sure they didn't go to the police. This was royally fucked-up.

The woman who had cursed me on her way out glared at me as she came closer. I waited as she came to stand in front of me, her voice hushed. "You're new. Why aren't you locked up with the rest of us?" She inhaled slowly and shook her head. "You weren't bitten."

"Right."

"You were born a wolf, but you're new. Did you leave your other Pack?"

I crossed my arms. "Something like that."

She peered around me in the direction Caldwell had taken Blake, then back up to me. "They made a mistake when they bit me. Did he tell you what I am?"

"A skin-walker. You can shift anytime, right?"

She almost smiled. "Except during the full moon."

I wanted to tell her I was going to get her and the others out. I wanted to tell her Caldwell was an asshole but his time on earth was nearing its end.

But I didn't. Because for all I knew, he left me alone here to test me.

"I'm Kaya."

"Good to meet you, Kaya." I didn't want to know the answer, but I had to know. "How long have you been in here?"

"Almost six months."

Shit. I shook my head. "Caldwell still doesn't trust you?"

A humorless chuckle escaped her lips. "I'm his secret weapon, and he wants more like me. Until I tell him about others, he'll keep me locked up."

I stared down at her, my voice a lethal growl. "Don't tell him."

"No chance."

I nodded. "Good."

She almost smiled. "You might be the first sane born wolf I've met."

"We *do* exist."

"Good to know." She walked away as Caldwell and Blake returned.

"Okay, Reynolds, help Blake get everyone back in their

units, and we'll get over to the bar."

Blake started barking orders as I watched Caldwell walking back toward his office. Alone. I turned back to the yard, the frustration and desperation plain on all of their faces. Blake couldn't kill them all if they attacked, but what kind of future would they have on their own? Maybe that was how he kept them from turning on him. As much as they hated him, they needed him.

Or at least they thought they did.

Blake locked doors and told me about feeding schedules and emptying the portable toilets in the units, but I barely heard him. For the first time in my life, I understood why humans might fear werewolves. If Caldwell continued down this path, it was only a matter of time until we really were hunted.

Chapter Twenty-One

Raven

I was wiping down the bar when Caldwell walked through the door. Seeing Luke coming in beside Blake in Bo's place jarred me a little. This was the plan. It was working.

But it also unsettled me.

Caldwell sat on a stool. "Is the deposit ready for me?"

I went to the register and opened the safe underneath. Luke's gaze followed my every move. Looked like I wasn't the only one shaken up.

"It's all here." I handed the money pouch to Caldwell, struggling to keep from looking at Luke. I ached to touch him, to ask if he was all right, but for now, Luke's safety depended on Caldwell believing in his loyalty.

He bounced it in his hand like he could judge the deposit amount by weight. "Good girl." He glanced over his shoulder at Luke and back to me. "Your guy is moving up the ranks."

I risked a peek at Luke. His jaw was set, tight. I focused on the bar again, but Caldwell caught my chin, forcing me to look into his eyes. "You're not happy about him working with Blake?"

Luke took a step forward, but Blake grabbed his arm.

I narrowed my eyes at my Alpha. "You established that my happiness doesn't matter right from the beginning."

He let go of me and laughed. "So I did." He gripped the money pouch. "Let's get over to the bank."

Luke and Blake waited on Caldwell to pass, but he stopped and turned toward Luke. "Aren't you going to kiss your precious mate good-bye?"

The venom in Caldwell's voice had goose bumps creeping up my arms.

"Plenty of time for that later," Luke answered.

"Is there now?" Caldwell's gaze slid slowly over to me. And I prayed a human customer would come through the door. Whatever he was planning, this wasn't going to be good.

The door didn't open.

"Raven, saunter your ass over here and show us how true mates kiss."

My heart raced, and Caldwell smiled. Sick bastard enjoyed knowing I feared him. I threw my towel on the bar and stormed around the bar, straight to Luke. I rose up on my tiptoes and pecked his lips, then glared at Caldwell. "Entertained? I have work to do."

His smile soured, his voice dropping to a guttural hiss. "You will fucking do as you're told, or I'll put golden boy Luke in the units with Kaya. It looked like she warmed up to him today. He could give her some strong cubs."

My chest constricted, jealousy licking at the raw wounds he was cutting into me. My gaze snapped to Luke. His blue eyes didn't stray from my face, but he also didn't deny anything. He took my hand and pulled me close, his lips fusing to mine as his other hand caressed my cheek, his fingers sliding into my hair. Our tongues tangled slowly, making me forget we had an audience. I clung to him, aching for the escape he offered.

Caldwell applauded, and Luke broke the kiss, his gaze locked on mine. Finally he turned to look at Caldwell. "Ready for the bank now?"

"Fair enough." The Alpha's eyes bored into me. "You could learn something from your mate."

He went out the door with Blake behind him. Luke hesitated at the door and turned back, his voice barely a whisper. "I love you."

And he was gone.

Alexandra came out from the kitchen and frowned. "Raven? Are you all right?"

"Yeah. Fine." My hands trembled. I was far from all right, but I went back to work trying not to think about the future, or the jealousy, or the fact that Caldwell owned us all.

Luke came back to the bar as we were locking up. I didn't know what to say. He didn't press, just quietly helped and then walked me out to my van. At the door, he reached for my hand. "This will be over soon."

I stared up at him, numb. "Every time I think I'm moving past all the hurt and fear, he steals another piece of my soul."

Luke shook his head. "I did meet Kaya today, and nothing happened. You're my mate, Raven. There will never be anyone else."

"Unless Caldwell gives the command." My voice broke. "When he gets tired of seeing us kiss, he'll order you to sleep with Kaya. He'll probably make me watch, and there won't be a damned thing we can do about it. If you don't do what he says, he'll have Blake put a bullet in your head. This is all a sick power trip to him."

Luke cupped my face, his thumb caressing my skin.

"Tomorrow is the full moon, then we make our move." His eyes searched mine. "I'm sorry we had to let him watch, but that kiss wasn't a show for anyone. I couldn't tell you with words how grateful I was to see you, to touch you. This Pack is a bigger shitstorm than I ever imagined. What he's doing, keeping all those wolves locked up…" He shook his head. "It's repulsive."

He paused, his tone softening. "But when I think I can't face anymore…you're my home, Raven. My peace."

His lips caressed my forehead. When he looked down at me, the moon shone in his eyes. "That kiss tonight wasn't for Blake, or Allen Caldwell, or this Pack, it was just me needing you."

I slid my hands up his chest and pulled him down, kissing him over and over, slow, hungry, my teeth grazing his bottom lip until he pressed me against the van. He ran a possessive hand up my side, his fingers splayed wide, setting me on fire with desire. When he broke the kiss, we were both breathless.

My lips brushed his as I whispered, "I'm sorry I let his comment about Kaya hurt me." I shook my head. "I've never been jealous before, but the thought of you touching another woman…I can't stand it."

He nuzzled against me, his breath warm on my cool skin. "I swear I'm going to get you away from here." Resting his forehead on mine, he whispered, "I give you my heart, my protection, and my life."

I swallowed the lump in my throat. "Sounds like some kind of…"

"Vow. A mate's promise. You're the other half of my soul, Raven. What I saw today…" He searched for words and finally shook his head. "It's going to end. And once we're sure your sister is safe and the bitten humans in the units are cared for, we're getting the hell out of here and we're never looking back."

I sniffled, my lips curving into a smile. "I love that plan." I stared up into his eyes and realized something. "I love *you*."

He laughed, scooping me up into his arms. "I am the luckiest bastard on earth."

We left my van at the bar. Luke got in the shower as soon as we got back. I couldn't blame him. I'd been to the units once. Everything about that place was wrong, and being powerless to stop it didn't make it any easier to live with the knowledge. You couldn't unsee those people, and there was no one to turn to for help.

Until Luke showed up, ready to take a stand.

I went in the kitchen and poured a glass of water, staring into the darkness. Part of me was quaking. I loved Luke. That word. I hadn't told a man I loved him since my father. It was the last thing I said to him. I hadn't realized he was saying good-bye forever. It hurt so bad that the twelve-year-old me promised I would never give a man that kind of power to wield against me.

Luke's voice echoed in my memory. *I give you my heart, my protection, and my life.*

And I believed him.

I stared at my reflection in the glass. I had my mother's cheekbones, her jaw, and her smile. She never smiled after our father left. That's when the drinking and the tranquilizers started. I'd spent my life hating her for giving up, for being weak.

But what if she had a secret we never knew? What if I let those moments I never understood steal my chance at happiness?

I turned out the lights and went into the bedroom. I lit a candle and got undressed. When I slid under the sheets, that telltale flush of dread wandered up my back, but I did my best to push it away. I was through letting my past decide my future.

Luke wasn't my father. I wasn't my mother. And our relationship was nothing like what I'd experienced with Blake and Bo.

The bathroom door opened, steam and heat filling the bedroom. Luke walked out in only a towel. And low in my belly, my body warmed in response.

His gaze flicked from the candle to me. "Everything okay?"

"Better than okay, actually."

He glanced at the bedroom door. "Should I take the couch?"

"No." I shook my head. "You should drop that towel and get in bed."

He didn't ask questions, just got under the covers and pulled me into his arms. Luke had a scent, wild and lush like a summer run in the moonlight.

"Bring me up to speed. I thought bedrooms are…tough." He kissed my hair.

I laid my head on the pillow so I could see his face. Even in the dim candlelight, the blue of his eyes was breathtaking. "They used to be. I'd like to make better memories."

A sexy smile slowly spread over his lips as his hand slid down my hip. "I'm a fan of that plan." He sobered a little. "But if you need to stop…"

I ran my finger along his jaw. "I love you." My gaze locked on his, and for once, I let my guard down and whispered, "I give you my heart, my protection, and my life. Whatever happens, I'll face it with you."

The candlelight sparkled in his eyes as he bent to kiss me. He rolled me over, his hips settling between my legs. My body ached for him, but he didn't push into me. I slid my hands down his back, my nails caressing the smooth curve of his ass.

He lifted his head just enough to growl against my lips, "I love you." He thrust forward, filling me completely, and didn't move. His teeth teased my ear. "My mate. Mine."

I bit at his shoulder, my wolf clawing closer to the surface. Instincts I didn't realize I had took over as my fingernails dug into his back. "I claim my mate."

Luke moaned, his thrusts deep, slow, and unrelenting. I ground my body into him, wrapping my legs up around his waist. We rolled over so I was on top, and I took the lead, working my hips harder and faster against him.

Our bodies were made for each other. Every move made the pleasure swell until he slid his fingers between us, rubbing me until I trembled. "Come with me, Raven."

My entire body was on fire as my orgasm rolled through me. He erupted inside me and I collapsed on his chest, trembling in his arms.

He kissed my shoulder. "That was…"

"…amazing."

"Not big enough."

A breathless chuckle escaped my lips. "True."

"How'd we do at making new memories?"

I grinned and stole a slow kiss, humming as I pulled back. "We rocked it."

...

We closed the bar early during a full moon. I put the MONTHLY STAFF MEETING sign in the window and locked the doors. Luke waited for me in the parking lot. I was dreading tonight. Once we shifted into wolves, Asher and I were tasked with keeping Luke away from Caldwell.

According to Luke, even though we were still alert and could sometimes influence the wolf when we ran, the animal instincts were in control. Luke's Alpha was up in Reno. His wolf wouldn't recognize Caldwell's dominance. If Caldwell demanded he bare his throat, Luke would probably attack.

At first, I'd thought this would solve all our problems. Luke was younger, faster, and stronger than Caldwell—he'd win in a one-on-one fight. But Caldwell was the Alpha of this Pack. Every wolf would protect him through instincts alone. Potentially even me.

The thought turned my stomach. Luke wouldn't stand a chance against an entire Pack.

But we had a plan, and I did my best to believe it would work.

I got in the car, and Luke started the engine. He reached over and ran his hand along my thigh. "Everything is going to be okay."

I puffed out a nervous breath. "What if we manage to keep you away from Caldwell but he goes after you?"

"Then I'll force my will as hard as I can and get my wolf to run. He'll never catch me."

I nodded, praying it would work out. When we got to the parking area by Bell Rock, we got out and walked toward the trail. Luke took my hand, our fingers entwining. He smiled down at me. "Our first run together."

I chuckled, shaking my head. "You make it sound romantic instead of life-on-the-line dangerous."

He lifted our hands and kissed mine. "I'll fight the change until you and Asher have shifted. It'll all work out. You'll see."

He sounded so damned confident, I almost believed him.

Chapter Twenty-Two

Luke

I put on a brave face for Raven, but inside my gut was churning. Adam hated my plan. He wanted me to find someplace else to shift, but that would mean leaving my mate unguarded with Caldwell and Blake, and that wasn't going to happen. No fucking way.

This would work. It had to.

Caldwell had a meeting spot in the middle of the red rock mountains, three miles from the nearest parking area and another two miles off the hiking trail. Apparently there was a cave that he shifted in, and tonight only Blake would be guarding it. Bo's broken ankle was going to leave him sidelined. Caldwell had locked him in the storage rec area. He wouldn't be able to escape, and Cole hoped it would keep him from running on his bad leg.

Personally, I hoped it hurt like a son of a bitch.

Asher was already waiting for us. He clasped my forearm, scanning the area. We were a good distance from the rest of the Pack. Everyone had their own place to change. Shifting from a human into a wolf was a gut-wrenching, indescribable pain, and none of us wanted an audience during the agony.

"Wait for us to get back here," Asher whispered. "If Caldwell gets too close, I'll distract him." He glanced at Raven. "If that happens, you lead your mate far from here."

She glanced my way. "No problem."

"Thanks, Asher."

He nodded and wandered into the shadows.

Raven leaned up and kissed my cheek. "Be careful."

"You, too."

She went behind the manzanita while I fought to repress my wolf. The pull of the moon's gravitation brought the wolf forward, so eventually I'd shift whether I wanted to or not, but I could hold it off for a little while.

Hopefully long enough for Asher and Raven to finish changing.

I'd never shifted without my Pack. Ever. I had no idea how disoriented my wolf would be when he realized our Pack was gone. And I prayed Asher and Raven could keep me away from Caldwell. If he demanded my submission, I probably wouldn't be able to keep my wolf from fighting—to the death.

Raven's groans on the other side of the bushes had mutated into whimpers. Joints popped, making me wince. I'd never witnessed anyone else changing, but I recognized the sounds. "Pain" wasn't a strong enough word for what Raven was experiencing right now.

Finally the brush snapped and cracked as Raven came through toward me. Her tongue lolled from her mouth, her sides still panting through the pain. She was a gorgeous black wolf with dark eyes. I smiled, and her head tilted.

"You're beautiful, Raven."

She came closer, and I held out my hand. The wolf was

cautious at first, but she recognized my scent, nuzzling into my hand. Sweat rolled down my face as I scratched behind her ears. "I can't hold off the call of the moon any longer."

The wolf didn't recognize my words, but deep inside her, Raven could. When we shifted, the human part of us was still alert, but the instinctive wolf had our consciousness. We could sometimes bend the wolf to our human will, but not always.

And this would be the first time Raven and Asher had ever tried. Yeah, Adam was probably right. This plan sucked. Fuck. Too late to back out now. I rounded the corner and undressed, leaving my jeans and T-shirt beside Raven's clothes.

The second I was naked, my back seized up, the pain dropping me on all fours. My gut wrenched, my muscles wailing as my bones grew, tearing my ligaments and reforming them. I ground my teeth to keep from screaming as my spine expanded, my tail growing. My teeth lengthened, my jaws jutting forward into a snout. Thankfully my human consciousness was drifting, taking a backseat as my wolf rushed forward, free for one night.

I rose up on wobbly legs and shook off the daze of the shift. Trotting around the manzanita bushes, my wolf skidded to a stop. Raven and Asher waited. In the depths, I did my best to calm the wolf, to push my understanding, but the wolf's heart rate raced as he tipped his head back, sniffing the wind.

He came closer, caressing our mate while simultaneously snarling at Asher. A howl in the distance had my wolf's ears pricked at attention. He tilted his head, not recognizing the Alpha's call.

Raven nudged my side in the opposite direction of the wolf's call.

A dangerous growl vibrated through my wolf's chest.

Fuck.

Before I could do anything, my wolf raced toward the enemy. Inside I fought the panic, trying to coax my wolf to turn back. Raven and Asher chased after us, but we were faster. Caldwell's scent was growing stronger, along with the rest of the Pack.

Another howl. The Alpha's call.

We bolted into the clearing, through the other wolves, growling at the large gray wolf in the center. Caldwell was formidable in wolf form, a good two inches taller at the shoulders than my wolf. But my wolf wasn't intimidated. My wolf only recognized Adam's dominance.

This was *not* Adam.

Raven jogged up next to me, nudging my sides. My wolf didn't take his focus off Caldwell. The gray Alpha bared his teeth. Beside me, Raven showed her throat in submission, recognizing him as her Alpha.

Behind me, Asher growled and bit my tail. The pain snapped my wolf out of the ritual hunger for dominance. We spun around and launched toward Asher. Raven bumped us in midair, and I rolled on the ground, scrambling to my feet. My wolf focused on her. Our mate.

Yes.

I pushed my will. *Follow Raven.* She chuffed and nudged me with her nose before bolting into the darkness.

My wolf gave chase. I followed her for miles.

...

When the sky started to lighten, we tracked the familiar human scent back to our clothes. She shifted first while my wolf kept watch. Before Raven finished, a tall man with a long black braid came toward me. I bared my sharp canines.

He smiled, his teeth bright white in the darkness. "Still pissed I bit your tail?" He shook his head. "I was saving your ass, wolf."

Asher. My wolf chuffed.

Behind me, Raven called, "Be right there."

She came around and stroked my head. We rubbed against her legs, and she knelt down to stare into my eyes. "Your turn. I'll wait for you."

She was true to her word. Once I was dressed, I found her chatting with Asher. They both turned my way, and she smiled. "You didn't make it easy, but we kept you safe."

I chuckled, my gaze moving over to Asher. "That bite probably saved me." The scent of blood stung my nostrils. My smile faded. Asher's sleeve was stained. "You're injured."

He glanced at his bicep and back to me. "I'll be fine. Cole can give me a couple stitches."

Raven frowned. "What happened?"

"After you led Luke on a chase, Caldwell turned on me."

Adrenaline shot through my bloodstream. "Fuck. He could've killed you."

"Nah." He shrugged. "I think he thought I was protecting him when I bit you—he was just pissed I let you get away. If he wanted to kill me, he would've gone for the throat."

I rubbed my hands down my face. "Thanks, man. For everything."

He nodded. "We need to get back to the others. Vance has a report from Reno."

My shoulders tensed. I had warned Adam about Vance's visit, but I had no idea if Adam had found the jaguar shifter or even which side Vance was really on.

The Sedona Pack all gathered in the oversize living room area of Caldwell's sprawling, desert-inspired mansion. I crossed my arms, struggling to keep my pulse from racing. Caldwell and Vance entered the room, but the Alpha headed straight for me.

His eyes narrowed as he leaned into my personal space. "Your wolf isn't as sure of your loyalty as you are." A muscle tensed in his cheek. "Next full moon, you'll be locked in one of the units. I don't have time for this shit."

There wouldn't be a next full moon. One of us would be dead.

I clenched my jaw, struggling to stay quiet.

He finally broke eye contact and circled the room. "Vance. Tell us what you learned so we can plan our attack."

I stared at the jaguar shifter, but Vance never met my eyes. All his attention focused on Caldwell. "Taking down the Pack in Reno won't be an easy task. Not only are the wolves well trained, but some of the females have psychic gifts. Dangerous gifts. Plus, Sasha Sloan was one of the best marksmen in all of Nero."

Caldwell crossed his arms. "We outnumber them more than two to one. We can take out some psychics, and Luke is going to take care of Sasha, right, boy?"

My gut soured as I nodded.

I'd never hurt her, and the lie that I would made me want a shower.

Caldwell spoke to Vance again. "So where are they weak? Did you find out where the Alpha lives?"

Vance rolled his shoulder back. "He has a horse ranch, Whispering Pines, just outside Reno. Without Luke there, it's just Adam Sloan and his wife and kids." He quickly added, "Adam is your target. Nero will collect his wife and children."

Caldwell raised a brow. "Antonio Severino seems very interested in his family. Why is that, do you suppose?"

I scanned the room for Isabelle. She met my eyes with an almost imperceptible shake of her head.

Vance shrugged. "I'm not paid to ask questions. I'm just passing on what I was told."

"I've done some digging of my own." Caldwell glanced over his shoulder. "Isabelle, come here."

She walked a couple of paces toward the two of them. "I gave you all the intel I could find."

He nodded. "I want you to share it with Vance."

She sighed and focused on the jaguar shifter. "She was abandoned on church steps as a baby and grew up in foster care. I can't find a connection to Nero except that she's attractive."

Vance chuckled. "Sebastian has no trouble with finding women on his own. He doesn't have to take an Alpha's widow."

This whole conversation was bugging the shit out of me. I couldn't keep my mouth shut. "None of this matters. If we're going to Reno, we need to know when, and we need a plan to get the Pack and weapons up there."

All eyes turned my way. Caldwell raised a brow. "You're eager. I like it." He sobered, his gaze moving around all of his Pack. "We leave in two days. Raven will drive the van; we'll load the weapons in the back. Bo will stay at the storage complex. He can watch over the women and children." He pivoted toward me. "Luke, I want you and Asher to work with Gage, Brock, and Ryan at the storage facility. I want them on the team in Reno."

I glanced at Asher and back to Caldwell. "We'll start tomorrow, but two days isn't enough time to—"

"It's what you've got," he barked. "No excuses. Teach them to fire a weapon, be sure they're loyal to the Pack, and report back to me. Understand, Reynolds?"

I clenched my jaw and nodded.

I had two days to end him. Shit.

Chapter Twenty-Three

Raven

I lugged cases of wine and flats of snacks into the bar. If Luke's plan worked, none of us would be moving in to attack the Pack in Reno, but until he took his shot, we had to keep up appearances. Caldwell had a weird connection to each of his Pack members. We had to be careful he didn't sense anything was off.

Luke barely slept last night. His tossing and turning kept waking me, and his moans in his sleep told me the dreams he'd been having weren't good. When I finally woke up, he was already working horses. Even though we hadn't been together long, I was starting to recognize that his coping mechanism was hard labor at the barn.

I'd wandered down before I left for the bar, but he'd been distant. Distracted. I never would have cared before, but this was all new territory for me. I loved Luke. And not being greeted with a kiss and a smile hurt a little. It shouldn't have, but it did.

We had bigger things to worry about right now.

But still.

I pushed it out of my head and helped Alexandra reload napkin holders and saltshakers. She grinned at me. "So do you have any big plans with Luke for the next week?"

Caldwell was closing the bar for a week. He claimed it was for taxes and inventory. Alexandra and Mike were excited for the surprise vacation. They had no clue Caldwell planned on killing werewolves up in Reno.

Man, my life had gotten strange.

"Not really. He still has to work. We'll probably go horseback riding and maybe see a movie."

She tucked a washcloth into the pocket of her apron. "Sounds wonderful! I'd love to go horseback riding someday."

Alexandra babbled on about their vacation plans—camping, hiking, and a trip into Phoenix for a couple days.

The door opened, interrupting her monologue. We both looked up at Caldwell.

He came in toward the register. "No one here to guard you, Raven?"

Dread crept up my spine, but I did my best to hide it. "Luke's training the guys, like you asked."

"Good." He popped open the drawer, packing cash and receipts into his bag.

I glanced around and frowned. "No Blake?"

"No." His silver eyes met mine. "He's watching Luke at the storage unit." Alexandra passed by, and he chose his words wisely. "After last night's little…show of aggression, Blake is being sure my assets are being attended to."

He laid the full money pouch on the counter and turned to Alexandra. "You and your boyfriend should take your lunch now."

She glanced at me and back to Caldwell. "All right."

Concern lined her eyes, but we all knew she needed this job, so she did as she was told. Once they were out, my pulse thrummed with anxiety.

Caldwell chuckled. "I'd like to think your heart's racing because you're aroused being alone in my presence." He took a slow breath. "But no. This is fear."

He shrugged, stalking through the chairs toward me. "Makes no difference—fear turns me on almost as much as the scent of a woman wet and ready for me."

I stood my ground, unwilling to give him the satisfaction of seeing me run. He'd catch me anyway. There was nowhere to hide from my Alpha.

He ran his finger up the outside of my arm, along my neck, and finally raised my chin. "Look at me, Raven."

"No, thanks." I stared past him to the other wall.

He tightened his grip until my jaw ached. "Look. At. Me."

His voice exuded Alpha power, pulling at the wolf inside me. I met his eyes. "I hate you."

"I know." He nodded with a cold smile.

He crushed his mouth against mine, his tongue thrusting through my tight lips. And instead of the familiar numbness, revulsion shot through me on an instinctive level.

This was *not* my mate. The wolf clawed forward, her strength adding to mine.

I slammed my knee into his groin so hard he squeaked and dropped to his knees. Scrambling back, I left him writhing, breathless on the floor of the bar. I was through being numb, through distancing myself from my body.

"Touch me again and I'll kill you." And I meant it with every fiber of my being. "I'm not your toy, and I'm not scared of you. Not anymore."

I turned around and walked out without looking back.

In the van, my hands trembled. Horrible timing for me to fight back. We were so close to getting out. Caldwell would retaliate. He'd never let my attack slide. But I couldn't help it.

I knew what it was like to be with a man who loved me.

And I was never going back to pretending I was someplace else and waiting for it to be over. He'd have to kill me.

I drove out of the lot toward Luke's place. I didn't know where else to go. My phone rang, and I almost screamed with surprise. The steering wheel was probably going to have grooves from my fingers by the time I got to Luke's place.

I hit the button to engage the Bluetooth.

"Raven? Are you all right?"

Luke's voice had never sounded so good. "Yeah. What's up?"

"I got this bad feeling. Just needed to know you were okay."

"I am now." I swallowed the lump in my throat. "I slammed my knee into Caldwell's balls and left him on the floor of the bar."

"Did he hurt you?" His tone was deep and menacing. "I'll kill him right now."

"I'm fine. For now." I watched the rearview mirror. "But we probably need to get your plan into action sooner than you planned."

Gunshots exploded in the background. "I'll leave Blake to finish up with these guys. Wait for me at home. I have a Glock in the bedroom closet. Remember how to load it?"

"Yeah." He'd only taken me shooting once so far, but I was pretty sure I could figure it out. "Be careful. If he calls Blake and gives him an order…"

"I'll watch my back." He paused and added, "I'll be home soon."

I loaded the Glock and laid it on the table. It should've made me feel safe, but I wasn't confident about shooting it. Now if I had a baseball bat, I could do some damage. Luke's Mustang purred coming down the drive, and relief swelled inside me.

He parked, and I met him at the door, fusing my lips to his. His fingers tangled in the back of my hair, his tongue twining with mine, erasing the memory of Caldwell. My heart raced, and not out of fear. Without breaking the kiss, he bent his knees and lifted me into his arms to carry me into the house.

Inside, he set my feet on the floor and looked me over. He brushed a kiss to my chin, and I tried not to wince.

His voice was barely a growl. "Did he hit you?"

I shook my head. "He squeezed it hard, but I'm okay."

His gaze wandered over my face. He didn't ask why Caldwell had my chin. He could probably guess. I held my breath. If he came unglued and ran for the bar, the whole plan would unravel. Fast.

Without a word, he pulled me into the safety of his arms. No judgment and no questions. I closed my eyes and breathed him into my lungs.

"Tomorrow." He kissed my hair. "This ends tomorrow."

...

It was almost midnight when Asher knocked on the door. Luke let him in, offering him a chair at the table.

Asher's dark eyes met mine. His mouth pressing into a thin line. I hadn't looked in a mirror, but judging by his expression, my chin was probably a nice shade of purple now.

He glanced at Luke. "What can I do to help?"

"Be available. I'm not going to show up at Caldwell's side in the morning. He shouldn't be surprised, since he hurt my mate. He'll need someone to back up Blake at the storage unit. Be sure it's you he takes."

He nodded slowly, but he didn't look convinced. "I hope you have a backup plan. There's no guarantee he'll choose me. You haven't been here long, but bitten wolves like me aren't as respected as the wolves born into their heritage."

The truth was, Asher and Ryker were the only two bitten wolves who had made it out of the units. Being bitten made them pawns for Caldwell, not members of the Pack.

Luke rubbed the back of his neck. "I'm going to be on the roof of the units. I can have a clear shot without human witnesses. Caldwell goes up to his office alone while Blake takes the others to the rec area. That's when I'll take my shot."

Before Asher could say anything, I added, "I'll be up there with Luke. If things go south, we face it together."

Asher raised a brow, a smile hinting at his lips. "That wasn't Luke's plan."

I shook my head as Luke's eyes met mine. "The plan's changed."

Luke nodded slowly. "Be sure you keep the others—namely Blake—occupied. I'll take care of Caldwell."

"I can do that, but if he chooses someone else..."

"Then I'll wing it."

I rested my hand on Luke's. "I can help, too."

He focused on me. "We need to get a message to Isabelle, too. See what she's found out about Caldwell's holdings."

"I'm on it." I started to send a text and stopped. "What about Blake and Bo?"

Asher got up from the table. "Blake has no friends in the units. With Caldwell out of the picture, no one will protect him."

Luke stood and clasped Asher's forearm. No one said the words out loud, but there was a better than average chance Blake would die tomorrow, too. I tried to muster some pity, or any emotion, but all I managed was dread. I wanted this to end. One way or the other.

Asher walked out and Luke locked the door. When he turned to face me, I realized one more thing.

I didn't care what happened to Caldwell, to Blake, to me, but Luke needed to live. And I'd do anything to be sure that happened.

Chapter Twenty-Four

Luke

I turned off my cell. Caldwell had sent a couple of texts, and the repeated phone calls were pissing me off.

He knew goddamn well why I wasn't answering his calls.

Raven hadn't said anything, but for her to knee him in the groin, he'd been too close to her. The bruise on her chin had rage festering in my gut, but it was the urgent, aching kiss when I got home that told me all I needed to know.

His scent was on her lips. That fucking asshole had tried to force himself on my mate.

But he hadn't expected her to fight back.

I carried the saddle back to the tack room, a bitter smile tugging at my mouth. Raven had hurt him. She'd protected herself. She'd surprised him. Maybe herself, too.

Raven came down to the barn, her arms tight around herself. "Isabelle replied. She said Caldwell has taken control of every bitten wolf's assets. Even Asher is giving him all the income from his touring company."

"If Caldwell checks them out first to be sure they don't have family nearby to miss them, no one would know. And the wolves have no one to turn to now that they can't go to the police."

He'd mutated his position as Alpha into a werewolf mob boss.

Her cell phone vibrated. She read the text and then showed it to me. Caldwell's name was at the top.

Come to the bar right now. Bring Luke with you.

She looked up at me. "I'm contemplating sending 'Fuck you' back."

I laughed. And *damn*, did I love her. "Go ahead. I'll grab my stuff and we can go stake out the storage unit."

She grinned and fired it off. "We better get out of here. Cole knows where you work. Caldwell could be here soon."

We didn't waste any time. I loaded my gear into the trunk of the Mustang, and we drove away. I parked in a busy coffee shop parking lot about a mile from the storage unit. Hopefully it wouldn't be noticed. Since I wasn't sure when Caldwell would be at the units, Raven got an Uber to take us over.

After casing the area for security cameras, we found a blind spot along the back fence. I slung my gear over my shoulder, and we climbed over the chain-link fence. Once we were inside, we stayed close to the building, hopefully dodging the security system.

If we had had another day, I could've learned about the building security, but Caldwell's actions the night before had escalated the plan.

We'd make it work.

We had to.

When we got to the unit closest to the office, I took a running jump for the edge of the roof. Clinging by my fingertips, I hauled myself up. Every muscle in my arms ached with the effort, but I made it.

I lay on my stomach and held a hand down toward Raven. "Jump. I'll pull you up."

She rubbed her hands on her jeans. "Maybe there's a ladder."

"No time." I opened my hand. "You can do this. You're a werewolf. Push your legs and jump."

She backed up and ran. When she launched herself into the air, she splayed her fingers wide, reaching for the roof. She caught it, but one hand slipped.

I grabbed her free hand. "I've got you."

Again, I was thankful for the extra strength the wolf gave me as I pulled her up with one hand.

Once we were both on the roof, we crawled to the edge, staring into the quiet storage area. Raven's heart was racing like a Thoroughbred.

I squeezed her hand. "This is going to work."

She nodded, and I opened my case, assembling my rifle and scope. Her phone buzzed.

"Oh, shit." The color drained from her face. She turned her cell around so I could see the pic.

Isabelle was tied to a chair in the bar with a gun pointed at her head.

A text followed.

If Luke Reynolds isn't here in an hour, your sister dies.

"Fuck." I stood up, frustration boiling over. "He's not even coming over here."

Raven's voice choked. "We're all dead. I can't let him kill her, but you know he'll kill us when we get there."

"Damn it." I shook my head, pacing. "I need to think."

I rubbed my hand down my face, fighting the urge to call Adam. He'd insist we wait for him to get down here. Isabelle would be dead by then. There had to be another way, I just needed to find it.

Banging started below us on the metal security door, followed by a voice I recognized. "Who's up there? Help us."

Gage.

I glanced over at Raven. "We're not going to the bar alone."

With my rifle over my shoulder, I dropped from the roof and looked up at Raven. "Jump. I've got you."

She crossed her arms. "Find a ladder."

I shook my head slowly, meaning every word. "There is no way in *hell* I'm going to let you fall."

"Not on purpose."

"Not ever," I growled.

Her gaze locked on mine as she sat on the edge. "If you miss…"

"Not gonna happen."

She took a breath, then scooted off. I caught her in my arms and set her feet on the ground. She smiled up at me. "Thanks."

"Any time." I banged on the door and called out. "Gage? It's Luke."

His voice came through the door. "Ready for more training."

I gripped the padlock and pulled with all my strength. The Master Lock didn't budge, but the latch ripped out of the sheet metal with a screech. I rolled the door up and stared at the men inside. "No more training and no more cages."

They looked at each other and then back at us. "He'll kill us all."

I shook my head slowly. "Not if we take him out first."

Gage clenched his fists. "I'm in."

Brock and Ryan weren't as gung-ho. "Can we hear the plan first?"

Raven rolled her eyes. "You'd seriously rather stay locked up here?"

Ryan grumbled and crossed his arms. "I'd rather stay alive."

"Fair enough." I tilted my head toward the rest of the units. "Help me get the others free and meet me in the rec area."

The others moved down the aisle to tear off locks and explain the situation. Raven and I broke open the unit with Kaya and the other two women with babies. My gut twisted at the fear in their eyes. "We're getting you out of here. Grab what you need for the little ones."

Raven went inside to help. For a second she and Kaya stared at each other. Finally Raven held out her hand. Kaya looked at it and back up to her eyes. She went to take Raven's hand, and Raven moved forward to clasp Kaya's forearm.

"This is how packmates greet each other."

The corners of Kaya's lips curved up. "Packmate sounds a hell of a lot better than prisoner."

Raven met my eyes, and something in my chest burned. God, I loved her. I snapped out of it and hustled in to help the redhead in the back corner. Her twins were already walking. It was tough to guess their age, since werewolves mature so much faster than human babies. A werewolf female gave birth after four months, and the babies grew physically and mentally at a rapid pace. It leveled out around five years old, but it kept our kids out of preschool for sure.

"I'm Luke."

"I'm Naomi." She handed me a wriggly toddler. "And that's Bart." Placing the other boy on her hip, she reached for the diapers. "And this is Ben."

Bart squealed. "Down! Mama…"

I didn't grant his request. "How old are they?"

She straightened up. "Eight months."

I bit back a curse. "You've been trapped here for…"

"I was bitten over a year ago." Her dark eyes hardened.

We started for the door, and Brock met us. He took Bart from me and put the wriggler up on his shoulders. Bart giggled, gripping handfuls of Brock's hair.

But both Brock and Naomi had dark eyes and dark hair. Little Bart's eyes were bright, almost silver. Familiar.

I frowned and glanced over at Naomi. "Is Brock their father?"

She shrugged. "I hope so."

I ground my teeth together. "Caldwell chose more than one mate."

"Yeah." Her gaze met mine. "Brock was one of them."

"And the other?"

She walked ahead, but her words were easy enough to catch. "Allen Caldwell."

Gage stopped me at the door. "Everyone is waiting in the rec area."

I half expected a "sir" at the end of Gage's report. "Were you in the military?"

He nodded. "Air force."

I clasped his forearm. "I know this wasn't the life you would have chosen, but once we finish Caldwell, this Pack is going to need you."

He gripped my arm tight, his expression resolute. "I've got nowhere else to go."

I shook my head. "Not good enough."

"I've been trapped in a storage unit, survived my body contorting into a wolf, and been at the mercy of a guy who gets off on pairing people up to see if they can pop out some babies." His jaw clenched. "I won't run away, but right now, that's all I have to give."

I released his arm and nodded slowly. "This ends today."

We headed for the rec area. What the hell was I doing? I wasn't an Alpha, but if we hoped to beat Caldwell, they needed one.

Raven came to my side and took my hand. "I don't know if this is a good idea."

I met her eyes. "We're running out of time and options. This is the best I've got."

She searched my eyes and tightened her grip. "I'm with you."

I pressed my lips to her temple and stepped into the center of the rec area. "Caldwell has a gun pointed at Raven's sister right now. We have to show up or he'll kill her, but you know him. When we get there, he'll kill all three of us. Then he'll take the men and lead you up to Reno to attack my Pack."

Crossing my arms over my chest, I scanned the group of bitten wolves. "My Pack is expecting Caldwell. They're armed and trained, and most likely, even though this Pack outnumbers them, they'll win. Caldwell is bringing you as shields to protect the born wolves."

Brock lifted the little one from his shoulders and handed him to Naomi. "Why should we believe you?"

My gaze locked on his. "Because I'm the one who broke the locks off the doors." Looking at the others, I went on. "I have my loaded rifle here, but it's not aimed at any of you. None of you will be forced to do anything. In fact, if you didn't at least consider telling me to fuck off, I'd be worried about your sanity, because what I'm about to ask of you borders on insane."

No one walked out. Good sign. I dropped my hands to my sides. "None of you should have been bitten. None of you should have been locked up. But the end result is the same. You're a Wolf Pack now, and unlike what that sadistic asshole might've told you, your strength doesn't come from fear." My eyes found Raven's. "It comes from love."

I turned toward Gage. "You all have survived in this hellhole. You've helped each other keep your wits. You're strong. It's time to pull together and take out the tyrant. Caldwell is *not* your Alpha. An Alpha loves his Pack above all else. An Alpha doesn't order his wolves to bite humans; he doesn't keep them as prisoners or threaten their lives in trade for their loyalty."

Gage interrupted. "What do you want from us?"

I lifted the strap holding my rifle over my head and handed the loaded weapon to Gage. There were a couple audible gasps. It was a risk, but none of them knew I still had my Glock holstered at the small of my back. I wanted to trust Gage and the others, but the truth was, I could get a shot off before he could even aim that rifle.

He took it, staring at the weapon, then me. "I could kill you and run."

I nodded. "You could, but as long as Caldwell is alive, he can find you. He's a powerful Alpha. But he won't be expecting all of us. I'm asking you to have my back. Raven and I will go inside the bar, but you'll surround it. If Caldwell makes it outside, end him."

Gage put the rifle over his shoulder. "What about Bo and Blake?"

"Asher took care of Bo. He won't be a problem. And if Blake gets in our way, he goes down, too."

Gage glanced at his cell mates and they nodded. He met my eyes. "We're in."

Naomi stood, holding the pudgy hands of her twin boys. "What about the rest of us?"

I turned toward Raven. "We need to stay together."

Kaya came forward, standing beside my mate. "I'll protect them."

Before our eyes, her form shivered, like a mirage coming up from the hot highway. Her features morphed, and in less than a minute, a large bobcat snarled. I'd never seen anything like it.

One of Naomi's little twins squealed and broke free. "Kitty!"

He hugged her leg, and the deadly cat licked his hair, grooming him. Again the air went electric, her shape wavering until she was Kaya again. "I shift sometimes in the unit to entertain the little ones." She smiled over at me. "You've never met a skin-walker."

I shook my head. "I didn't know they were real."

"We are. And if things go south at the bar, I'll keep them safe."

"Thank you." I took Raven's hand. "We need a way to transport everyone."

She peered around me toward Brock. "You used to work on cars, right?"

He nodded.

"Caldwell has a cargo van up by the office. Think you can hot-wire it?"

He almost smiled. "I know I can."

Oh, shit. This might actually work.

Chapter Twenty-Five

Raven

The unmarked white van followed us to the bar. We were praying Caldwell wouldn't already sense the others were free from the storage units, but we had no way of knowing the limits of his Alpha senses.

Brock parked at the strip mall across the street. They would all come to the Wolf Pack Bar on foot, but Kaya would keep the women and children in the parking lot behind my van. I gave her the key in case they needed a quick getaway, but for now, we were safer in numbers. None of them had ID or money, and they couldn't go to a hospital or the police, so our options were limited.

As Luke and I headed to the door, I stopped. He turned my way. "What's wrong?"

I almost laughed, but it strangled in my throat. "Besides everything?"

He ran a finger down my cheek. "Whatever happens, I have no regrets. Finding you has been the best thing that's ever happened to me, and I wouldn't give that up for anything."

Tears welled in my eyes. "You owe me at least twenty years to love you, so no getting killed today."

"Deal." He bent to kiss me, and my breath hitched as I drank in his taste. He pulled back slowly, gaze locked on mine. "Let's finish this so we can go home."

Home. I hadn't had one in so long. "I like that plan."

He opened the door and I stepped inside. Against the back wall, Asher and Ryker stood together, tense. By the bar, the born wolves, Dex and Deacon and Chase and Cole, were beside Bo.

Isabelle tugged at her bonds, shouting behind her gag. Where was…

I turned just as Blake buried his fist in my stomach. I fell to my knees with no breath to scream. He grabbed my arm and dragged me to a chair.

What happened to Luke?

I tried to twist to see, stars igniting on the edge of my vision. Furniture crashed, and a gun fired. The silence magnified the lifeless thump. My voice strangled in my breathless chest. Suddenly Blake dropped me on the ground, leaving me heaving for air.

Bo lay in a crumpled heap, a puddle of blood expanding around him as his brother knelt at his side. Luke had his Glock pointed at Caldwell.

Sadly, the Alpha was now behind my sister, the barrel of his gun buried under her chin.

Power thrummed in Caldwell's voice. "Seems you have three choices, Reynolds. Either you shoot through your mate's sister to get me, or you wait for me to kill her first, or you do the right thing and *put your fucking gun down*."

Luke didn't move.

Caldwell chuckled. "Good. Your mate can see what a heartless bastard you really are. Either way I win."

I crawled around the back of the chair toward my sister and pulled out my phone. I fired off a single text.

Now!

The front and back doors both exploded open at the same time, Gage and Brock in the front and Ryan at the back.

Caldwell shouted, "Dex and Deacon, take the back. The rest of you, grab those useless bastards."

Time slowed to a crawl, like an action movie sequence, only this was real. Gunpowder stung my nostrils as the rapid fire deafened my ears. Bodies flew through the air, furniture tumbled over, but my focus stayed on Isabelle. It was my fault she was here.

Since our father walked out, I'd wasted so much of my life looking for someone to save me.

Time to save myself and make things right with my sister.

Caldwell kept the pistol under Isabelle's chin, but with his free hand he cut her bonds. "One wrong move, bitch, and I'll make your sister clean your brains off the ceiling."

He yanked her out of the chair, clutching her close like a shield as he made his way behind the bar. The bastard was trying to get out the back door.

I followed, but I needed a weapon. Scanning behind the bar, my heart sank. Napkins, straws, plastic stirrers—but then I noticed the ice pick next to the ice drawer. It would have to do. I snatched it by the handle and kept moving. He was almost to the door. Time was running out.

"Let her go!"

He turned, his lips curving into a twisted smile. He moved his pistol from my sister's chin to point it at me. Isabelle didn't hesitate. She slammed an elbow into his ribs. One shot hit the floor before he dropped the pistol. Isabelle bolted, but he grabbed a fistful of her hair, slamming her head into the steel door. Isabelle crumbled to the ground; then he took a step toward me.

"Did you and your new boyfriend think killing your Alpha would be easy? Think again." His eyes narrowed, and power flooded his deep baritone. "Open the door for me, Raven."

I blinked, shaking my head.

"Now."

Pain shot through my head. The wolf inside me whimpered. I walked toward the door and the agony eased.

"That's it."

The sunlight assaulted my eyes as I held the door wide-open for Caldwell to pass through. He took the ice pick from my other hand. "Turn around and put your hands on the building."

My heart pounded in my ears, my fingers trembling as I struggled to break his spell.

"Now, Raven."

I ground my teeth, fighting to resist, but it was useless. I pressed my palms to the painted wood.

"Good girl." He gripped my ass, his hot breath on my cheek. "Stay right here. I'll be back for you."

He slammed the ice pick right through my hand, burying it into the back wall of the Wolf Pack Bar. I screamed, pinned in place.

His teeth grazed my ear. "Say my name."

His erection pressed against me, and something snapped. I reached up with my other hand and jerked the ice pick free. In one swift movement, I swung it behind me, burying the tip into the side of Caldwell's neck.

When I turned around, he dropped to his knees. "Bitch."

But his voice choked, blood bubbling up on his lips. He fumbled to grab the handle of the ice pick. I backed away, stunned by the gore. My sister groaned, snapping me out of the horror. I spun away from the visceral scene, rushing to her side.

She sat up, her hand pressed to her head.

"I'm so sorry, Isabelle." Hot tears ran down my cheeks.

She frowned. "You're bleeding."

I lifted my left hand and glanced back. Caldwell didn't move. As the adrenaline ebbed, the pain blossomed.

So did my worry for Luke.

"Wait here," I whispered.

Blood dripped from my fingertips as I crept back into the bar. The rich odor of blood mingled with the gunpowder now. Dread coiled inside me. I peered over the bar. Broken glass, pieces of furniture, and battered men littered the room. Asher and Cole were both bleeding as they tended to Ryker. He wasn't moving.

I scanned the room, unable to breathe. Where was he?

Something moved in the corner. Luke. Relief swamped me as I rushed to his side. He clung to one of the tables, pulling himself to his feet. He clutched me to him, his hands shaking, chest heaving. "Thank god. I thought he took you. You're all right." He kissed my hair and froze. "You're bleeding."

I held my hand up. "Flesh wound."

He turned it over and winced. "Fuck. I'll kill that bastard. Slow."

I shook my head, tremors moving into my hands. "Already did."

His eyes softened. Did he know I'd never watched someone die before, let alone delivered the killing blow? Nausea swelled. I stumbled away, losing everything I'd eaten. Luke hobbled behind me, his arm around my waist steadying me. When I straightened up, he almost lost his balance.

I glanced at his leg. "What happened?"

"I'm pretty sure my knee is broken. Chase took me out with a stool."

I turned around, looking for Chase. But something caught my eye. Bo was missing. His blood still covered the floor, but no body. A trail of blood led to the front door. It had to be Blake. There was no way Bo could've walked on his own.

No sign of Blake, either.

Then I noticed Chase on the floor in the other corner. Motionless.

Cole stopped compressions on his brother. He met my eyes. He didn't have to say anything. The pain on his face told me all I needed to know. Chase was gone.

The front door opened, and we all froze.

"Ah, fuck." Vance closed the door behind him and locked it. "What the hell happened?"

Isabelle leaned on the bar, the side of her head swollen, one eye already discolored. "Caldwell's dead. Tell your boss this is over. We're not going to Reno. He can take care of his vendetta on his own."

Vance blew out a breath, taking in the carnage. He shook his head, crossing his arms. "First things first, we need to clean this up. Fast. If the police show up right now, we're all screwed."

The police. Reality pierced through the shock. I took in the aftermath, but I couldn't formulate a solution.

Asher came forward, pressing one of the bar rags to the cut on his forehead. "Where are the others?"

It took me a second to realize who he meant. Then it clicked. "The women and children are out back in the van. Kaya was guarding them."

He nodded slowly, his dark eyes scanning the room. When no one else spoke, Asher pushed on. "Someone needs to take them to Caldwell's place while we clean this up. We'll meet them there."

I wasn't leaving Luke. Plus, I was bleeding. Did we have anyone who wasn't bleeding? I glanced around, and Isabelle straightened up. "I'll fish the keys out of Caldwell's pocket and take them over."

Luke stood tall, but his weight was heavy on my shoulder. His voice was strong, though. No sign of weakness. "Caldwell is dead. If any of you are loyal to him, get the hell out. We won't follow you. Just go."

I held my breath, but no one moved. Finally, Cole turned around, his eyes rimmed in red. "My brother and I hated the path he was leading us down, but…" He shook his head. "Blind loyalty." He cursed under his breath, breaking eye contact. "Chase is…I'm not losing anyone else."

Dex crossed to Cole and turned toward us. "I'm staying, too."

"Me, too." Deacon cradled his wounded arm.

Asher placed his hand on Cole's shoulder. "Can you tend to the wounded while we clean up?"

Cole cleared his throat and nodded. He'd have to mourn later.

I helped Luke to a chair while he waited for Cole to brace his leg. He caught my uninjured hand as I turned away. "Wait."

Tears welled in my eyes. "I need to clean this up."

"In a second." He searched my face. "It's over. You did what you had to do."

I swallowed the lump in my throat. "I know."

He was right. But I couldn't stop hearing Caldwell's last word in my head. *Bitch*. The blood liquefying his voice. I didn't want to think or talk about it—I just wanted it to end.

My fingers slid free of his, and this time he didn't stop me. I went to the bar and wrapped my hand. Cole could take a look at it later. There were others who needed medical attention more than I did. I tried not to notice Vance and Asher carrying the bodies out back. We'd lost Ryan and Chase, and Cole was still working on Brock.

Behind the bar, I pulled out my cell phone, surprised to see it was not only still on but unscathed, the time and date blazing like I hadn't just killed a man. I watched Luke, the muscle in his cheek tight, his fists clenched.

He wouldn't like what I was about to do, but it didn't change that it needed to be done. I sent a text to Logan, since he was the only member of the Reno Pack in my phone.

Caldwell is dead. Luke might have a broken leg. He told me you have a doctor in your Pack. We could use him.

I hit send and pocketed my phone. The ache in my hand pulsed as I mopped up the blood where Bo had been shot. Maybe he'd been alive when Blake pulled him out of the bar, but this was a lot of blood. Without a hospital…Bo was probably dead, too. He and Caldwell could both rot in hell.

Vance grabbed a broom from the back and cleaned up all the glass, while Asher carried the broken furniture out back. Soon, you'd never know there had been a bloodbath in the Wolf Pack Bar.

Sadly, I didn't think I'd ever be able to forget.

Chapter Twenty-Six

Luke

I could move my toes, but my knee was so swollen now that my jeans were tight around it. Not a good sign. But I'd live.

It didn't look so good for Brock. He was still breathing, but he hadn't regained consciousness.

Blood was soaking through the towel Raven had tied around her hand. For a second, I forgot my own wound and started to get up and go to her. *Damn it!* I sank back into the chair. My hands shaking with the pain.

Cole came toward me, his face all business. "Where are you injured?"

I pointed at my knee.

He glanced down and back up. "Be right back." He returned with a box cutter. Exposing the razor blade, he cut along the seam for a couple of inches and then tore the fabric open just past my knee. Starting at the bottom, he put pressure on the swelling. "Pain?"

I shook my head. "Not really."

He moved his hand up closer to my kneecap. "Now?"

"Fuck!" I blinked away stars clouding my vision. "Yeah. That hurts."

He rocked back on his heels. "It's too swollen for me to get a good idea if it's broken or a torn ligament. I can take an X-ray at my office later; for now I'm going to get some ice. You need to keep it on your knee, okay?"

I nodded, and Cole headed behind the bar. If I had just lost Logan, there's no way I would've been able to tend to other people. Maybe it made it easier for Cole if he kept busy. Either way, I appreciated his help.

Vance came over while Cole was busy filling a bag with ice. "We've got the bodies in the back of Raven's van." He scanned the bar. "And this place is as put together as it's going to get."

I looked up at him. "What's Nero's next move?"

He chuckled. "That would be way above my pay grade."

I almost smiled. "I am *not* used to hearing jaguar shifters laugh."

"If you tell anyone, I'll deny it."

I shook my head, sobering. "Thanks for your help here."

"No one wants the humans to find out shifters exist. We can all agree on that much."

I stared at Raven pulling the trash bags free of the cans.

Vance nudged my shoulder. "You taking the lady back to Reno?"

"As soon as we can."

But even with the physical mess cleaned up, I wasn't sure Raven and I could just walk away. The shifters left behind, and the babies…they needed to pull together. They needed a Pack.

And an Alpha.

I couldn't drive with my bum knee—hell, I almost couldn't get into the damn van. We opened all the windows, but we couldn't escape the stench of death. Raven didn't complain. In fact, she barely spoke.

We were taking the dead to Caldwell's estate. Back home, we cremated our dead out on Adam's ranch where humans wouldn't disturb us. It also didn't leave any evidence for a medical examiner.

These bodies, riddled with gunshot and puncture wounds, meant we had to be extra careful the authorities didn't discover them.

Isabelle let us in the gates, and Raven drove along the back toward a second garage. Her phone buzzed as she turned off the engine.

She stared at the screen, then over at me. "Is your cell on?"

"I didn't turn it off." I pulled it out, but the screen was black, the glass cracked in many places. I held it up. "But I guess my knee wasn't my only casualty."

She didn't smile. "You're not going to like this, but it was for your own good."

I raised a brow and waited for her to go on.

"I texted Logan that you need your Pack doctor."

"Shit." I glanced out the window. "I told you I don't want them mixed up in this."

She got out of the van and came around to my side. I was already out, keeping my weight on my good leg. She slid her arm around my waist, but I didn't move.

"Cole can handle this. I just need a brace and a crutch."

Raven tipped her head back, her eyes narrowing a little. "Caldwell is dead. The threat is over. Let your Pack help you. Why are you being so hardheaded about keeping them from coming here?"

Good question. I wasn't sure I knew the answer. It had

started out being the danger of Caldwell bringing his Pack to Reno. I knew Adam couldn't spare anyone when they were so outnumbered.

But now?

Grudgingly, I let Raven help me inside the house. Although we were at the far end of the sprawling mansion, the squeals of the little ones, free for the first time in their lives, warmed my heart. "Wait."

Raven looked up at me. "Do you need to sit?"

"Not yet. I have to tell you something." I swallowed the lump in my throat. "I'm not mad. You made the right call. It's just…" I shook my head and stared out the window. "Ever since I got to Sedona, with my new job, you, this Pack, I've been Luke Reynolds, head trainer, mate, leader of a rebellion…" I chuckled, shaking my head. "As soon as Jason and Logan get here, I'm Logan's little brother. The moody one, youngest guy in the Pack."

I met her eyes. "I like who I am *here*. And in spite of all our injuries, I hear those little guys laughing, and I helped make that happen. I did it on my own."

She reached up to cup my cheek. "You are so much more than Logan's little brother. You showed us the way a Wolf Pack should be. Because of you, we all pulled together and believed we could be free from Caldwell."

Her dark eyes searched mine. "I'm not in love with the baby of a Pack." Her full lips curved into a sexy smile. "I'm in love with this amazing man who made me believe I matter. I've never met a better man with a bigger heart and the courage to match. No one can ever take that from you."

My vision blurred as I blinked hard and pulled her close, kissing her slowly. Resting our foreheads together, my gaze locked on hers, I whispered, "You were worth waiting for."

"I love you." She kissed me once more. "And that text said Logan and Jason just landed in Phoenix. They'll be here in a couple hours."

"We better get busy. There's still a lot to get done."

Raven got me settled on the couch, and Cole put more ice on my knee, elevating it while Asher gave me an update.

"Vance and Jett are at the bar assuring the police the noises people heard were illegal fireworks, not gunfire."

I raised a brow. "I didn't see Jett at the fight tonight."

Asher nodded. "He works for a security company as a bodyguard. He was on a job."

"Okay." I met his eyes. "What about Brock?"

He sighed, keeping his voice low. "Still unconscious. Cole's worried he has internal bleeding."

Not good. "Any sign of Blake?"

He shook his head. "Blake and Bo are still unaccounted for, but they've probably left town. Without Caldwell, they have no power here."

"Where's Gage?"

Asher tipped his head toward the other room. "He's with Samantha. Caldwell mated her to Chase and Gage, with Chase gone…"

"He's a good man." I crossed my arms. "Are the twins his?"

He shrugged. "We don't know."

"You're going to have to rebuild this Pack the right way. Just because a woman is bitten and can carry a shifter's baby doesn't make her his mate. The wolf inside decides, not the Alpha." He still seemed puzzled, so I added, "If she finds her true mate and touches him, it won't matter how well Gage treats her, she'll need her mate. Same goes for him."

"And the one who hasn't found their mate yet…"

"…will be hurt they leave."

He nodded slowly. "I understand."

"You've got a lot to fix here."

"*We* have a lot to fix."

I frowned. "This isn't my Pack."

His gaze met mine. "But it could be. I already talked to Dex and Deacon. We want you and Raven to stay. You can be our Alpha."

Chapter Twenty-Seven

Raven

I left Luke on the couch with Asher and went to find my sister. Tracking her scent, I found her behind Caldwell's desk in his office. She set a folder down and got to her feet. We met in the middle of the room, hugging each other tight.

When she stepped back, her gaze held mine. "How are you holding up?"

"I killed a man today." My voice wobbled, but I got the words out.

She pointed to my bandaged hand. "In self-defense."

I nodded. "Yeah, but still…"

"If it didn't freak you out, I'd be worried about you."

I smiled and sat in a leather chair; she took the one next to me. Picking at my nails, I whispered, "I'm sorry I got you mixed up in all this."

"None of this was your fault. Bo bit you."

I lifted my head. "I realized today that ever since Dad left, I wanted someone to save me, Mom, men, you…" I shook my head. "I'm through with that."

She smiled. "You're like Dorothy in *The Wizard of Oz*. You had the power all along."

I rolled my eyes. "I wish I had discovered that a few years ago."

"Time travel isn't possible yet, so ease up on yourself." She gripped my knee. "Just make the future count, okay?"

I nodded. "I plan to."

Her gaze wandered to the door. "Have you thought about what happens next?"

"We haven't made any real plans. I'm excited to go to Reno and get a fresh start." I was sure I already knew the answer, but I had to ask. "Will you come with us?"

She sighed and went over to the desk. "I can't. Caldwell kept everything rolled into his corporation, so I need to get some paperwork filed and set up a power of attorney. I'll also have to get the word out that he's gone abroad, pondering retirement. Then I'll carve out all the businesses he stole and get them back to their rightful owners."

I shook my head. "You got roped into this mess—you shouldn't get stuck cleaning it up."

She looked up from the paperwork. "There's something else keeping me here."

I frowned. "What?"

"Dad."

My jaw went slack. "Dad? How so?"

She rested back into the chair. "When I was digging into Lana Sloan and Luke mentioned Nero's breeding program and the school for psychics…" She stared at the ceiling. "Mom graduated from Brightwood. You and I have a connection to Nero somehow. I can feel it in my gut. We're missing a big piece of the puzzle. They wouldn't just let her walk away."

"Can't you research in Reno? Luke's Pack has more intel about Nero than anyone here."

"Wrong." She shook her head. "Vance is here for now, and when he tells Severino that his buddy Caldwell is dead, he'll probably send Sebastian back to get even, or take over, or who the hell knows. But this Pack was in bed with Nero. I've got a better chance at finding the information I'm looking for if I stay here."

"I'm going to miss you." My chest burned.

A soft smile warmed her lips, and for just a moment, she reminded me of our mother before our dad left. "Reno isn't that far. We'll visit and Skype. And once I have everything I need, I'll head in your direction."

"Deal." I got up. "Logan and Jason, the doctor from Luke's Pack, should be here soon to help out. You should let him look at your head. You could have a concussion."

"He can check it, but I'm sure I'm fine. I've got a hard head."

"I love you."

She came over and held me tight. "I love you, too." She pulled away and went back to the desk. "And you're not leaving tonight, right? We've got a few more days."

I nodded. "Yeah. I don't think Luke is good to travel yet."

"So I'll keep working here, and if I can find answers, I'll start looking for work in Reno."

I opened the gate for Logan and Jason's SUV to pull through. Logan parked and got out, staring at the snow-topped peaks of the red rock mountains. Finally, he shook his head and turned my way.

"My brother didn't tell me it's so damned beautiful here." Logan wore his hair longer than Luke, but otherwise, it would be tough to tell them apart. He covered the distance between us in a few steps and opened his arms. I gave him a quick squeeze, trying not to be starstruck.

But holy crap, Logan from Logan and the Howlers just hugged me!

He grinned. "Great to finally meet you, Raven." He turned to the man behind him. "This is Dr. Jason Ayers."

Jason wasn't like any doctor I'd ever met. He was rugged and probably got mistaken for Hugh Jackman in airports. He had a duffel bag in one hand and offered me the other. I passed his hand and clasped his forearm.

He smiled, gripping my arm. "I forgot you're already a wolf." His attention shifted to the house. "Where's my patient?"

I took them inside, and Luke got up despite Cole's instructions not to move. Logan rushed forward and clasped his forearms before tugging his brother into a tight embrace.

"Good to see you." Logan helped Luke back onto the couch. "You didn't tell me your mate was gorgeous."

Luke chuckled. "Didn't want to make you jealous."

They elbowed each other, reverting to ten-year-old boys, while Jason opened his bag.

Cole came around the corner and froze. "You must be Dr. Ayers."

Jason stood up and nodded. "Yeah. Are you the Pack doctor here?"

"Pack medic." Cole cleared his throat. "I'm actually a veterinarian, but I'm all we've got."

I was expecting judgment or an aloof dismissal; instead Jason smiled and clasped his forearm. "Good to meet you. My dad is a vet, too. He was the Pack doctor up in Reno until I finished med school."

"I'm Dr. Cole Vega." His shoulders relaxed. "When you finish with Luke, maybe you can help me with one of our other guys. And Raven's sister might have a concussion."

Luke added, "Be sure you check Raven's hand, too."

"Sure." Jason knelt in front of Luke. "Let me have a look at your knee, and then I'll make the rounds with Cole for the others."

While Jason worked on Luke, I went into the kitchen. Exhaustion weighed me down, but we had a houseful of werewolves who were going to be starving once the shock of the day wore off. I pulled open the fridge, scanning the contents, when I realized suddenly that I was inside Caldwell's house and I wasn't tense. The noises all around me didn't have me jumpy, waiting for the other shoe to drop.

It was over. I was free.

Sniffling, I fought back the wave of emotions threatening to drown me. I was *not* going to lose my shit in the middle of making dinner. I took out two large packages of hamburger meat and two big skillets. Tacos would be easy.

As I lit the burners, Kaya came around the corner. "Can I help?"

I plopped the hamburger meat into the pans. "Sure."

While I seasoned the meat, I waited for a pang of jealousy, but it didn't come. That was Caldwell's doing, too. Kaya was beautiful and seemed intelligent—powerful, being a skin-walker—but in my heart, there was no doubt of my mate's loyalty and love.

Kaya grated the cheese and glanced my way. "I guess this place will be yours now."

"What?" I almost dropped the wooden spoon. "Why would you think that?"

"I thought... Sorry, there's already whispering that Luke is going to be the new Alpha. I just figured you guys would move in here. It's big enough for all of us to meet up. Made sense..."

Luke was going to be Alpha? Was that why he didn't want his Pack coming down to Sedona?

I started stirring to keep the spoon from shaking in my

hand. "We haven't really talked about it yet, but his Pack is up in Reno."

She set the grated cheese aside and started chopping lettuce. "He already has a job and a place to live here, right? Now he wouldn't have to give it all up. He could join this Pack. Lead it."

I hadn't thought about his job on the ranch. He was proud of being the head trainer, and one of the horses had a chance to be a champion once show season started. What if Luke wanted to stay? He could always visit his family in Reno.

I went to the fridge to grab the tortillas, my throat tightening up at the thought of living in this house. No amount of renovations would erase the memories here. I put the tortillas in the warmer and popped it into the microwave.

Kaya set out all the taco fixings and glanced my way. "You and Luke would be good leaders here."

I struggled to change the subject. "What's next for you?"

She rested a hand on her hip. "First, I call the manager of my restaurant and find out what kind of bullshit story Caldwell fed him."

"You own a restaurant?"

She nodded. "Yeah. Coyote Café."

One of my favorite restaurants in Sedona. My eyes widened. "I should've let *you* cook dinner."

She chuckled. "Nah, I'm probably out of practice after all these months in that damned unit he locked me in."

"Do you have family here?"

"No. My blood relatives are dead. Maybe that's why he chose me in the first place. But Caldwell didn't know I was a skin-walker. I'm sure the others have been searching for me, but they wouldn't involve law enforcement, either. If he convinced the manager of the restaurant I was fine, there'd be no one to report me missing."

"Will you stay with the Pack here?"

She shrugged. "Skin-walkers are usually loners. We know the others exist, but we don't bother each other. We're not territorial like werewolves." She leaned back on the counter. "Now I've got a foot in both worlds, and I probably don't belong in either."

"Those kids love you. And until things settle down, they're going to need you." I started opening cupboards until I found paper plates. I set them on the counter and met her eyes. "I'm sorry that I didn't do something to get you all out sooner."

"We all knew it was Caldwell." Her gaze met mine. "You didn't have any more power than we did, just fewer walls."

I almost smiled, nodding slowly. "True."

One by one, the werewolves who could walk followed the scent of tacos into the kitchen. Samantha and Gage came in with the little ones, loading up plates of tacos. He looked over at me and winked. "Thanks for the food."

"Thanks for helping us today." I shook my head slowly. "We never would have ended Caldwell without your help."

The group was battered, but we were far from beaten. I picked up a plate and made some tacos, then left the others and went into the living room. Luke's knee was wrapped tightly, with an ice pack sitting on top. His eyes tracked my every move.

I sat beside him, and he leaned over, kissing my temple. "Missed you."

"You were busy making plans." I offered him a taco.

"Plans?" He took a bite and groaned. He swallowed and grinned. "Best taco I've ever had."

"You're just really hungry." But I had to admit, it was a damned fine taco. Maybe I was starving, too.

He polished off a second taco and glanced my way. "Jason is pretty sure the bone isn't broken. We're going to take an X-ray at Cole's office just to be sure, but I probably tore the ligaments."

"How long will you be laid up?"

He shrugged. "I guess it'll depend on whether or not my kneecap is broken. Hopefully the bone is fine. If it's just ligaments, maybe a week or two."

I swallowed another bite. "Then you'll be good to travel?"

"Travel? Where are we going?"

My heart thumped. "I thought we were going to Reno."

"Oh." He nodded, focusing on the tacos. "Yeah. There's still a lot to settle here first."

I set the plate aside. Not sure if I wanted to know the answer. "How long do you think you're going to want to stay here?"

He took my uninjured hand. "We don't need to figure that out tonight." He tightened his hold. "Tonight we mourn the ones we lost and celebrate a future without Caldwell."

I nodded and handed him another taco.

Suddenly, I wasn't very hungry.

Chapter Twenty-Eight

LUKE

Jason went out and bought me a crutch while the others cleaned up the kitchen. Jett made it back and let us know the police gave the bar a noise violation. For now, we were in the clear.

Asher and my brother went out back to prepare the bodies while I hoisted myself up onto my feet. With the crutch under my arm, I was careful not to put weight on my injured leg as I moved through the house.

I checked room by room, but no Raven. Finally, I opened the front door and found her sitting in a chair, staring up at the moon. It was still pretty bright, just beginning to wane. Before I could get to her, she called over.

"You should be resting." She didn't take her eyes off the moon overhead.

"I can rest later. It's you I'm worried about." I hobbled out to her and sat in the other chair. "Talk to me."

She finally met my eyes. "I'm all right. I think." She

shrugged. "Just not sure what's coming next."

I reached for her good hand. "You still need to let Jason fix up your hand."

"I know. Maybe after…" She shuddered and crossed her arms. "How's Brock?"

"Not good. Jason's got him comfortable, but without exploratory surgery in a hospital, he can't find where he's bleeding internally."

She turned her face to the moon again. "He's dying."

I wished I could give her better news, but I wasn't going to lie. "Probably. There's always hope that his body will heal on its own, but…Jason isn't sure he'll survive the night."

She swiped a tear from her cheek. "I didn't even know him." She pressed her lips together, pulling in a deep breath. "But he didn't know me, either, and he still ran into that bar to help us. He could've run away and left Sedona behind. He'd still be alive."

I caressed her cheek until her eyes met mine. "He's a good man. They all are."

"They just need an Alpha."

Her tone was dry, like an accusation. I frowned. "What's going on?"

"Nothing." She dropped my hand and stood up. "Everything." She turned toward the house. "Kaya told me they want you to be the new Alpha here. That all this would be ours." She swung her arm at the surroundings. "You'd be crazy not to take it."

I raised a brow and hauled myself back up on my feet. "This isn't like a job offer, Raven. It's supposed to be passed from father to eldest son, but Caldwell didn't leave a grown heir, so someone in this Pack will need to rise up and accept the responsibility and the power that comes with it."

"And they want it to be you."

"Tonight they do." I glanced at the house. "Tomorrow it

might be someone else. Nothing is being decided right now."

Her heart was racing, but I had no clue why. Frustration brewed inside me, fed by the throbbing pain in my leg. If I wasn't careful, I'd probably say something that would come back to bite me in the ass.

I held out my hand. "Let's go honor the fallen Pack members, then we can get everyone settled in here and we'll go home. Just like we talked about."

She nodded and walked toward the house, her arms wrapped tight around her middle. "Back to your place at the ranch. I don't have a home."

The door closed behind her, leaving me alone in the dark with no idea why.

Out back, Asher and Logan had Chase and Ryan's bodies on wooden pyres. One bitten and one born wolf. Both dead. Their skin glistened in the moonlight, the oil already covering them.

Caldwell hadn't passed on any of our traditions to this Pack, so I stood at the end by their heads. Usually the Alpha led the ceremony, and for now, I would stand in.

Logan and Asher held torches, ready to light the pyres. My gaze traveled around the circle, taking in all the battered faces. "We offer our brothers back to the moon and the night. May their spirits be lifted, free to run with the pack of our ancestors and watch over those they left behind."

I glanced at Cole on my left. "It's tradition for each Pack member to speak before the pyre is lit."

Cole cleared his throat, but his voice was gravelly, broken. "My brother, my blood, my best friend." He shook his head and wiped his eyes. "I miss you already."

One by one, each member of the Pack said a few words.

Gage spoke up for Ryan. "We were trapped in that unit, but you never lost faith that we'd get out. You stood up to Caldwell more than once, and he rewarded you with solitary confinement and no mate, but it never shook your hope for the future." He paused, clearing his throat. "Caldwell is never going to hurt anyone else. Because of you. I'll never forget you, Ryan."

When we got to Raven, she tipped her head and looked up at the moon. "I didn't know Chase or Ryan well, but I know they didn't deserve to die. I hope wherever they are, they're without pain or worry."

I nodded, and Asher and Logan touched the torches to the pyres. The fire blazed forward, roaring as the oil fed the flames. One by one, everyone retreated into the house. I stayed behind with Cole. Usually the Alpha would watch over the pyres. I would have to do for now. Raven took my hand, our fingers lacing together.

The heat from the fire knocked us back a few steps as the smoke curled its way up to the heavens. I looked down at her and whispered, "You can go inside. We still need to burn Caldwell's body, too."

She nodded. "I'll see you soon."

It would be hours before the flames died down. Cole went inside before we lit up Caldwell's remains. We didn't have a ceremony for him. He'd betrayed his Pack, and werewolves in general. He was no hero, his death no tragedy.

Through it all, my twin brother and Asher were at my side. Silent sentinels.

By the time I got in the house, my knee was swollen and throbbing. Raven had drifted off, curled up on the leather sofa. I settled down beside her, lifting her head onto my lap. She snuggled in without waking as I stroked her hair.

We weren't going anywhere tonight.

Someone was sobbing. I woke with a jerk, scanning the room for the source. Raven was still sound asleep, her head on my lap. Careful not to wake her, I got up, grinding my teeth to keep from cursing. My knee hurt like a motherfucker. Shit!

I grabbed my crutch and followed the sniffling.

Jason met me at the doorway, his voice low and all business. "I did all I could short of opening him up, but…we lost Brock."

I peered around him. Naomi sat at Brock's side, wiping her nose. Samantha had all four little boys over by the window.

I clasped Jason's forearm. "Thanks for trying."

His eyes were red and swollen. Had he slept at all last night?

He glanced over his shoulder and back to me. "Trying wasn't enough this time."

"Go rest. I'll stay with them."

He nodded and walked down the hallway. I went inside and dragged a chair over to the other side of Naomi. "I'm sorry."

She looked over at me, drying her cheek. "I'm not sure why I'm crying. I barely knew him. We slept together a few times when Caldwell ordered it, comfort in a horrible situation." She stroked his hair back from his forehead. "But he was always kind to me. And he loved those boys. He never wondered if they were his. He didn't care."

"He was a good man, and you'd still be locked in those units if he hadn't helped us with Caldwell."

She opened her mouth to speak when glass broke. We both looked up as Samantha fell to the floor. Blood blossomed on her white T-shirt, a single bullet into the heart.

"Get down!" We all hit the ground just as another silent bullet burst through the window and slammed into the wall.

Naomi crawled to the boys, pulling them all down onto their bellies.

"Stay here." I used my elbows to drag my body across the room; Logan was already in the hallway.

"Are we under fire?"

I nodded. "Someone's out there." When we had a wall between us and the window, Logan pulled me up to my feet. I grimaced but kept my balance.

He frowned, looking me over. "Are you hit?"

"No. But I think Samantha's dead." I hobbled into the living room to check on Raven. "Close all the blinds. I'll grab my rifle." I glanced at Logan. "Did you bring yours?"

He shook his head. "TSA would've shit themselves."

"Right. Okay, ask Isabelle if Caldwell has a gun safe. I can't imagine he stayed here unarmed."

Logan rushed through the house, careful to get the blinds closed. Raven frowned. "What's going on?"

"I think Blake's back. He got Samantha through the window."

The color drained from her face. "Shit."

"Yeah. Stay low and away from the windows."

She crept over to my side. "What can I do?"

"I've got my rifle and scope here, but I need some help getting up to get a clear vantage point."

She crossed her arms. "You are *not* going up on the roof."

"Got a better idea?"

She groaned. "Can't Logan take your rifle and do it?"

"Someone who is more mobile than me needs to stay here and protect the house. Give my brother my Glock."

She rolled her eyes. "This is crazy."

"I don't have time to argue with you." I grabbed my rifle from the counter where Gage left it the night before. "Fuck."

"What?"

I stared at the front door. "My ammo is out in the van."

Chapter Twenty-Nine

Raven

My thoughts were a tangled jumble. Samantha was dead or dying somewhere in the house, Luke was going to drag himself up on the roof with a bum knee, and now we needed someone to get to the van while avoiding fire from a crazed werewolf gunman outside.

Isabelle came in with two handguns and a few clips of bullets. "Logan told me to grab weapons."

Luke turned her way. "Yeah, the extra ammo for my rifle is in the van."

Logan came up behind her. "I'll get it if someone can cover me."

"No." Luke tensed beside me. "There's got to be a better way."

Isabelle pulled the slide back on the Glock. "I'll cover you."

"Maybe there's another way." My pulse pounded in my ears as all the attention focused on me.

"Rave, we can't stay in here hiding." Isabelle gestured toward the window. "We're sitting ducks."

I yanked out my cell phone and hit Blake's number. He answered on the first ring.

"Bo's dead."

I swallowed the lump in my throat. If I could keep him on the phone, he wouldn't be able to shoot at us. "So are Caldwell, Chase, Brock, and Ryan. None of it will bring Bo back."

"Maybe not, but when I kill Luke Reynolds, I'll know you're hurting, too. That's all that matters."

All the wolves in the room could hear the conversation, but I gestured for them to keep quiet. "Caldwell's dead. You don't have to fight his battles anymore."

"Everything was fine until Reynolds came to town and claimed you as his mate."

Rage smoldered deep in my belly. "*Nothing* was right *until* Luke came to town. I know you hated sharing me with you brother. That was all Caldwell's doing. You can still find your real mate. She's out there somewhere."

"It's too late for that."

"No." I met Luke's eyes. "It's never too late."

He nodded slowly and gestured to Logan. While they headed for the back door, I kept Blake talking. "Blake? Did you hear me? You can join us. Help us heal this Pack, and find your mate. Caldwell's dead. His rules don't apply anymore."

"Spare me your sunshine bullshit. You'd kill me yourself if you got the chance."

I shook my head. "I know you had no choice. We were all pawns in Caldwell's game."

"He was like a father to me!" he shouted, his voice choking up at the end. "My whole family is gone now. Because of *you*. I want you to hurt like I do. First I'm going to kill Reynolds, and then your cunt of a sister."

"You sack of shit!" I was screaming now, but I didn't care.

I embraced the rage. "You don't give a crap who you hurt. Samantha's dead. Because of you, her babies have no mother now. She never asked to be bitten or be a part of this sick excuse for a Pack. You killed an innocent, unarmed woman. Do you feel good about that, you bastard?"

"Casualty of war."

"War?" I paced, walking off some of my frustration. "This isn't a war. This is a loose-cannon asshole who thinks killing other people will make the hurting stop. Well, guess what? The hurting never ends. It infects every part of your life and turns you into someone you don't recognize anymore."

Logan came back in, and Luke was already loading his rifle.

"Spare me, bitch. I'm coming for you."

He ended the call. I turned around as Luke hooked the rifle over his shoulder.

I sighed. "You're sure about this?" He nodded and came forward to embrace me. I clung to him and whispered, "Be careful."

He kissed my hair, his lips against my ear. "I love you, Raven."

Logan helped him out through the kitchen. A bullet crashed through the closed blinds in the living room. We all hit the floor. Outside, Luke pulled himself up onto the roof. I tried Blake's number again. It went directly to voicemail.

Logan stormed through the house and opened the front door, taking cover inside against the doorframe. Two bullets flew through the opening, breaking glass in the kitchen. Logan leaned into the doorway and fired off rapid-fire shots before taking cover again.

Above us, Luke thumped on the roof.

Another bullet came through the door and was answered by a loud bang from the rooftop. I held my breath. We all did.

Logan peered outside and fired one more shot. He took

cover. We waited.

No return fire.

Luke was on the move. Finally he shouted from the edge of the roof, "Need some help over here."

Logan supported Luke's weight as he came down from the roof. The rest of us tentatively got to our feet. With all the gunfire, we were lucky Caldwell's estate covered acres of land on the outskirts of Sedona. There weren't any neighbors to report the noise, so we probably wouldn't have a visit from local law enforcement.

I crossed the room to help steady Luke. "One shot?"

He held me a little tighter. "He made it easy. No cover, just firing at the house in the open."

I led Luke to the couch while Logan grabbed a holster and put it on. Once he had the gun holstered, he headed for the door. "I'll bring his body around back."

Jason came out from the back room, carrying Samantha. His voice was barely audible, but every wolf heard. "It took her instantly. No pain."

He kept going out the back door as tears stung my eyes. Luke wrapped an arm around my shoulders, and I watched my shoes, surprised to see they looked the same. So many people had died in the past two days, but my shoes hadn't changed. There was a twisted comfort in it.

He massaged my shoulder. "It's over now."

I lifted my head. "Is it?"

Shaking my head, I walked out. None of this was Luke's fault. I wasn't even sure if I was angry with him. But I *was* angry. I hated this place. Caldwell had poisoned the soil and the air until I couldn't breathe.

Luke hadn't been here very long. He hadn't lived with that tyrant, with his threats, being paired with "mates" who made you their property. How could I make him understand?

And how the hell could I ask him to quit his job and walk

away from this chance to be Alpha? I had no doubt he'd be an amazing leader—he already was. He'd banded us together and showed us what this Pack could be. The others believed in him. Some gave up their lives for his vision of the future. For freedom.

I swiped a tear from the corner of my eye. Was I really selfish enough to take that from him and force him to turn his back on this Pack when they desperately needed a strong leader?

Shit. Basically I either had to suck it up and stay here, suffocating in the memories, or ask the man I loved to give up his dreams so I could run away. What kind of mate could hurt the other half of her soul like that?

"Raven?"

I turned around to find Luke on his crutch in the doorway, concern in his bright blue eyes, and in that moment, the decision was made.

I'd get through this. I'd put him first. We weren't going anywhere.

I went to him, taking his hand. "I'm all right."

A sad smile tilted the corner of his mouth. "Liar."

"Okay, so I'm barely holding it together." I rolled my eyes. "Better?"

"At least it's honest." He bent to kiss my lips, his touch so tender it bound up the pieces of my broken heart. He opened his eyes, staring into mine. "Please don't shut me out."

The pain in his voice broke me.

I tangled my fingers in his hair, crushing my lips to his. He growled, holding me tighter against him, our tongues twining, urgent. All the fear, sadness, and even hope poured into the kiss, speaking the words I couldn't give voice to.

When I pulled back, my voice was a breathless whisper. "I love you, Luke. It's the one constant." I searched his face. "You're my mate, and if you're walking through hell, I'll be right there at your side."

His eyes shone with tears he hadn't yet shed. He pressed his lips to my forehead. "And I'll be at yours, too." He drew back. "But you have to let me."

Before I could ask him what the hell that was supposed to mean, Asher came up behind him. "Luke…Brock, Samantha, and Blake are…ready."

Luke sighed and nodded. "I don't want the little ones there."

"Naomi and Gage are keeping them busy." Asher looked down the hall. "Samantha's twins are only a few months old. Hopefully they won't remember this day."

"We're all praying for the same thing." Luke made his way outside, slow and steady. I wasn't happy about staying in Sedona, but I was damned proud of my mate.

Chapter Thirty

Luke

I washed my hair three times, trying to get rid of the stench of smoke. Death. Maybe it was all in my head. Hell if I knew. When I came into the front room, Logan was sitting on the couch with Raven.

He looked up and smiled. "I was worried we wouldn't get to say good-bye."

"You guys need to go back already?"

He nodded. "Yeah, Jason's missing his little ones, and I have a concert later tonight."

"All right. I'll walk you out." I still had the crutch, but I was upright. It was as close to walking as I was going to get right now.

Logan and Raven stood. He hugged her tight. "Take good care of my baby brother."

She smiled at me over his shoulder. "That's definitely my plan."

He pulled away and grabbed his bag while I leaned in to

snag a kiss from Raven. "Be right back."

We went out to the rental car, and Logan turned around to face me. "She's amazing, bro."

"Yeah." I nodded. "I never would have found her if I hadn't taken this job."

He shook his head. "I thought it was a horrible idea for Adam to sign off on this move, but…" He rested his hand on my shoulder. "I'm proud of you. If you hadn't gotten involved, most of these people would still be locked up."

"We also wouldn't have been burning six bodies."

He kicked at the dirt. "No one said being an Alpha was easy." He lifted his head. "You're not coming home, are you?"

I glanced up at the house and back to my brother. "I don't know yet."

He raised a brow. "Even I've heard the whispers about you being their new Alpha."

"I know." I wasn't sure how to articulate the mass of emotions brewing in my gut. "And part of me wants it. It's different here than back home. I'm just Luke. I've got a good job. I'm no one's assistant, or the baby of the Pack."

"So what's holding you back?"

Did I know? I met his eyes. "You were going to leave our Pack for Vivi."

"Yeah." A crease lined his forehead. "She wasn't ready for our world, but she was *my* world. It wouldn't matter where we ended up as long as we were together."

"I feel the same way about Raven."

"Okay." He frowned. "She was living here before you got here, right? I'm not following you."

I rested on my crutch. "When we first realized we were mates, I couldn't wait to bring her home, to meet my family and my Pack. She seemed excited about it."

Logan leaned on the car. "So come home and visit."

"Not that easy." I sighed. "Caldwell made Raven's life hell

here until the moment he drew his final breath. If I agree to be their Alpha, I'll be asking her to pass up a chance at a fresh start back home in Reno."

"And if you come back, you'll be giving up your job and the chance to lead this Pack."

"Either way, one of us loses, I guess." I shook my head. "Thing is, I don't really give a crap about being Alpha. Not really. Helping this Pack out of their mess was the right thing to do, that's all."

Logan crossed his arms. "So what are you asking me?"

"I'm asking what you would do if you were me."

He looked up at the house and then met my eyes. "I'd talk to her. She loves you. She's not going to ask you to quit your dream job so she can leave town."

"What if I can't get her to talk to me?"

"You're on your own there." He started to smile. "You'll figure out something."

I clasped his forearm and pulled him in for a tight embrace. "Tell everyone I miss them."

"Will do." Logan nodded as Jason walked toward us. My brother opened the car door and turned back. "Taryn and Jared are getting married at the cabin in Lake Tahoe next month. You should be there."

"Whatever happens here, I won't miss it."

Jason and I said our good-byes. I promised to take it easy on my leg for at least a week, and finally the car rolled down the drive. When I turned away, Raven was standing in the doorway of the house, the wind blowing her dark hair in front of her face. My heart pounded in my chest at the sight of her.

I headed for the door, and she met me halfway. Still no smile. I took her hand, lifting it to my lips. "I'm ready to get out of here. How about you?"

She nodded. "You still need to work a few things out before we can go back to your place."

"Like what?" We started making slow progress toward the house.

"Other than Asher and Ryker, none of the bitten wolves have a place to stay. Kaya's aching to get back to her restaurant, and Isabelle has some paperwork she wants to show you."

I stopped walking, waiting for her to look up at me. "Can I take you to dinner tonight? Just us?"

She tilted her head a little and started to chuckle. "Seriously? We've got a lot to take care of here."

"And there are plenty of Pack members who can handle it."

She pondered it for a minute. I waited her out. Gradually she started to nod. "Yeah. I'd like that."

I smiled. "Me, too."

Once we had Gage, Naomi, and the little ones set up in Caldwell's house, Raven and I walked out to her van. She waited for me to get inside and comfortable before she started the engine.

"How's your knee?"

I buckled the seat belt. "Not as bad as it was this morning."

She smiled, and my battered knee ceased to exist. I wanted to spend the rest of my life making her smile.

"Where to?"

"I was thinking Ken's Creekside." I'd only been there once, but they had an outdoor patio overlooking the creek, and I was betting since it was winter, we'd have it all to ourselves.

The hostess fired up two of the heaters on the outdoor patio. Like I'd suspected, we were the only ones braving the winter chill. A single candle flickered in the center of the table, and strings of little white lights crisscrossed above us.

Instead of sitting apart, we were huddled close together. It seemed like an eternity since we were alone. I put my arm around her, and she settled into my chest, eyeing the menu. I breathed her in, pressing my lips to her temple. "Is it too cold out here?"

She shook her head, meeting my eyes. "Gives me an excuse to snuggle in."

"You don't need an excuse." I chuckled. "I'll never get tired of having you close."

We placed our orders, and I held her hand, our fingers entwining together. "Now that we're not constantly looking over our shoulders, I was thinking about the future."

She nodded, sobering. "I have, too. I think you should be the Alpha. They need you."

I brought her hand up to my chest, covering my heart, and waited for her gaze to meet mine. "It's just us right now. I want to know what *you* need."

She rolled her eyes, but the candlelight shone on the tears welling up. I ground my teeth. I was sick of seeing her in pain.

"I learned something in all this. I'm done with wanting someone to rescue me." Her hand tightened into a fist.

"This isn't about needing someone to swoop in and solve your problems." I frowned. "Hell, you took out Caldwell, not me. And it was you who distracted Blake so we could get the ammo from the van." I shook my head slowly. "You definitely don't need any rescuing from me."

Cupping my cheek, she whispered, "Every decision I ever made led me here to Sedona. It's my own fault I'm here."

Shit. I wasn't going to give up. Not yet. My eyes locked on hers. "We're in this together."

"I know."

"Do you?" I raised a brow. "It doesn't have to be all or nothing. If there wasn't a Pack here, what would you want?"

"I'd want to see you happy, like you are when I watch you

with the horses."

It was a start. I tried to be patient. We hadn't been a couple for long, but long enough for me to know if I offered to give everything up for her happiness, she'd fight me kicking and screaming.

That was part of why I loved her. She was every bit as hardheaded as me.

"Okay. I want to keep training horses, too, but there are stables all over the country. Sedona isn't the only place I could find a job."

Her lips pursed, and her eyes sparkled. "But Sabrina is going to be a champion this year."

"Yeah." I nodded slowly. "I think she will."

"You did the work. You should get the glory."

I grinned. "Very tempting, but if I'm half the trainer I think I am, she won't be my only champion. There will be others."

"Fine." She nudged me, trying not to smile. "But we'll never be able to afford a palatial estate like Caldwell's on a horse trainer's and a bartender's salaries."

"True." I tried not to smile. "But do you really give a shit about a mansion?"

Her laughter warmed me from the inside out. "Nah, I'd rather have a little place so I can keep accidentally bumping into you."

I grinned and stole a kiss. Couldn't resist. "Okay, so we'll rent a tiny house. They have those up in Reno. We could find one together."

"We can't just run away to Reno." Her smile faltered, fading away. "What about everyone here? They need money and a leader. Who will open the bar next week when Alexandra and Mike get back?"

"You said yourself that Ryker can tend the bar. Kaya owns a restaurant, so she can probably help with bookkeeping and payroll. And Isabelle is getting the paperwork together for everyone to regain control of their businesses."

I waited for her to counter, but her gaze went distant, toward the creek in the darkness. I frowned, squeezing her hand. "What's wrong?"

She chuckled and wiped a tear away at the same time. "Was this your plan the whole time?"

"What plan?"

"Moving home. Getting me out of Sedona." Her eyes met mine. "I thought you wanted to be Alpha."

"I was honored." I shrugged. "And the guy who was sick of being the baby of the Pack was eager to prove himself." I kissed her lips and whispered, "But if I'm honest, all I really want is to be your mate and make you happy. Sedona has too many bad memories. What I really want, if you're willing, is to make some new ones."

Her kiss was tender at first, but as her hand slid up my chest and mine moved along her thigh, her lips parted. Our tongues swirled, her fingers tightening in my hair. Vaguely I heard the waitress return. There was some nervous throat clearing, but she finally gave up and left our food on the table.

I tilted my head, deepening the kiss and sliding my hand higher on her leg. Raven moaned, and her stomach growled in answer. She laughed against my lips. Her cheeks were flushed with color when she straightened up.

"Apparently I'm hungry."

I smiled. "I'm hoping that kiss was a yes to moving to Reno."

She nodded, and her eyes shone in the candlelight. "Maybe later I'll give you an 'Oh yes'…"

Damn, I couldn't eat fast enough.

Chapter Thirty-One

Raven

We'd spent the past ten days tying up loose ends. Asher had been a godsend. Somehow, in addition to running his own business leading hiking tours and campouts, he managed to keep the new Pack focused on the future. Even though he was a bitten wolf, the born wolves seemed to like him. Asher also had a knack for sensing when someone was struggling.

Best of all, he supported Luke's decision not to become Alpha and to move back to Reno.

When we told everyone our plan, I expected Asher to fight us, but he understood. And beyond that, he believed the wolves would all come together, easing Luke's worries for the Sedona Pack.

Luke worked with Asher and Cole on Pack law and helped present the information to the others so the whole Pack was on the same page when it came to hiding our existence from humans. He hit them hard about no biting or converting any humans against their will and the importance of finding your true mate and letting them decide if they wanted to be changed.

For my part, I trained Ryker. He was a hard worker and now had a pretty good handle on running the Wolf Pack Bar. Isabelle went through her channels to get documents for the little ones, legally labeling Naomi as the mother of Bart and Ben, and Gage as the father of the infant twin boys.

Kaya didn't abandon the Pack. She helped babysit and even cooked a few Pack meals for all of us at Caldwell's place. I hadn't thought it would be possible, but the Sedona Pack was coming together. Born wolves, bitten wolves, and a skinwalker.

We didn't know if there was another Wolf Pack like it in the world, but I had a good feeling they'd be all right. Maybe their diversity would even make them stronger.

Time would tell.

I knocked on the doorframe of Caldwell's office. My sister's head popped up from the paperwork. She smiled. "Hey. Good to see you."

I came in and sat across from her. "We're leaving tomorrow. Are you coming with us?"

"Not yet."

I sighed. "You've done all you can, right? They have money, Caldwell's assets—what more is there to do?"

Isabelle held up a yellowed document. "Caldwell has old records on Antonio Severino. Our dad's name is on some of these."

"What?" I couldn't wrap my head around what she just said. "Dad ran an air-conditioning company in Phoenix. What could Nero have wanted with him?"

"Mom never told us she was a psychic, either. It's safe to say there's plenty we don't know about our folks." Isabelle set the paper down. "I'm staying here until I get some answers."

I sat back in my chair. "Maybe it's a mistake."

"You think there are many guys named Solomon Wood out there?" She raised a brow. "He's listed here as one of their top assassins and a trainer for Nero."

I puffed out a breath, struggling to reconcile my memories of my dad with the new image my sister was painting. He'd always been loving to us and kind of goofy. I couldn't picture him as a hired hit man. "So the air-conditioning business was just a cover?"

"I can't tell yet." Isabelle shrugged. "I don't see his name listed anywhere on these newer documents."

Ugh. I was way beyond giving our father the benefit of any doubt. I glanced at the door. "So if you stay here, you're counting on Vance and Sebastian to come back."

"They're my only connections to Nero. We killed Severino's ally. By my count in the bank records, he paid Caldwell over a hundred grand to lead a Pack to Reno and kill Adam Sloan." She lowered her voice. "He's not going to be happy about losing his investment."

I leaned forward, resting my elbows on my legs. "You think they're going to take the Pack to Reno anyway."

"I hope I'm wrong."

"How can you expect me to leave you here?"

"Look, if I'm right, this Pack is going to need me. I'm a bounty hunter, remember? Dealing with badasses is my day job." She crossed her arms, shaking her head slowly. "If they do come calling, this way I'll be able to send you a heads-up to warn Luke's Pack."

"These aren't bail jumpers." Worry burned a hole in my stomach. "They're trained killers with heightened senses."

"And I'm a werewolf bounty hunter." She grabbed my hand, squeezing it tight. "I'll be fine. And as soon as I figure out what happened to Dad, I'll come up to Reno, okay?"

I sighed and stood up. "Dad walked out on us. That's what happened."

"But what if there was more to it, Rave?"

The pleading in her voice stabbed at my heart. I'd been a self-absorbed twelve-year-old when our father walked out of our lives. Isabelle had just graduated from high school. Back then, eighteen had seemed so grown-up to me. For the first time, I realized my sister had never given up hope that she might find him again.

"Even if there was a good reason at the time, if he wanted us, he'd be here now. We haven't changed our names. He could find us if he cared."

She got out of the chair, shaking her head. "I wish I could just stay perpetually pissed at him like you, but I can't help thinking something happened. He wouldn't have left us like that. And Mom..." She met my eyes. "He never would have hurt her. Not like that."

The conversation picked at old wounds I didn't want to reexamine. I hugged my sister tight. "I hope you find what you're looking for."

She pulled back. "I know it's a long shot, but I have to try."

I'd closed that door ages ago. "Be careful."

"I will." She smiled. "And tell Luke if he doesn't take good care of my baby sister, I'll come up to Reno and kick his ass."

I chuckled. "I don't need anyone to take care of me. But he does make me happy."

"You deserve it."

"Thanks. I love you."

"Love you, too, Rave. Call me when you get there."

I got back to the ranch before Luke. Good. I had one last loose end to handle before we left town. Once I was out of the van, I headed for the barn. The wind whipped around me, freezing my ears and stinging my cheeks.

The tack room door was ajar, and I hustled inside. Gabby was waiting.

I tried to catch her eye. "Thanks for meeting me."

We hadn't had an instant friendship. Tough when you both wanted the same guy. But we also didn't have any bad blood between us, either. That's what I was counting on.

"I'm only here for Luke." She lowered the hood on her jacket. "He's a great horse trainer."

I wasn't going to argue. "Did you talk to Adam?"

She nodded. "Yeah. My folks are going up to check out Whispering Pines this week."

"Sounds good. Thank you."

She crossed her arms. "We're not doing any of this for you."

"I know." I put my hands up a little. "I appreciate you keeping it on the down low, too. If it doesn't work out…I just don't want to get Luke's hopes up."

Her stare weighed heavy on me, sizing me up. "You really love him."

"Yeah, I do." A smile warmed my lips. "Very much."

"He's a good guy. I'm glad someone's looking out for him." She sighed. "I better get going." Neither of us moved as awkward silence descended. Finally she turned for the door. "Have a safe trip."

And she was gone.

I waited a couple of minutes. The last thing I wanted was to bump into her again. I wasn't going to apologize for falling for Luke, and aside from that, Gabby and I didn't have much else in common.

When I figured the coast was clear, I opened the door and bumped right into Luke. He caught me before I fell and held me close. "I didn't expect to find you down here."

His knee was almost completely healed now. No more

crutch, but he wasn't exactly running just yet, either. I smiled up at him. "I'm full of surprises. So are you ready for the trip home?"

He bent to kiss my lips and whispered, "Almost."

I hummed against him and stepped back. "Almost? We leave in the morning."

He nodded with a playful spark in his eyes. "So we've still got tonight."

"To pack…"

"Already packed."

I raised a brow. "So what's left to do?"

A sexy, lopsided grin lit up his face, and my heart fluttered as I ran my hand up his chest. "You sure your knee is up to it?"

He swooped me up into his arms. "What knee?"

I laughed and nuzzled into his neck as he carried me toward the cottage. His pulse pounded in my ears, and I lifted my head. "I can walk."

He chuckled. "I'm fine."

"Your heart is racing."

"Not because of my knee." He set me on the ground at the passenger side of the Mustang and opened the door. I got in and noticed sleeping bags and a backpack in the backseat.

He got in the driver's side and answered me before I could ask. "Thought one last dinner at the vortex might be fun."

I blinked. One of my few happy memories in this town. "Sounds perfect."

It was dusk by the time Luke donned the backpack. The trail was rocky and uneven. I shook my head, eyeing all the rocks. "Maybe this isn't such a good idea."

He handed me a sleeping bag. "It's a great idea."

His grin won me over against my better judgment. If he ever started using his sexy powers for evil, I'd be in trouble.

"Fine, but if you hurt your knee again…"

"…you have my permission to I-told-you-so me all the way to Reno."

I rolled my eyes, trying not to laugh, and headed for the vortex.

By the time we reached the top, I didn't need my jacket anymore. The chilly wind invigorated me. For the moment. Luke stripped off the backpack while I started to unroll the sleeping bag.

"Just a sec." He dug into the pack and removed cold pizza, a couple of beers, and finally an air mattress.

My eyes widened along with my smile. "Nice upgrade."

He laid it out flat before hitting the battery pack switch to inflate it. "It's the only thing I'd change about our first time up here."

We munched pizza and stared at the tapestry of stars above us. Luke glanced my way. "Thanks for coming up here with me tonight. I know the weather's not…ideal." He smiled. "But before we go home, and you meet the Pack and my family, I wanted one more night of just us."

I finished my beer and set the bottle aside, trying not to grin. "It didn't have anything to do with the vortex energy up here making us…"

He chuckled and put my hand over his heart. "I already told you it wasn't pounding because my knee hurt."

I laughed as he laid me back on the mattress and grabbed the other blanket. "I had plans for you."

"For me?"

He nodded, his lips brushing mine. "Big plans."

His hands ran down my body, his touch hungry and possessive as our tongues wrestled together the way I ached for our bodies to join. He made quick work of the button and zipper on my jeans. I lifted my hips, and he slid them off.

"Yours need to go, too."

He obliged my request, and judging by his erection, the cool temperature didn't seem to have any effect on how badly he wanted me. I held the covers open for him to get inside with me, but he lifted the sleeping bag near my feet and slipped underneath.

I squeaked as he spread my legs. "You're cold!"

"And hungry for you." His breath was hot on my inner thigh. His cool lips made their way up, teasing me until my back arched, aching for his attention.

He pressed his mouth against me, his tongue sliding deep into my core. I buried my hands in his hair and bent my knees, opening myself to him. Luke growled, and the vibrations rocked through my bloodstream. He nibbled little higher, and my entire body shuddered.

"Right there," I gasped.

He slid his fingers inside me while his tongue worked faster. My heart pounded in my ears. My hips writhed into his fingers.

From under the covers he murmured, "Let me taste you. Come for me, Raven."

My orgasm consumed me. My body, my heart, my soul were all his. He withdrew his fingers as my inner muscles clenched tight, his mouth tender and slow against my sensitive flesh. I trembled, staring up at the stars and thanking whatever god or fate or destiny made Luke my mate.

His head poked out the top of the sleeping bag cover, passion still burning in his eyes. He sat up and tugged off his T-shirt. "Come here."

I straddled his lap, enjoying the way he groaned as his erection entered the warmth of my body. God, he fit perfectly. He lifted my shirt off over my head and unfastened my bra. The cold air had my nipples rock hard before his lips covered my breast. I arched my back, watching the sensual way he fed on my body. He looked up at me from under his dark lashes as he ground his hips into me, sending another flood of heat through my veins.

I dropped my head back, moaning his name up to the heavens. He held me tight, the friction teasing us higher. I slid my hand between us, my fingers rubbing in time with his thrusts.

He kissed my shoulder. "I want to make love to you all night."

My teeth grazed his ear. "We'll freeze."

A husky laugh escaped him. "Then we better come… now…"

Hearing him cry out my name as he erupted deep inside me sent me right over the edge with him. We shuttered through the aftershocks, clinging to each other under the fathomless universe of stars.

"I love you," I whispered. "Thank you for finding me."

He leaned back enough to meet my eyes. "I would've searched forever."

I kissed him as he turned us, lying over me on the air mattress without separating our bodies. Already he was stiffening again, and I had to admit…

I might miss the vortex.

Chapter Thirty-Two

Luke

Coming home hadn't been anything like what I expected. A small part of me, a selfish part, had loved being my own man in Sedona, but something crazy happened when I got home.

I was still the same guy here.

Maybe it was all a state of mind, but I left Reno as the baby of the Pack, or so I thought, and now...I was no longer Adam's assistant trainer. When we got back to Reno, he presented me with business cards.

Luke Reynolds
Head Trainer, Whispering Pines Ranch

Adam was quick to let me know he wasn't retiring, but I was welcome to start bringing in my own clients and taking on more responsibility at the stable.

After I introduced Raven to all of the Pack, Taryn, Jared's mate and owner of Goldstone Properties, found us a great rental house with two bedrooms and just enough space that

Raven could bump into me whenever she liked.

My parents and Raven hit it off from the moment I introduced her. She took over tending bar at the Full Moon Bar and Grill and enticed my brother to commit to bringing Logan and the Howlers back for another intimate show in the restaurant.

The best part was seeing Raven happy. I thought she was gorgeous from the first moment I met her, but the shadows in her eyes were gone now, no more fear and anger. She smiled and laughed, and every time her gaze caught mine, I felt like the luckiest son of bitch in the world.

My only small regret was giving up the horses at Valley Farms back in Sedona. Especially Sabrina. I'd get new clients. I already had one. But Sabrina was something special. She was going to win championships, but it would be for someone else now.

I turned off the spigot at the end of the barn and rolled up the hose as Adam came down the barn aisle. "Did the corner stall on the right get new bedding?"

I nodded and straightened up. "Yeah, it's ready. Is a new horse coming in today?"

He nodded. "Something like that."

His cryptic answer made me smirk. "What the hell does that mean?"

Raven's van pulled down the drive. She came down, all smiles. "Am I late?"

Adam shook his head. "Nah, just in time."

It was like I just woke up in the damned Twilight Zone. "Is someone going to clue me in here?"

Raven grinned, coming to my side and sliding her arm around my waist. "It's a surprise."

"What is?"

Adam cocked his head; then I heard it, too. A diesel engine. A red Dodge dually with a matching horse trailer turned into the drive. I recognized it instantly.

"Valley Farms. What are they doing here?"

Adam stared at my mate and back to me. "Raven suggested to their daughter that Sabrina should stay in training with you at least through the upcoming show season. They came up last week while you were house hunting, and I showed them around. They thought it would be a good fit, and Gabby is going to come up one weekend a month for lessons."

I looked at Raven, struggling to wrap my head around this. "You talked to Gabby?"

She nodded with a smile. "Don't look so surprised."

I chuckled, shaking my head. "You two weren't exactly best friends."

"True, but we both agreed on one thing." She took my hand. "You're an amazing trainer, and it wouldn't be fair to Sabrina to stick her with someone else."

I embraced her and swung her around, drinking in the sound of her laughter. When I set her down, I focused on my Alpha. "Raven got you involved, too?"

He nodded. "She convinced me Whispering Pines could handle two trainers, and when she told me her plan to get Sabrina's owners up here, I had to help." He glanced at the truck as they killed the engine. "They told me they hated to lose you. You were the best trainer they ever had."

I stared at Raven and vaguely registered Adam in the background.

"I'm heading up to help unload the mare."

His footsteps faded as I kissed her. Resting my forehead on hers, I smiled. "I can't believe you did this."

She shrugged. "You were giving up everything to bring me back here, and I couldn't stand it."

I ran my finger down her soft cheek. "Thank you."

She shook her head slowly. "Remember that night when we met at the rest stop and you told me I wasn't alone anymore?" Her eyes searched mine. "Well, you're not, either."

My heart pounded in my ears. I finally understood what my brother and the other wolves in the Pack had been talking about. My mate wasn't only mine—I was hers, too.

And whatever the future held, I'd never be a lone wolf again.

I headed up to meet my new clients, and the devil himself couldn't have wiped the damned smile off my face.

God, it was good to be home again.

Acknowledgments

First off, I have to thank all my readers for your love of the Wolf Pack and for telling your friends about the series. I couldn't do this without you! I also need to thank my editor, Jenn Mishler, for helping me polish this one, and to Bridget O'Toole, Tera Cuskaden, and the entire Entangled Publishing team for all your support for the Moon Series! I also need to thank my fabulous agent, Laurie McLean, for always believing in this series and helping me find a home for it!

Big shout out to my intrepid beta readers: Denise Fluhr, Heather Cox, and Elizabeth Neal! You guys always keep me on track and inspired to write more. Thanks SO much!

I'm also super grateful to my amazing Night Angels Street Team! You really are the BEST readers in the world. I'm so lucky to have you all in my corner helping spread the word about my books!

Lastly, I couldn't do any of this without the support of my family! I love you Panda and Reno! And to my husband who was such a good sport when I drove him all over Sedona and out to the Hopi Nation for book research. He endures me asking every living breathing person a million questions, and never rushes me. And at least this time we didn't get caught in a blizzard… I love you!

About the Author

Lisa Kessler is an Amazon Best Selling and award winning author of dark paranormal fiction. Her debut novel, *Night Walker*, won a San Diego Book Award for Best Published Fantasy-Sci-fi-Horror as well as the Romance Through the Ages Award for Best Paranormal and Best First Book. Her short stories have been published in print anthologies and magazines, and her vampire story, "Immortal Beloved," was a finalist for a Bram Stoker award. When she's not writing, Lisa is a professional vocalist, performing with the San Diego Opera as well as other musical theater companies in San Diego. You can learn more at authorlisakessler.com. She loves hearing from readers—LdyDisney@aol.com

Discover more Entangled Select Otherworld titles...

HIS FAKE ALIEN FIANCÉE
an *Out of This World* novel by Patricia Eimer

Alien Princess Perripraxis has to find a fiancé—and fast—so her father doesn't drag her back home. Bartender Brandt Turner didn't need all those years in the army to teach him never to leave a man behind. If his alien friend needs someone to play the lovesick fool to convince her dad to let her stay on Earth, he'll let the world think Cupid finally took him out. Unfortunately, neither realizes Daddy Dearest has his own plans.

THE WEREWOLF WEARS PRADA
a *San Francisco Wolf Pack* novel by Kristin Miller

Melina Rosenthal worships at the altar of all things fashion. Her dream is to work for the crème de la crème fashion magazine, *Eclipse*, and she'll do pretty much anything to get there. Even fixing up the image of a gorgeous, sexy public figure who's all playboy, all the time. Even if he's the guy who broke her heart a year ago. And even if Melina has no idea that Hayden Dean is actually a werewolf...

THE HUNT
a *Shifter Origins* novel by Harper A. Brooks

Prince Kael has just lost his father to an assassin, and he's the next target. A murderer is on the loose, the kingdom is in disarray, and Kael is determined to make the person responsible for killing his father pay. But falling for the beautiful Cara, panther-shifter assassin and main suspect his father's murder, wasn't part of the plan. He's not at all sure she did it, and he finds himself going against everything he's ever known just to claim her.

Discover the* Moon *series…

MOONLIGHT

HUNTER'S MOON

BLOOD MOON

HARVEST MOON

ICE MOON

BLUE MOON

Also by Lisa Kessler

NIGHT THIEF

NIGHT WALKER

NIGHT DEMON

NIGHT CHILD

BEG ME TO SLAY

CPSIA information can be obtained
at www.ICGtesting.com
Printed in the USA
LVOW11s1620160317
527463LV00001B/24/P